Praise for
Dark Lie

"Nancy Springer's first foray into suspense is a darkly riveting read, featuring a scarred heroine whose past is shrouded in a shameful secret she would kill—or die—to protect. The pages swiftly fall away, along with layers of secrets and lies, to reveal the pulsing heart of this compelling thriller: the primal bonds between parent and child, between man and woman—and the fine line between love and hate."

> —Wendy Corsi Staub, national bestselling author of
> *Nightwatcher* and *Sleepwalker*

"A fast-paced, edge-of-your-seat thriller that will have you reading late into the night and cheering for the novel's unlikely but steadfast heroine, Dorrie White."

> —Heather Gudenkauf, *New York Times* bestselling author of
> *The Weight of Silence* and *These Things Hidden*

"A page-turner of a thriller with a truly unique and fascinating heroine. I found myself rooting for Dorrie White as she was forced to confront not only a brutal killer but the dark secrets of her past."

> —Alison Gaylin, national bestselling author of *And She Was*

DARK LIE

NANCY SPRINGER

 NEW AMERICAN LIBRARY

NEW AMERICAN LIBRARY
Published by New American Library, a division of
Penguin Group (USA) Inc., 375 Hudson Street,
New York, New York 10014, USA
Penguin Group (Canada), 90 Eglinton Avenue East, Suite 700, Toronto,
Ontario M4P 2Y3, Canada (a division of Pearson Penguin Canada Inc.)
Penguin Books Ltd., 80 Strand, London WC2R 0RL, England
Penguin Ireland, 25 St. Stephen's Green, Dublin 2,
Ireland (a division of Penguin Books Ltd.)
Penguin Group (Australia), 250 Camberwell Road, Camberwell, Victoria 3124,
Australia (a division of Pearson Australia Group Pty. Ltd.)
Penguin Books India Pvt. Ltd., 11 Community Centre, Panchsheel Park,
New Delhi - 110 017, India
Penguin Group (NZ), 67 Apollo Drive, Rosedale, Auckland 0632,
New Zealand (a division of Pearson New Zealand Ltd.)
Penguin Books (South Africa) (Pty.) Ltd., 24 Sturdee Avenue,
Rosebank, Johannesburg 2196, South Africa

Penguin Books Ltd., Registered Offices:
80 Strand, London WC2R 0RL, England

First published by New American Library,
a division of Penguin Group (USA) Inc.

ISBN 978-1-62090-671-2

Printed in the United States of America

PUBLISHER'S NOTE
This is a work of fiction. Names, characters, places, and incidents either are the product of the
author's imagination or are used fictitiously, and any resemblance to actual persons, living or
dead, business establishments, events, or locales is entirely coincidental.
The publisher does not have any control over and does not assume any responsibility for
author or third-party Web sites or their content.

For my beloved husband,
Jaime Fernando Pinto

DARK LIE

ONE

As usual, I had to tell myself I wasn't doing anything wrong. Every other minute of the week I lived for my husband and his business, my elderly mother and father, family values, et cetera. Surely I could be allowed my bittersweet secret on Saturday afternoons. If my husband ever found out . . . But I'd told him no lies. I'd told him I was going to the mall, and there I was.

I stood at the window of the plus-size store, pretending to scan the display of boxy blazers with matching elastic-waist skirts. Despite my uneasy conscience, I felt pretty sure that, in my old brown car coat and my favorite dress with its full blue corduroy skirt, I looked like any other overweight, middle-aged housewife in search of clothing that would disguise her thunder thighs.

Middle-aged? I was only in my thirties. But an "affliction," as my parents called it, had roughened my face, scarred my skin, stiffened my joints, and made me look and feel a decade older. It was just lupus, and I'd met other people with lupus who danced through it, but my case had attacked like the wolf after which it was named. And the steroids my doctors had prescribed gave me chipmunk cheeks and hippopotamus hips.

Actually I could have used some new clothes, if only for retail therapy.

But instead of really studying the plus-size fashions, I watched the reflections in the display window's glass. That way, I could surreptitiously look down the mall.

There were not as many shoppers as usual on a Saturday because this was the first sunny, warm day after a miserable Ohio winter. Anybody with good sense was out digging in the garden or flying a kite. But I continued to watch and hope, because the spring formals were coming up and the mall was having a well-promoted Prom Time sale, so maybe—

"Dorrie!" Somebody behind me called my name. "Dorrie, hi!"

"Oh, hi." Turning, I forced a smile. The speaker was an overly perky woman from church. Fulcrum is not such a small town—we have a branch campus of University of Ohio—but it's still a one-mall town, and in that mall on a Saturday afternoon I could expect to meet people I knew.

"Sam let you out of his sight?" teased the woman, an annoyingly skinny redhead who worked as a teller at the People's Bank of Fulcrum. "All by yourself?"

I made myself keep smiling, although I wasn't amused. Sam was a nice guy, no worse than her husband or anybody else's. Like most of them, he was not much to look at, just another standard-issue male with a big blunt pink face as plain as a pencil eraser, and hands that were clever when it came to machinery but klutzy when it came to romantic caresses. Like most of them, he didn't dance or ask for directions, he left his wet towels on the bathroom floor, he required full-time care and feeding. But as husbands went, Sam was as good as most and better than some. Didn't drink or fool around, did his best within his limits to make me happy. Not his fault if I wasn't.

I tried to reply lightly. "Yeppers. Sam let me out all by myself."

"What's he doing? It's such a beautiful day. I hope he went golfing."

"No, he's at the machine shop." As usual. Right out of college Sam had taken a management job at Performance Parts & Gears, and now, only eleven years of shrewd hard work later, he owned and operated the place. Sam made good money, but he paid the price in long hours and penny-pinching and headaches. I would have loved to have gone on a cruise to Bermuda, Alaska, Panama, anywhere, but Sam couldn't leave the shop that long, or so he said.

"He's there almost twenty-four/seven, isn't he?" What was that edge in the redhead's voice? Sarcasm? Envy? Disapproval? "And so are you, aren't you, Dorrie?" True, although my helping out in the office was supposed to have been temporary, until Sam could afford to hire somebody. Which he could now, but he didn't want to spend the money. The redhead burbled, "Working with the hubby—I don't know how you do it. I'd go insane."

I stiffened. "Not at all." But if anyone knew how much I lived in a secret world of memories and daydreams . . .

I changed the subject. "Want to see what I bought?" I held up my plastic shopping bag. As usual, I'd purchased something lightweight I could carry around so I'd blend into the mall ambience.

The redhead peeked at my purchase du jour. "Wire baskets? Graph paper? For Sam?"

"Baskets for Sam's desk. Graph paper for me. In case I go back to teaching."

"Really! Is that what you're planning—?"

I cut her off. "I'm not sure." Actually I'd gone into teaching only to appease my parents, and was surprised to find I was good at it and I liked it, if it weren't for the administration, and some of the parents I had to deal with, plus the grading system and the politics. . . . I didn't really want to go back. But I felt I had to do something with myself. Life stretched ahead far too empty. Some churches might have social activities other than the occasional covered-dish supper, but not mine. Some bodies might enjoy yoga or Zumba or a membership in the gym, but not mine. Some husbands might take their wives on interesting business trips or vacations, or bring them flowers for no reason, or have long, soul-searching conversations with them, but not mine. Sam and I used to talk, but not so much lately. Maybe if we had been able to have children, things would be different, but—

"But what about your health problems? Will you be able to hold a job?"

Annoyed, I glanced at my wrist as if I had to be somewhere. Except there was no watch there. I never wore a watch to the mall on Saturdays. Didn't want to notice or care how much time I spent there. My wrist showed me only a display of irregular white splotches, unpigmented skin, caused by lupus.

"Two hairs past a freckle," teased the redhead.

Pertinacious woman, did she have to notice everything? I showed my teeth in what I hoped passed for a grin as she consulted her own wristwatch and told me with digital precision, "It's two thirty-seven."

"Um, thanks."

And at that moment I felt my face forget all about its polite smile as a movement far down the mall caught my eye. The lilt of a certain walk amid hundreds of walkers. Barely more than a hint at the distance, but my heart beat like butterfly wings. I'd know that coltish stride anywhere.

"Um, excuse me," I told the redhead, hurrying off.

Limping, rather. Lupus made every movement painful, but if I let it slow me down, it would get even worse. At least today I wasn't having the knock-me-flatter-than-roadkill fatigue. It was a good day. Actually, a wonderful day now that I had spotted the person I had come to see.

Not to talk to. Just to see. Secretly.

There. I caught sight of her more plainly now: a slim teenage girl striding along, her dark eyes shining as she laughed with her friends. A boy kept glancing at her; was he in love with her? He ought to be. The whole world ought to love this delicate girl with her sleek dark hair pulled back from an Alice in Wonderland brow, her small head poised high on a balletic neck. Capering, she broke free of the group for a moment to skitter like a spooked filly—no, she was lovelier than a filly, I decided as she circled back to the others. She was a deer playing in a cow pasture, set apart from the other teenage Ohio corn-fed stock by every fawnlike, long-boned move, every lovely feature of her fair-skinned face.

Juliet.

Juliet Dawn Phillips.

My daughter.

Who didn't know me.

Whom I was not supposed to know. Whom I had given up for adoption sixteen years ago.

When I'd married Sam, we'd thought we'd have children. We'd bought a house, big and rugged, kind of like Sam, to accommodate all our dream children. More children than most people. Maybe four or five or six.

It hadn't happened. Lupus had happened instead.

Sam and I had been married for ten years now, and it had taken about eight of those to diagnose the lupus. My parents had muttered darkly of STDs at first, behind Sam's back. Doctors had postulated hypochondria or depression. Even Sam had believed it was all in my head or, rather, my hormones, some kind of woman thing, and what I needed was a family. But it was my irregular menstrual cycle and my inability to conceive that had made the doctors stop murmuring vaguely of chronic fatigue syndrome, Lyme disease, possible lead poisoning, or whatever, and finally order the blood tests that had confirmed the lupus.

For ten years now it had been just me and Sam, Performance Parts & Gears, and our house—lavishing my frustrated maternal instincts on the house, I had made it a warm and welcoming place, as much unlike my parents' home as possible.

Welcoming, but empty. Barring miracles, Juliet was the only child I would ever have.

Hiding behind a MALL INFORMATION sign, I gazed at her and let the sight of her transport me into the memories that seemed more real and alive than my weekdays, my husband and his forever work, my married life:

Me, Dorrie, age sixteen, and I am balletically slender with my long dark hair pulled back from my Alice in Wonderland brow, but I do not realize I am beautiful until Blake tells me so.

My parents will not let me crimp my hair, put makeup on my face, or wear jeans, ever, for they wish to save my soul. But they are not unkind. They have let me put aside the prayer bonnet except for Sundays, and they hope this will help me make friends at school and avoid being jeered at as before. Always after school my mother is waiting with cookies warm from the oven. We talk little but she often prepares the meals I like best, hamburgers or spaghetti, as if to tell me something she cannot say.

Evenings I spend at home. Mother and Father will not let me go to the amusement park or the video arcade. They won't let me date, or stay out after dark, or talk on the phone unsupervised, but they try in their ways to make me happy despite the many restrictions. My father is interested to hear what I have learned in school, and my mother keeps offering more cookies. Yet for some reason I remain thin.

Blake Roman is one of the older boys at my school in Appletree, Ohio, my hometown, which—although I do not know this—I am soon to leave, never to return. If Blake is aware of my parents' rules at all, he bypasses them entirely. He doesn't ask for my phone number. He doesn't ask for a date. He doesn't even say hi to me before the day he joins me as I walk home from school, takes the books from my arms, and places them on a park bench. He says, "I know your name. You're Candor Birch. I'm going to call you Candy. You're going to be my Candy."

My parents call me Candor, and everyone else calls me Dorrie. Once an aunt tried to call me Candy. My parents stopped inviting her to the house.

I have not particularly noticed Blake before. He is ordinary look-ing. But the moment he speaks to me, his voice transfixes me. Unlike him, his voice has black, black hair and a handsome passionate Latin face. His voice possesses such princely power that the simple words he is saying sound wonderful, romantic. His gaze, like his voice, issues out of his ordinary-looking face, out of his brown eyes, with a force of focus that is—more than powerful, more than princely. The author-ity and intensity in that boy's gaze—I recognize it. I've seen it in all the masterful leading men in the only movies my parents will let me watch, the old classics. Rock Hudson. Humphrey Bogart. Alan Ladd.

Blake says, "I know who you are. Candy. You are beautiful like

Cinderella. My Candy. I love you." Right there on the sidewalk in the full stark March daylight he takes my face between his strong hands and touches his lips to mine, softly, tenderly, his touch radiating throughout my body to linger there as a physical memory. It is Clark Gable sweeping away Vivien Leigh, it is John Wayne grabbing Maureen O'Hara, it is Spencer Tracy putting the moves on Katharine Hepburn. It is a perfect, perfect kiss, and it is my first.

The memory played back in my mind as clearly as a DVD. But as Juliet and her friends drifted down the mall, I paused the video in order to follow, feeding upon the sight of her.

Luck, careful snooping, and a talkative teenage neighbor had let me know Juliet spent some of her Saturday afternoons at the mall. About half, but a fifty percent chance of seeing her was good enough for me. I had missed Juliet's childhood and puberty entirely. My parents had led me to believe that she had been adopted by an anonymous couple far, far away, in California or someplace, and I would never see her beyond a single look at her in the delivery room. I carried that memory like a snapshot in my mind: the strong bloodstained baby, arched and stiff with indignation, lying on my belly with her tiny fists battling the air. The nurse who had placed her there said, "You've given someone a beautiful daughter for Christmas." It was Christmas Day 1995.

Peace on earth and goodwill for me that year had been my parents pretending my baby daughter had never happened, encouraging me to go on with my life while upholding the same pretense. Which I had tried to do. Having no idea my little girl was right here in Fulcrum with me.

Fifteen years later—a bit more than a year ago—I'd found out accidentally, from the bureaucrat who'd taken my application to renew my teaching certificate. "Small world," he had remarked to me across his desk in the Department of Education building in Columbus. "I know Don Phillips. He and I went to law school together. How are he and Pearl doing?" Faced with my blank look, he'd added, "According to the transcripts your college faxed to me, Phillips paid your bills. We're talking about the same Don Phillips, right? District attorney, lives in Fulcrum?"

I don't remember what I said, but I'm good at being vaguely agreeable.

"Is he your uncle or something, paying your tuition?"

I had no idea. News to me.

But I'd always wondered why my parents had sent me to college, uncomplaining about the expense, when they were the type to scold about "money up a puppy's rectum"—honestly, those are the exact words they used—if I broke an orange juice glass while washing the dishes.

Driving back to Fulcrum from Columbus, with my hands clenched tighter and tighter on the steering wheel, I had headed straight for my parents' brown shingled house.

I suppose I ought to call it a Cape Cod, but it lacked the implied coziness and charm. It was just small, that's all. Rife with restriction, like the people who lived in it.

Walking into the entry, where plastic covered a rag rug that covered the carpet that covered the floor, I saw Dad in the living room, watching *Jeopardy!*; he waved but did not look at me. I headed in the opposite direction and found Mom in the kitchen, a sterile white place with no nonsense or fridge magnets, just as the other rooms held no whimsy or dust catchers, just as Mom wore no personality or jewelry except her wedding ring, ever.

Standing at the kitchen sink, Mom was cutting up whole

raw chickens, undoubtedly purchased in bulk at a bargain price. Immobilizing a plump chicken leg over the index finger of her left hand, Mom wielded her favorite old wooden-handled butcher knife, neatly severing the drumstick from the thigh as she sliced unerringly through the joint. I shuddered. Big sharp knives always gave me a sick feeling in the pit of my stomach. I didn't know why.

"'Lo, Mom." I heard the tension in my own voice.

But nodding back at me, Mom seemed relaxed enough, her gray hair smoothed back under a crocheted prayer bonnet instead of a starched linen one. My mom was fifty-five, but she looked seventy. Being born old seems to run in my family.

Of course she asked me whether I would like some freshly baked "hermits," applesauce-and-honey pastry cut into bars, and I declined because always and forever I was dieting. Quite truthfully I told her that I wished I could still gobble her warm-from-the-oven baked goodies the way I used to. Sitting at the kitchen table, I made small talk for a few minutes, then said, "Mom, I need to get in touch with the adoption agency from, you know, back when I was a teenager. . . ."

Mom dropped her knife into the sink with a clatter and swiveled to look at me as if I'd morphed into a warthog. Foreseeing such a reaction, I'd rehearsed an explanation.

"The doctor says I should, because of the lupus," I told her levelly. It's easy to lie to your parents when they've trained you to hide your true feelings, to live a lie. "The baby may have inherited a predisposition for autoimmune disorders from me. So the adoptive parents need to be notified. Which agency was it?"

Mom told me, "You'll do no such thing."

"You don't want me to do what's right?" I don't think I'd ever argued with her so coolly. I was able to do it because at that moment, having spent hours thinking about what she and my father had done, I hated her.

And maybe she sensed something deep underneath the calm words. She left her work to sit at the table facing me, wiping her hands with a dish towel, faltering, "If your affliction . . . If God sees fit to punish . . . God's will . . ."

"I just want to inform the agency," I lied. "But if you won't tell me the name of the agency, then I'll have to try to find the child and notify her myself. It's not so hard anymore, you know, on the Internet. I—"

Mom interrupted. "There was no agency."

"No agency? But you always said 'the adoption agency' this, 'the adoption agency—'"

"It was a private adoption. You can't notify any agency or trace it on your whatchacallit, computer. So just put any such nonsense out of your mind, Candor Verity." Her use of my full name signaled the finality of this pronouncement.

Candor? Verity? She and Dad had named me Truth, Truth, yet they had been lying to me for years.

"You are not to speak of it again." Broomstick straight and rigid, Mom stood up and marched to the sink, where she picked up her knife to dismember another chicken.

I wanted to grab the big butcher knife away from her and stab her right in the—but the thought, the impulse, frightened me even more than the sight of the knife did. I got up and left the house.

Over the next few days I had found out what I needed to know from public records and news archives on the Internet. Don and Pearl Phillips had a single child, a daughter, Juliet Dawn Phillips. Her birth date: Christmas Day 1995. And yes, she was adopted. A gubernatorial hopeful who touted right-to-life and family values, Donald Phillips had made public reference several times to the blessed adoption process that had given him and his wife their beloved daughter. He hadn't gone into detail about the private adoption, which, from what I had just learned about where my college tuition money had come from, had probably skirted the edges of legality. While he hadn't exactly bought a baby, my parents had certainly made lemonade in the shade.

So that was what I learned last year . . . but even now, on a sunny Saturday afternoon in the Greater Fulcrum Shopping Mall, I still clenched my teeth just thinking how my parents had shamed me for getting pregnant, snatched me away from the only home I had ever known, arranged for the disposal of my baby, and then "let" me attend U of Ohio right here at Fulcrum, still under the parental thumb.

"Hypocrites," I whispered through my teeth as I accelerated past a Hallmark store and a jewelry store, anger lengthening my stiff, painful strides. "Lying hypocrites." I hoped Juliet was planning to go to a real college and have a career—

It looked like Juliet and her friends were heading for the food court.

Yes. Swerving like a flock of starlings, they swarmed the taco stand. I sat down on one end of a mall bench, forgetting my anger, once again intent on just watching. Juliet stood hugging herself, rubbing her bare arms with her hands. The child was underdressed for the weather; what were her adoptive parents thinking, to let her out of the house in that skimpy top, with her sleek little belly bare? Didn't they care whether she caught pneumonia or, even worse, boys?

Didn't they realize she might make the same mistake—

No, my dreaming mind took over. It hadn't been a mistake and it couldn't happen to Juliet because there was not, would never be, and never had been another boy like Blake.

• • •

I am sixteen and living a fairy tale. I have been a good, good girl for years and now it is all happening, I am Cinderella and Snow White and Sleeping Beauty all awakening as one, and Blake is my miracle prince. Every day in school he gazes into my eyes and gives me the most special flower, a white rose folded out of notebook paper, with a red candy nestled deep inside. Hiding in a stall of the girls' room, I suck on the cherry candy as I unfold the rose to read Blake's secret message to me. His angular printing sprawls all over the paper; each line seems to dive off the edge of a cliff. "My sweet, sweet Candy," he writes, "I am going to open you and suck your sugar." I have no specific idea what this means, but it warms my whole body with the most wonderful feeling. "I am going to taste you with my mouth and my tongue. Meet me in the back stairwell at beginning of lunch period. I am starving for you, my love."

A girl I barely know stops me in the hallway. "Listen, stupid, stay away from Blake Roman," she tells me, hard-eyed. "Where do you think he learned those slick moves of his?"

What I perceive as her jealousy sets me aglow with joyful defiance. Missing lunch, I meet Blake in the back stairwell, because I am like a heroine in one of the romance novels I read on the sly; I have been swept away. I am caught in a kind of carnal rapture. In the shadows under the last flight of stairs, Blake starts to pull my top up. "But someone might see us," I whisper.

"Yes," he agrees, "and that makes me hungry like a wolf. I need you. Do you love me?"

"Yes!"

"Then you will do this for me." Expertly he lifts my bra to bare my small breasts. He is so sure of every move, so masterful that I know he is more than my prince; he is my love angel, born knowing how to do these things just for me. I obey him as I have always obeyed

those with authority: God, the preacher, the teacher, my parents . . .
no, I try not to think of my parents. I sense clearly enough that what
I am doing is so deeply forbidden that I cannot even imagine what
would be my punishment. But my parents' authority has been super-
seded by a more compelling one, Blake's, because nothing, nothing in
my life or my dreams, has ever felt so wide-eyed spine-curling shock-
ing electrically good as what he does to me.

"I'll be waiting for you right here after school," Blake whispers as
he twitches my bra back where it belongs, "and we'll go somewhere
and I'll unfold you like a white flower, my Candy, my love."

Sitting there in the mall, I realized I'd better stop playing that
particular memory or it would show in my face. I refocused on
Juliet. She and her friends had settled at one of the sticky plastic tables in the food court, and right beside it was another
table, empty. Back-to-back with Juliet's chair stood an empty
chair. I stared at it.

No. I had promised myself I would keep my distance. I knew
in my heart that my being here constituted questionable mental
hygiene, that there was something unhealthy about the way I was
acting. Imagine if anyone were to find me scouring the Internet—
the Fulcrum Area High School home page, the Phillips family
Web site, Facebook, MySpace—imagine if anyone were to find
the downloaded pictures of Juliet that I kept in a scrapbook hidden under my mattress. Imagine if anyone had seen me trying to
get my first sight of her, watching summer band practice with
binoculars from my car. Anybody would think I was sick, pitiful,
even a bit psycho—and now I wanted to sit close to her to eaves-
drop on what she was saying? No. Maybe someday, somehow,
I would hear the sound of her voice, but not today.

Maybe someday, somehow, we would talk face-to-face.

Often, trying to fall asleep at night, I fantasized about a revelation, a reunion, how she would embrace me and I would whisper "Daughter" and she would reply "Mother" and we both would cry. But that was a wish-fulfillment fantasy, nothing more. In my real life it was enough—it was going to have to be enough—to attend Youth Symphony concerts and see her playing all the flute solos, to drive past her high school (I couldn't drive past her house; it was in a gated community), to watch her talking with her friends as she ate her burrito.

I hadn't gone places with friends when I was her age. I'd been a shy nobody, unfashionably dressed in the modest tops and skirts, some of them home sewn, that my mother had provided. Worse than being the only girl in my school who wore kneesocks instead of panty hose, I was too well behaved. I was hopelessly uncool.

Blake hadn't had friends either. He'd worn slim black jeans instead of saggy pants, black boots instead of Converse sneakers. Other boys had stayed away from him and that seemed to be the way he liked it. Rebel. Loner. A misfit, like me.

But it looked to me as if Juliet was normal. Popular, even. She and all her friends were laughing about something. I wondered what was so funny. Were they being mean, laughing at someone, or was it the good kind of laughter, warm laughter? I wondered what Juliet was like, really. Did she go "awww" over puppies and kittens and lop-eared bunnies? Did she give her adoptive mom and dad a hard time? Did she dream about horses? Was she smart, a good student? Did she cuddle babies? What kind of music did she listen to?

She stuck something into one of her nostrils, some sort of gimmick—maybe from the party store?—that flashed like a tiny sapphire blue strobe. The kids laughed so hard a blond girl nearly choked on her soda.

I smiled, feeling an odd, aching pride. My daughter, clowning around? I'd never been like that.

She removed the blue flasher from her nose and placed it into one of her ears, then stood up to stick it into her navel. She posed like a fashion model. Perhaps some ribald things were said. Juliet grinned at one of the boys, put the tip of her thumb to her teeth, and gestured subtly with her fingers. The boy slumped in his seat amid howling and hooting. Whatever the exchange of insults had been, apparently Juliet had won.

I tried not to beam too obviously. *My daughter.*

Juliet looked at her wristwatch, removed the sapphire strobe from her navel, exchanged a couple of good-bye hugs with her girlfriends, and walked away while the others stayed where they were. Juliet had to go somewhere, evidently. I wondered where. Some sort of lesson? Flute? Gymnastics? Voice? Had she inherited my love of singing harmony?

At a distance, I followed her out of the main mall entrance to the front lot where everybody parked; the back lot got used only at Christmastime. Standing on the mall apron, in the shadow of one of the pink concrete pillars holding up the portico, I watched as Juliet walked into the sunshine. Sashayed, rather. Or skylarked. Always that balletic lift in her step. Sunlit, her long, dark hair shimmered almost golden as she strode toward the red and white checkerboard MINI Cooper her parents had given her.

There didn't happen to be anyone else going or coming at the time. Not that anyone would have noticed me anyway, just another housewife waiting for her husband to bring the car around.

Wait, there was one other person out here. As Juliet strode across the parking lot, a middle-aged man limped toward her, leaning heavily on a thick wooden cane. Disabled. From his other hand, the one not gripping the cane, hung several heavily pendulous plastic shopping bags.

He spoke to Juliet, and I saw her smile and nod. She followed him to a neutral-colored van. Watching, I felt my chest swell warm, warm as she opened the side door for him. Yes, my daughter was a nice girl, yes, my daughter had a good heart, helping a handicapped man. She took the heavy plastic bags from him, turned, and leaned far into the van to place them where he wanted them.

And the man stood up straight, swung his cane like a club, and struck her with it, hard, on the back of the head. She fell into the van. He threw the cane in on top of her, shoved her dangling feet inside, and closed the sliding door with a slam. Then he walked briskly around the front of the van, climbed into the driver's seat, started the engine, and drove away.

TWO

Juliet.

My daughter.

Being taken away.

Shock froze me so stupid I couldn't react, couldn't think, couldn't conceptualize *captured, kidnapped, abducted.* All I could think, incredulous, was *He hit her. He hurt her.* I should have screamed, yelled for mall security, run to head off the van, but I'd been secret and ashamed and silent for so long that I couldn't react. I just stood there watching the van roll toward the parking lot exit.

My daughter.

I still couldn't scream, but I jerked into action. Sprinting to my car—I wouldn't have believed my aching body could move that fast—I fumbled in my purse for the car keys, couldn't find them; the confounded things always burrowed in the sludge at the bottom, and whoever had invented handbags deserved to be hung by the ears. . . . There. Keys. Hands shaking, I unlocked my blue Kia, jammed myself into the driver's seat, started the car, and thank God there was nobody parked in the space across from mine. If I'd needed to back out, it would have been too late. But as I floored it and slewed across the parking lot in wild defiance of designated traffic patterns, I caught sight of the van at the mall entrance's traffic light.

Turning left.

Heading out of Fulcrum on the state highway.

But when I got to the light it was red, and several cars stood between me and that left turn. Meanwhile, I could see the van maybe a quarter mile away, accelerating toward flat, open Ohio countryside.

I'd never in my life run a red light, not even by mistake, not even as a teen driver. I didn't know *how* to run a red light. But stopping was not an option. Bearing down on the gas, I aimed my car toward—I'm not sure. I think I shot between the cars waiting to turn left and the cars waiting to go straight. I heard metal clash against metal; I think I tore somebody's mirror off. I know I hoped somebody would call the cops and report me as I swerved left, other people's brakes screeching and horns protesting on both sides of me.

Call. Police.

Taking off after the van, I groped in my purse for my cell phone, found it without too much hassle, flipped it open, and brought it to my ear. Dial tone. Yes. Peering through my windshield for glimpses of the van far ahead of me, trying to get over into the left lane, and trying to locate the 9-1-1 buttons on the phone, I cut somebody off, swerved as his horn trumpeted in my ear, and very nearly sideswiped the car I was passing. This was the first time in my life I'd committed such blatant vehicular offenses. Where were the police when I needed them? If only an officer would pull me over, I could call out the cavalry, send them after the van. But no, all I got was a monotone, staticky voice in my ear saying, "County Control; what is the nature of your emergency?"

"Juliet Phillips has been abducted from the mall parking lot by a man in a van," I said rapidly and, I thought, cogently.

"Ma'am? State the nature of your problem, please."

"I *told* you. Juliet Phillips—"

"Is that your name, ma'am? Julie Smith?"

It would have been funny if it weren't that something was roaring like an animal inside my ears, my head hurt, my insides seemed to have turned to water, and I felt as if I might throw up. "That's the *girl's* name!" I found myself yelling. "She's been abducted. *Kidnapped,*" I corrected myself. A kidnapper would want money, that was all. The Phillips family could pay. The kidnapper would let Juliet go. He would not—do anything to her; he would not hurt her. She was being kidnapped, not abducted. "Kidnapped," I repeated. "A man in a van hit her over the head with his cane and took her away."

"Describe the man, please."

"Um, Caucasian, maybe in his thirties or forties, not fat or anything, kind of average . . ."

"And where—"

"At the mall! The Fulcrum mall."

"Is that where you're calling from, ma'am?"

"No! I'm following them. They're heading south on the Old Buckeye Pike. You need to get somebody to stop that van."

"What van, ma'am?"

"The kidnapper's van!"

"Make and model?"

I had no idea. Had never paid much attention to cars. "I can see it from here," I said, hating myself for sounding like a child. Far ahead of me the van's rear looked like a square of bread. In any normal place with hills, I wouldn't have been able to see it at that distance at all. "It's kind of beige," I said, "or silver. A light silver brown. Kind of taupe." Excitedly my mind seized upon the exact comparison. "Actually, it's the color of a Weimaraner."

The dispatcher sounded unimpressed. "License number?"

"I don't know! It's a big van. It has kind of darker brown stripes on the sides."

"Ohio plates?"

"Um, I don't know. It has a wheel cover on back," I supplied helpfully, "with a design that looks kind of like one of those diagrams in a doctor's office of the female reproductive tract—you know, the ovaries and the uterus and . . . and stuff."

The dispatcher's tone of voice declared me a nutcase. "Recent model?"

I felt tears stinging in my eyes. "Listen, I'll call you back when I get closer." I started to set the phone aside.

"Ma'am! Ma'am, I need you to stay on the line. Your name and location?"

"My name, um . . ."

Nobody was supposed to know about me.

Thumbing buttons blindly, I tossed the phone onto the passenger seat. I blinked hard. No time for tears right now. Clutching the steering wheel with both hands, I stepped on the gas. And if the car was shaking, so what? So was I.

This was definitely my day for new ventures into automotive danger. I pushed the Kia up to ninety, ninety-five, a hundred, and still nary a police cruiser appeared in my rearview mirror. But I was getting closer to the van, and I could see it better now, including its Weimaraner-colored wheel cover with the white design that looked like ovaries, et cetera, on it.

And probably the driver, if he was looking at his rearview mirror, could see me tearing after him.

Did I want him to know I was following? If I got close enough to read the bastard's license plate, he was sure to notice me. And then what would he do, and what might happen to Juliet? How could I keep her safe? What was I going to do until County Control got its act together and the police showed up?

I had no idea.

Slowing down, I blended back into the right lane, three cars behind the van, and tried to think.

But all I could think was *Juliet. Daughter.* Was she still unconscious? Or awake and crying? Or trying to talk the driver into letting her go? I didn't have any idea how Juliet might be reacting. Would she get hysterical? Would she do something impulsive and dangerous, break a window, try to jump? Would she get angry, mouthy? Or would she be thinking, watching, ready to seize a chance to escape?

I didn't know.

I didn't know my own daughter.

If I sped up and hung by the van's left rear corner till I could call the cops with the make, model, and license number, then the kidnapper would notice me for sure. And then what? He'd get away, that was what. He wouldn't wait for the police to come and stop him. He'd go tearing off, maybe take a side road, and being male, not to mention being criminal, he'd probably had a lot more practice at speeding than I had. Plus I had a feeling a big van could go faster than a Kia.

Unless . . . maybe I could get in front of him quick, cut him off, make him slow down so Juliet could jump . . .

And break her neck, probably. Get run over. Killed.

I stayed where I was, following the van from a discreet distance. I thought of phoning Sam, my husband, but how could he help and what could I say? He knew nothing about this—my other life, my daughter. I would call him as soon as I had figured out what to tell him. Meanwhile, I trailed that van like toilet paper stuck to a shoe. It was all I could do.

• • •

Three hours passed. Three hours and forty-one minutes, actually.

I kept telling myself that as long as he was still driving the van, he couldn't have hurt Juliet. Or not much.

And sometime he was going to have to stop for gas.

I still had more than half a tank. I'd started off the day with a full tank, and on the highway the Kia got forty miles to the gallon. The van couldn't possibly get mileage like that. He'd have to stop soon.

On the other hand, the van probably had a much bigger tank of gasoline than my car did—

I bit my lip to discipline the doubt away.

About that time I saw green highway signs ahead, and a jumble of motels, fast-food restaurants, gas stations. We were coming up to the interstate.

I stiffened as I saw the van's right turn signal flashing. Now what? Where was he taking her?

Into the Exxon.

I breathed out.

And swerved into the BP just before the Exxon.

I pulled around back of the building and lurched out of the Kia, leaving it running, leaning against its door with one hand until I could stand upright. My lupus doesn't affect my organs—yet—thank God, but it gnaws at my skin, my muscles, my connective tissue, and my bones, especially my spine. After so many hours in the driver's seat, my back was screaming.

When the pain subsided enough so I could walk, I limped around the corner of the BP building, head down, fumbling in my purse for a pen while I looked for the van through a screen of my own limp hair. Not like Juliet's anymore, my hair, not sleek and brown with golden lights, but faded and grayed to the color of a squirrel.

There. The van had pulled in for gas with its rear end and passenger doors toward me, the pumps on the other side. The driver stood over there pumping gas. I could see him only indistinctly, through a blur of the van's window glass, but I could clearly see the license plate, and I could see—

I choked back a scream.

I could see Juliet sitting in the passenger seat.

She was conscious. Sitting up.

To me she looked as pale and fragile as a porcelain swan. How could everyone not see she was in trouble?

Yet, because there she was in full sight, everyone assumed she was all right. Sitting there in the front seat. Not duct-taped or handcuffed or anything.

But—but if she wasn't physically injured or tied hand and foot, why didn't she run, flee, escape? This was her chance, with the kidnapper on the far side of the van from her. Why didn't she dash into the Exxon and tell somebody to call the police?

Maybe she was thinking about it. She turned her head slightly. I saw her frozen face.

I understood. Or thought I did.

She was the way I had been.

A good girl. Obedient.

I wanted to run to her, shake her, yell at her to snap out of it and run, run—

Already the chance had passed. The kidnapper was hanging up the gas nozzle. As he screwed the lid onto his gas tank, I peered at his license number and wrote it down on the palm of my left hand. The chrome lettering on the van, I saw, read DODGE RAM.

Aaak. That white design on the Weimaraner-colored wheel cover was supposed to be an abstract front-view rendering of a ram's head. I had given it a Rorschach inkblot interpretation.

The kidnapper strode around the rear of the van.

Hastily I turned away so he wouldn't see me watching him. With my back to him, I opened a door in the side of the BP station and walked in.

I found myself in a rather rudimentary bathroom, and suddenly realized how badly I needed to use it.

Quickly, though. A minute later, when I peeked out, the van was still at the pump and Juliet was still sitting woodenly in the passenger seat. I hadn't lost them.

The kidnapper seemed to be paying for his gas inside the Exxon. He would be smart to do that, use cash so as not to leave a paper trail. If I could get to Juliet—

No, already it was too late. Here he came.

With one eye to the crack in the door, I watched as he strode across the parking lot to his vehicle. I wanted to have a description of him to give to the police. But I saw little more than before. Nothing special about his build, his weight, his height. Average, average, average. Khaki slacks, blue Windbreaker, baseball cap. Face mostly turned away from me, shadowed by his hat. About all I could see was the pale outline of one cheekbone, yet I felt a chill snake up my spine and coil in the hair at the nape of my neck, making me want to hide. I fought an impulse to close the door and stay in the bathroom.

Juliet.

Where was he taking her? Farther down the Old Buckeye Pike? Or onto the interstate?

Couldn't hide. Had to follow.

The kidnapper, with his back to me, had almost reached his van. Closing the bathroom door gently behind me, I trotted around the corner to where I'd left my car running. It was still there. Sighing with relief, I wedged my hind end into the driver's seat, put the Kia in gear, and nosed it out from behind the BP just in time to see the van pulling away from the Exxon pump.

I waited. Didn't want the kidnapper to see me following. After he'd made his turn onto the highway, I pulled forward just enough so that I could see past the Exxon to watch the interchange. The kidnapper could either continue south on the state route or head east or west on the interstate.

He pulled into the left turn lane to head up the ramp on the other side of the overpass. Interstate, eastbound.

It was time to call the cops again. They'd have to pay attention now.

I pulled out of the BP, positioned myself in the correct lane with several cars between me and the van, stopped to wait for the traffic light to turn green, then reached toward the passenger seat for my cell phone.

It wasn't there.

Excuse me?

I peered at the passenger seat where I'd tossed the phone, then at the passenger-seat foot well. No phone.

I saw my purse plopped on the seat, my plastic shopping bag plopped on the floor. I lifted the purse. No phone under it. I leaned over and clawed at the bag to move it in case the phone had fallen on the floor. A horn sounded behind me.

No phone.

I dumped my purse onto the passenger seat. An embarrassment of private items fell out, but no cell phone.

Three or four more horns added their plangent tones to the first.

Blinking at the green light and open road ahead of me,

I stepped on the gas and turned left onto the interstate's eastbound ramp, trying to think. I'd lost sight of the van, but it couldn't be very far ahead of me. What had become of my phone? Had it slid under the seat, or slipped down between the seat and the passenger door? I couldn't look either of those places without pulling over and stopping the car. Meanwhile, the man in the van would be taking Juliet farther and farther away from me.

My right foot made the decision for me, pressing on the accelerator as I roared up the ramp. I needed to catch up with that van. Needed at least to get in sight of it. A giant hurtful fist of need had clenched around my heart, making it cry like a toddler when the parent threatens to leave it behind. I had to find Juliet.

And in order to do that, I was going to have to drive even faster than before. Traffic on the interstate averaged around seventy miles an hour. Merging, I pushed the Kia up to seventy, seventy-five, feeling it shaking, poor little car; I could actually see the hood vibrating. I moved into the passing lane. Seventy-eight, seventy-nine—

POW, like a gun blast, and simultaneously a sound as if the Velcro that held the world together had just ripped apart. Everything in front of my eyes went crazed and blank. Hurtling along at eighty miles an hour, I couldn't see the road—had I gone blind? No, blindness should be black, not ribbon blue. In no way could I comprehend what was happening, but my right foot, once again more intelligent than my mind, pumped the brakes as I ducked to peer through an inch or two of daylight at the bottom of the windshield. Something huge had crashed into the rest of it, covering it, and all the glass had alligatored, would have shattered if it hadn't been held together by a layer of safety plastic. I could just barely see to keep the Kia under control as I braked while swerving toward the median, coaching myself: *Slow down—don't roll it, Dorrie!* Wrestling with the steering wheel, I bumped onto the grass and blundered to a downhill stop.

I turned the car off.

For a moment I just sat there, listening to the sound of my own heavy breathing and the whoosh of cars swishing by at seventy miles an hour. And staring at my own car hood, which for some reason had just tried to enter the passenger area via the windshield. Maybe it wanted to sit on my lap.

Nothing made sense.

And that man still had Juliet.

The thought got me moving while my heart was still pounding like my father thumping his Bible. Fighting my own shock, I opened the car door, lurched out, then leaned on the door, staring so hard I barely noticed the pain in my lupus-eaten joints. Why would my car hood fly open and turn itself inside out on top of my Kia's windshield and roof? Sam was going to be furious when he saw the damage.

All I could do now was call the police with the frustratingly little information I had regarding Juliet's whereabouts. And ask them to send a tow truck for me. I limped around to the other side and opened the passenger door to get the phone, which had to have slipped under the seat or beside it.

But it still wasn't there.

And I still couldn't believe it. I got down on my knees and peered under the seat, searching with my hands. Phone.

Not. There. On my knees in the grass by the passenger seat, I packed wallet, checkbook, pill bottles, pens, junk ad infinitum back into my purse in case I had somehow missed seeing the phone. But I bared the seat and it still wasn't anywhere.

It was gone.

Cell phones don't just walk away by themselves.

I stood up, lips pressed together, starting to comprehend. "That bastard," I whispered between clenched teeth.

If you loosen somebody's hood latch, what happens when they accelerate up to eighty?

"That consummate bastard."

The kidnapper. Smarter than I'd given him credit for. Had seen me tailing him, even though he had no reason to think anybody might be following. During the minute I'd spent in the bathroom, he had taken care of me very quickly and simply.

And efficiently. I could have crashed. I could have been killed.

Now I'd lost him.

Where was he taking Juliet?

Sam White hardly ever got out of the machine shop before seven p.m., even on a Saturday, but today he made a point of leaving before six. Dorrie would be pleased. Driving home in his freshly washed Chevy Silverado, Sam thought about taking her out for dinner. He hated to waste money on restaurants, especially those overpriced steak-and-seafood places Dorrie favored, but he knew he ought to do it anyway. He'd noticed Dorrie had been acting kind of quiet lately, a little bit down, and once again he was getting that stupid feeling she wanted to leave him.

A feeling he had never mentioned to anyone, of course, not even to Pastor Lewinski and especially not to Dorrie, because it was nonsensical. Even when she was really angry at him, which happened seldom, she had never threatened to leave him. And she'd never shown the least indication of possible infidelity. Sam knew where she'd be and what she'd be doing just about every hour of every day, and whenever he'd phone or stop by, yep, there he'd find Dorrie, right where she'd said she was going to be, at the church or the grocery or whatever. She'd never given him any reason to worry the way he did. It was just . . . sometimes, even though she was right by his side, he felt as if she were far, far away. Sometimes, looking at her, Sam wondered what she was thinking, but he was afraid to ask.

Like when she sang in the church choir on Sundays. All the other women would be watching the director and smiling, but Dorrie would be staring sad-eyed out a window, gazing at something only she could see.

He wished she would sing to him. It was her voice that had startled his heart like a song he could never forget.

Her voice, even before he saw her, even though her words were ordinary. College. Finishing his bachelor's in business administration, Sam had been sitting in Appreciation of Modern Art, which he had been taking only because three credits of "culture" were required for graduation. He had been thinking about what lay ahead, a job of some sort, when a softly resonant voice speaking from the other side of the classroom had captured all his attention.

Something in him deeply recognized something in the voice, and he still remembered the exact words. "It bothers me that they put Monet in those heavy, ornate frames when his water lilies are so light and free. The frame kind of imprisons the painting. To me, anyway."

Sam, to whom none of this made much sense, had looked over to see a girl whose beauty he recognized at once, unlike any lipstick advertisement and unlikely to be noticed by anyone fashionable, but ineffably like the beauty of the Mother of God, modest and innocent.

"How would *you* frame the Impressionists, Miss Birch?" the professor had asked.

"With feathers," the girl said, and then laughed at herself, melodious as a wood thrush. "I don't know. Why must their art be framed at all?"

Gazing at her, memorizing her, Sam failed to follow the rest of the conversation. But on the way out of class he caught up with the girl, who wore her hair simply and her skirt long. "I liked what you said," he told her.

She smiled readily and looked up at him with the most amazing eyes, brown-green with hidden depths, like a still pool in a forest. The way she walked, the way she turned her head to talk with him, she made him think of a deer, while every other girl seemed like a cow to him. She asked him, "Do you like Monet?"

"I don't know yet. I never heard of him before today." This, Sam realized, was not the most intelligent-sounding thing he had ever said, but Sam White did not know how not to be honest.

The girl's smiling mouth quirked at the corners, somehow tender. "You're taking the course to fill a distribution requirement."

"Yes."

"What would you rather be doing?"

"Building something. Fixing my car."

She nodded with utter acceptance. That was one of the things that he soon came to love best about her, that she never made him feel klutzy, uncool, a doofus, the way most girls did. Her modesty meshed perfectly with his honesty.

"I bet there's art in fixing in a car," she said.

"How?"

"Well, liking art fixes me every day."

"It *does*?"

"Sure. I get to *see* more."

He had never met anyone else like her. Dorrie Birch. And she had helped him see more, ever since that first meeting. With her.help and companionship he had seen the shape of interspace, he had seen Seurat beyond the dots, he had seen green sky in sunsets, he had seen the brilliant white and tan of a pinto-barked sycamore tree against a cobalt sky, he had seen the different colors in the pebbles beneath his feet. What he could not see, dating Dorrie, was why she still lived at home with her parents, who seemed not to trust her or even like her much. He sensed some sort of mystery there.

Remembering this, driving the Silverado home from work, Sam felt dismally that the mystery had deepened, if anything, over the years. "God," he asked as if he were talking to a passenger in his Silverado, "could you help me understand my wife?"

Sam often talked to God in this spontaneous way, because he had been raised to believe in the power of prayer. He prayed routinely twice a day, in the morning driving to work and in the evening driving home, times when he was alone, and prayer strengthened him in his purposes; he expected no other answer.

He did not tell Dorrie he ever prayed about her, because she would not have liked it. Her parents had prayed over her too often the wrong way, like Pharisees.

"What is it, God?" Sam murmured. "What's making her sad?"

There was something otherworldly about Dorrie. Something deeply innocent, something that made him feel as if she required protection. Not that she wasn't smart. She'd been a straight-A student when he'd met her, and even more impressive, she seemed to really get something out of Pollock and Matisse and that weird guy, whatsisface, Escher. Dorrie understood paintings and music and books, stuff like that, but sometimes she didn't seem wise to the real world.

And at the same time, paradoxically, Sam couldn't help feeling as if she knew something he didn't. He sensed something hidden about Dorrie. Something fugitive.

Nothing new, Sam reminded himself as he steered the Silverado. It was a mystery, an enigma, that had attracted him to her in the first place. Dorrie shy yet bold, Dorrie who would sing softly but skylark true as they walked across campus, sad songs with strange words he had never heard before. "I wish I were a tiny sparrow, and I had wings, and I could fly. I'd fly away to my own true lover, and all he'd ask, I would deny." And there were other ones: "She'd her apron wrapped about her and he took her for a swan," a girl whose lover shot her dead with an arrow, and "Black, black, black is the color of my true love's hair," with a red rose growing up from his grave.

Odd.

She still sang those songs and others sometimes, in the pickup cab with him, around the house, even walking in the mall. And she still wore long, swinging skirts—Sam's Mormon upbringing made him cherish the conservative way Dorrie dressed, rare and commendable in this day and age. Then there was something secret about her, silent and almost ashamed, that had piqued his curiosity, had made her seem even more beautiful than she was—and Dorrie had indeed been beautiful, in her own distinctive swanlike way. A quietly, classically, darkly beautiful girl.

It was too bad that lupus had messed up her skin and made her put on weight, but it bothered him only because it bothered her. He sympathized with her discomfort, but heck, he was getting a bit hefty in the belly himself, and as far as he was concerned, Dorrie had gotten big in all the right places. Sam considered her womanly, guitar shaped, her firm-waisted figure good to look at and heavenly to hold. So what if the lupus had changed her face, turning it round and puffy with some scars from itchy rash, some white patches from loss of pigment? It could do that, but it could never change her eyes, amazing to gaze into. Nothing about her appearance could make Sam love her more in the deepest way, love her for who she was: a lyrical woman who sang folk ballads, a beauty-hungry woman who loved anything with wings, a brave woman who seldom complained, didn't want any special treatment, kept on keeping on.

"God, is it the lupus that's making a silence between us?"

Dorrie had lupus really bad, so bad that it could possibly give her systemic problems that might eventually kill her. Maybe it was a sense of her own mortality that gave Dorrie a faraway look sometimes. Maybe he was worrying about what was on her mind when he should be worrying about her dying.

Maybe *she* was worried about dying.

Sam shook his head hard. *Don't go there.* But at the same time he whispered, "God, I promise I will make more of an effort if you please don't take her away." Definitely if Dorrie hadn't started supper preparations, Sam would ask her whether she wanted to go out to the Red Lobster or Hoss's or someplace.

One of these days he ought to bring her flowers. . . . Well, he'd consult God before making that sort of a change. Up until now, flowers, cards, hugs and kisses, that stuff just made him feel uncomfortable, didn't seem to fit into the context of their churchgoing lifestyle or their marriage. But Dorrie ought to be able to tell he loved her, which he did. And that he was faithful to her, which he was. He gave her a nice home, and she could call off work whenever she wanted, and his insurance took care of her medical bills. He and she got along. They didn't quarrel. Well, maybe once in a while because he wanted kids and she wouldn't agree to adoption, but still, she'd never just walk out on him. Not the way she was raised.

"God, why?" This time it was more of a complaint than a prayer. "Why do I keep getting this miserable, neurotic, paranoid feeling she's not happy with me?"

That was not a good way to end his consultation with his invisible passenger, but there was no more time. He turned the Silverado onto the street where he and Dorrie lived.

There. The house. Kind of rustic with a real fieldstone fireplace and chimney, big tulip poplar trees, five bedrooms, three baths, three-car garage. Real estate was the most secure investment, and anyway, Sam considered himself a family man. He'd planned on kids. Dorrie joked at him sometimes about the size of the place, said if he wouldn't get her a cleaning service, she'd pay for it herself by opening a bed-and-breakfast—

Sam stiffened and stared, his grip tightening on the steering wheel.

Dorrie couldn't have put the car in the garage. She always parked it outside, because she couldn't raise the garage door manually, not with her messed-up back. He kept meaning to fix the garage door opener, or get her a new one if he ever saw one on sale.

It was getting dark. Dorrie's car should have been in the driveway.

But it wasn't.

THREE

I lunged into motion, reacting more than thinking: I grabbed my car's hood and tried to yank it off the roof and windshield.

Naturally, it refused to move. The metal was a bit stronger than I. It cut my hands.

A female voice called from behind me, "Are you all right?"

Automatically I yelled, "Yes, I'm *fine*," the socially correct lie at such times, as I turned to see who it was: a weary-looking woman in an ancient Hyundai, with several kids piled into it, their round eyes staring over her sagging shoulders. People in stylish cars zoomed past without a glance, but this harried soul had pulled over on the median shoulder to check on me.

I hollered at her, "Call the police!" Too panicked and angry to be sensible, I neglected to tell her anything about being in pursuit of a predator who had abducted a teenage girl. Somehow this woman's motherly ESP was supposed to have picked up all she needed to know about Juliet and me.

She flapped a hand out her open window in reply. "And a tow truck," she yelled. "Will do." She pulled away.

What? She was thinking in terms of a disabled vehicle, nothing more? "Wait!" I screamed after her.

Too late. She was gone.

Irrationally my anger turned on her. Dim bulb, she could just go ahead and call her contemptible tow truck, but by the time it got here, I'd be *gone*. I marched to the Kia's trunk.

Struggling to exert leverage with various inscrutable tools, I gradually freed my car's passenger compartment of the rumpled hood's embrace. Some time later I managed to slam the hood down, but it no longer fit the car the way it was supposed to; it had turned inside out, with its edges up in the air. I whammed at them with a folding shovel from the trunk, waxing more furious and stubborn with each blow. If I'd been thinking, I would have abandoned the Kia, tried to flag down one of the vehicles whizzing by, and borrowed a cell phone or begged a ride. But I didn't. Juliet's abduction had solidified a kind of atavistic compulsion in me, more desperate than obstinate, that made me stand there hammering at my car's ruined hood. The despicable thing refused to lie flat. I wanted to tear it completely off the car and fling it aside, but my body, yowling with pain, gave me pause.

Okay, I needed a different approach. Tie the hood down with something.

Scowling, I peered into the back end of the car, looking for wire or whatever, suddenly aware that it was getting hard to see what was in there; day had turned to dusk. My God, how long had I been fooling around in the middle of this godforsaken highway? Sam was going to be worried about me—not that he didn't always worry anyway. It was funny sometimes to watch his worry at war with his stinginess. He'd equipped my car with a safety gadget, a combination flashlight/tire gauge/air pump I was supposed to plug into the cigarette lighter, but he'd found it at a yard sale, and the cord was too short to let the thing reach all the tires—

But that electric cord was plenty long enough to tie down the hood.

And strong.

I grabbed the ingenious device, then wasted more time trying to find something I could use to cut its cord off. Sam had given me one of those everything tools to keep in the glove box, but I'd lost it as quickly as possible because it had included a sharp knife. Knives, ick. I would tolerate spiders, admire snakes, pick stranded earthworms off the pavement after a rain, but knives made me profoundly uncomfortable, even afraid. I hid my very few kitchen knives deep in a drawer, and I used them as little as possible. I bought my veggies presliced and my stew meat pre-diced and anything else in a freezer bag. Trying to help me get over my childish phobia, Sam kept giving me cute little pocketknives, sometimes disguised as key chains, and I kept "accidentally" dropping them down storm drains.

Anyway, I carried nothing that resembled a knife in my car, and there I stood beside the darkening highway trying to yank the electric cord off the air pump with my bare hands. I never did get it off. Eventually I somehow managed to tie down my hood with the electric cord while the bulky gadget dangled between my front wheels.

At last, I thought, I could get going. I ran to the driver's seat, keys in hand, hurled myself behind the steering wheel—

And realized I could not possibly see the road through the crazed safety glass of the windshield.

Grabbing my purse, swinging it by the strap, I flailed at the shattered windshield. Glass lumps sprayed outward as I walloped a considerable hole to see through.

Finally.

I turned my key in the Kia's ignition just as headlights pulled in behind me.

Annoyingly strong halogen headlights high off the ground, glaring into my rear window. And overhead, an official-looking yellow light going flashy flishy flash.

"You need help, ma'am?" a male voice called from the near-darkness.

I wanted to smack him; I felt so furious that he had shown up now that I had done all the hard work. And he was just the tow truck operator. I needed a cop.

"May I use your cell phone?" I screamed back.

"No, ma'am, it's against company policy, but—"

"But nothing." Retaining just enough sanity to turn on my headlights and my hazard flashers, I gunned my miserable car up the slope of the median and back onto the interstate.

Within moments I realized I was an idiot who should have asked the nice man in the tow truck for a ride to a police station. On my own, I was pathetic. With no functioning windshield, I had to mosey along at thirty-five miles an hour, and even at that poky speed the force of air in my face whipped tears from my eyes. I could barely see where I was going. Didn't notice I'd just passed an exit until some cowboy in a pickup truck merged in front of me. I'd missed my chance to find civilization, and maybe God knew how far it was to the next exit, but I sure didn't. I had no idea where I was.

By now it was dark. Traffic whizzed past me as indifferent as ever. Anybody could see I had my blinkers going, but nobody seemed to notice or care that I was driving with a rumpled hood, an air pump dragging between my front wheels, and no windshield. Nobody was likely to offer me help again.

I wanted to cry, and the stinging heat at the back of my eyes made me realize that there was something wrong. Physically, I mean. Or more so than usual. I felt weak. Light-headed.

Catching sight of a highway sign in my headlights, I slowed down and blinked my eyes clear in order to read it.

EXIT, it said, APPLETREE, 2 MILES.

Appletree. My hometown.

I had never been back.

In that moment my emotions felt as wide open as my windshield, blown around like my hair. Just the sight of that town name, APPLETREE, spun me into a flash of memory as vivid as a fever dream:

Blake, my dark love angel Blake, and he has taken me a little further each time until here we are on a sofa in a back basement lounge of the Appletree Public Library. Somehow Blake knows the back stairwell that says EMPLOYEES ONLY. *He has taken me down to a mostly underground room I have never seen, where muted light filters in from a single small window right up at the ceiling. This lounge, the place where the librarians go for lunch or on break time, is empty at this time of day, because school has just let out, kids need this, that, and the other for their homework, all the librarians are busy upstairs. As Blake positions me on the sofa, I look at that window and see people's feet go by on the parking lot, feet in sneakers, in Docksiders, in high heels. It would be funny if the sneakers were on a businessman, the Docksiders on a kid, the high heels on my mother. She would never wear fashionable shoes. She wears black stockings and black oxfords.*

Lying on the sofa, I turn my face away from the window, averting my eyes from the light.

My mother would die on the spot if she saw me here.

I wonder whether Blake's mother wore high heels. When he had a mother. He has no parents anymore. When I asked him about grandparents, he said he had a grandfather, but then he laughed in a way that stopped my questions.

"Grandpa knows all about it," he had said.

All about what? Us?

Like God, the white-bearded grandpa in the sky, watching?

Kneeling on the floor beside me, deftly Blake sets my nipples yearning with hands and mouth. When he does that, I forget all thoughts of Mother, others, the window, the light. I start to pant with desire; I cannot help it. He is touching my breasts, yet I feel that touch in the most private sanctuary of the temple that is my body, and he knows it. With one hand he reaches under my skirt.

"No," I whisper, panting. "No. What if someone comes down here—"

"Even more exciting," he murmurs.

"No, Blake—"

"You like it, Candy." He slips his fingers under my panties. "Don't try to tell me you don't like it."

Like it? I love it so much I can't stand it. I could weep with ecstasy.

But his touch goes away and he stands up, looming over me. "Unzip my pants."

This has not happened before. I freeze, staring up at him, air cold on the wet bits of my naked chest.

"You have to do it, Candy," Blake orders. "Unzip me. Take my pants down."

"No, Blake. What if—"

"What if I kill myself?" He pulls something out of one pocket and flips it open. It is a jackknife. A big one. My gaze fixes on the blade, a thin grooved hungry metal animal with a stark spine. Blake is saying, "I have to have you, Candy. I'll kill myself if I can't have you." He raises the knife. "If you love me, you'll do it, or I'll slit my wrists right here, right now. You must do it or it would be rape. Unzip me."

His passion aggrandizes him, makes him seem like a hero in an *old movie, the white-hat cowboy seizing the rich rancher's virginal daughter. The girl is supposed to be frightened; her fear heightens the drama of her surrender. Terrified and exalted, transported into a more vivid life where only he can take me, I do as Blake says. But I am not quite brave enough; I can't really look. As he lies on top of me, pushing my panties to one side, I close my eyes.*

What he does with me hurts a little, but that's only because it is my first time, Blake tells me. Next time I'll adore it, I'll come to him with a spasm of rapture; he knows how to make me come that way. "Take your panties all the way off," he murmurs to me, "and give them to me for a souvenir."

I shake my head. My mother will want to know what happened to them; she inventories laundry items.

"But I need to have a souvenir, Candy!"

"Something nicer," I whisper, slipping out from under him and sitting up, blinking, dizzy. "I'll think of something." My heart pounds. The world looks strange, incomprehensible, the seemingly bodiless feet passing at the window strangest of all. My own hands look alien to me, disconnected, as I straighten my bra and smooth my dress.

When I get home late from school, my mother gives me the usual welcoming snack—today, warm molasses cookies—but also a hard look. "Candor, where have you been?"

"At the library," I tell her. I know she would see it in my face if I lied, but I am safe, because I am telling her the truth.

The next day I try to play sick, but my mother will not allow me to stay home. At school I try to avoid Blake, but he hunts me down. He kisses me in the hallway, with other kids watching, in defiance of school rules. I know now that he carries defiance of school rules in his pocket. The knife. And I know how much defiance he hides in his black jeans. "Candy," he murmurs, "my Candy, my love. Meet me after school. You know where."

I am a coward. "No, Blake, I . . ."

He puts a finger to my lips. "There's even more we can do. I'll open you like a red rose. Be there."

"But—"

"Be there, Candy, or that is the place where they will find my dead body, and I will write your name on the wall with my blood."

Every day for the rest of that week and into the next, I remembered, I went with Blake to the library after school. But my habitual daydreams did not include every detail of those days. My memories of that time had been washed out by a kind of white light.

EXIT, read the highway sign, APPLETREE, 1 MILE. I needed to get off at that exit, of course, and find a telephone, and my mother and father didn't have to know, but still, I felt my buttocks tighten, cringing. I'd been forbidden ever to enter that town again.

That was the way my parents had done things all my life. Sometimes they had let me get away with little things out of kindness, but when push came to shove, they had laid down the law. No explanations. No discussion.

The exodus from Appletree had been that way, a no-questions decision made by my parents, although even for them it had been quite abrupt. I had come home late one afternoon from school—well, from the library—and I'd found my mother and father in a fury of activity, piling boxes and suitcases into the old station wagon. My father should have been at work. My mother should have been in the kitchen giving me chocolate-chip cookies soft and warm from the oven as she started supper. Neither of them was acting normal, but neither of them offered any explanation or even so much as looked at me.

My mother ordered, "Get in."

"What's going on?"

"Shut up." My father had often spoken to me harshly, but never so vulgarly. "Get in the car."

I needed to go to the bathroom, and I wanted to put down my schoolbooks, put on the sweatshirt and baggy slacks I was allowed to wear at home, and have my snack; why was I not to be allowed my usual snack? But I did not dare to talk back. I crawled into the backseat of the station wagon, and with a clash of metal my father banged a box of pots and pans onto the seat next to me. They grated like the sound track in a movie when the jail cell clashes shut. My father slammed the car door and barked at my mother, "Let's go."

"My African violets—"

"Forget about them." An enormity: African violets are difficult, fragile, but properly cared for, they can live forty years. Abandoning them was like abandoning children. But Father barked, "Let's *go*."

So we drove out of Appletree and passed through dusk into darkness along a bewilderment of country roads. I looked at my father's black narrow-brimmed hat, my mother's stiffly starched white prayer bonnet. I wondered whether they had packed any clothes for me. Neither of them turned around. No one spoke.

Finally I ventured, "Where are we going?"

"Shut up." My father.

Then I knew for sure that whatever had happened was my fault. And although I did not yet allow myself to think it, I sensed that I would never see Blake again.

Somehow my parents had found out.

How, I had no idea. They didn't tell me. They didn't accuse me, they didn't threaten me; they didn't speak to me at all. Once we stopped at a drugstore for a few things. Famished, I stared at a display of junk food cupcakes in plastic wrappers, but I didn't dare to ask for any. We drove on in the dark, and no one suggested supper. I had not yet fully realized that I would never see my home again, but somehow I already knew they had left my T-shirts and sweatpants, my teddy bear, my pink plush fla-mingo wearing a magenta tutu—everything dear to me.

Except the very dearest.

But only because they didn't know.

I still had my love notes from Blake; those I carried with me in a pocket of my three-ring binder, always, and they were all that would remain of everything I cherished. I sat in the back-seat of the car clutching myself and shivering—

Stop it, Dorrie, I ordered myself, gripping the Kia's steering wheel. *That was a long time ago.* Now I was the one in the front seat, and not just a passenger like my mother either, but driving. Driving the car long after dark. On my own. I was thirty-three years old, for gosh sake; why did I still feel weak and shivery?

"Because you haven't eaten, dodo head," I told myself aloud.

Yet I couldn't eat, not with my stomach wadded into a fist of anxiety. I wouldn't be able to think of eating until I found a phone and called the police and got them moving. I had to make sure they would find Juliet before—

Before nothing. It was a kidnapping. There would be a ran-som demand. That was all.

The interstate felt lonely now. I turned off my four-way flashers.

APPLETREE EXIT, read the sign, with an arrow pointing the way for me in case I didn't remember how to get there.

I crawled along country roads for the next twenty minutes and never passed a gas station, a convenience store, anything except benighted farmhouses and fields. And I began to wonder whether I'd taken a wrong turn, because, actually, I didn't remember how to get to Appletree.

I'd repressed a lot since we'd left. The last thing I remembered clearly was my mother bursting into the motel bathroom the next morning as I peed, thrusting a paper cup between my legs to catch the urine. Utterly startled and embarrassed to tears, I clamped my legs together a moment too late.

"When's the last time you had a period?" my mother demanded.

Sobbing, my hands folded over my lap, I shook my head. I didn't know. Mom probably knew. Trust Mom to keep track of my periods.

Mom opened a box and dipped a kind of paper stick in the urine. PREGNANCY TEST, the box read. I just sat on the commode—that was what my parents called the toilet, "commode"—because I didn't want to wipe in front of her. She lifted the strip and looked at it.

Her face went ugly. My mother, ugly. "You *slut!*" she screamed at me, and she slapped me so hard she split my lip.

After that, my memories got really blurry. I vaguely remembered pleading with my mother and father that the boy loved me and he would marry me. But my father hit me when I tried to speak Blake's name. I'd never seen Father so furious. I was never to speak of, or to, "that sinful, fornicating young man" again.

But—but Blake and I were in love. He was my prince. We were supposed to be together forever.

Instead, I was to be locked away like a princess in a tower.

I hadn't even given him some little thing to remember me by. A keepsake.

We hadn't even said good-bye.

What would become of him?

He would be so distraught he might kill himself.

It was all my fault.

I was not allowed to contact anyone in Appletree to tell them where I was or what had happened.

Somehow there was a strange new house. I spent months locked in a strange new bedroom lacking any of the amenities of a princess's tower. Then there was the baby, born and given away the same day. Then six more weeks locked in the room, although by this time my mother was once again baking warm treats and offering them to me. Then a strange new high school, and once again Father asked me what I had learned, but he locked my room after I went to bed, and I was never allowed out of the house at night. As if night had ever had anything to do with it.

Then college, much the same. No driver's license. No car. My mother didn't have a license or drive a car; why should I? I took the bus to campus. My father picked me up at an appointed place and time to drive me home, asking what I had learned in class. My mother gave me cookies or brownies or pastries just as delicious as ever, then sent me to my room. Rather than eat them, I flushed them down the toilet, then dreamed of Blake.

I wondered what had happened to him. Was he alive? Was he okay? Had he graduated from high school? What was he doing? He was a poet, I fantasized, living somewhere at the edge of the world, in the wilds of Alaska or on an island in the ocean. He didn't need to grow up and be like my father, wear a narrow-brimmed hat, spend his days selling prefabricated farm and storage buildings. Blake would never work for anyone. He didn't seem to need to eat, or follow any of the usual rules. It was as if he had been created, not born. No way was he imprisoned by family as I was.

Living at home was more like just existing. I didn't really live except inside my mind. Nothing I felt was valid to my parents—the only people close to me—so I no longer allowed myself emotions.

No wonder the months are mostly blank in my mind. Years, really. Until I got out of my locked room and away from my parents by marrying Sam.

As soon as he had let himself into the empty house, Sam phoned Dorrie's cell. But she didn't pick up. He got her voice mail, her gently musical voice telling him she couldn't take his call right now.

Why wouldn't she pick up? She always picked up. Her phone seldom left her purse and her purse never left her arm.

He tried three more times before he left a typically under-stated message: "Hi, Dorrie, it's Sam. Got home from work, wondering where you are? Please call me."

He wished the darn phone wouldn't switch over to voice mail after only five rings. Wished it would keep ringing and ringing until she *had* to answer. But he failed to consider what might be the implications if a cell phone rang in the weeds behind a BP station and nobody heard.

After the first few minutes, Sam found that he couldn't sit down. Pacing the empty house, he phoned some neighbors and some women Dorrie knew from church, asking whether they had seen Dorrie or knew where she was. No, they hadn't, and no, they didn't, but Sam could tell by the extra courtesy in their voices that he was overreacting. Dorrie probably had a flat tire or was stuck in traffic, for gosh sake. A couple of hours late meant nothing.

But she was hardly ever late, even by a couple of minutes.

Forcing himself to stay off the phone for a while in case she was trying to phone him, Sam walked into the bedroom to change clothes, pulled off his tie and tossed it onto the bed, then forgot what he was doing and walked out of the room still in his business suit and wing-tip shoes. Downstairs again, finding himself in the family room, he sat on the edge of his lounge chair and tried to watch the news on TV. Stock market down. Floods in Georgia. Suicide bombing in Pakistan. In late-breaking local news, possible abduction of the daughter of District Attorney Don Phillips . . . but the details were sketchy, and Sam couldn't focus or sit back and relax or even sit still. He got up and emptied the clean dishes from the dishwasher, stacking them by size in the cupboards. Then methodically, starting in a sensible way at the back, he loaded the dishwasher with dirty coffee cups from the sink. He found himself pausing, teaspoons in hand, to listen for the sound of Dorrie's car in the driveway.

The phone rang. He jumped to answer it.

Telemarketer.

Sam slammed the phone down on the guy's spiel, then stood breathing deeply, surprised at himself. Never before in his adult life had he been so rude. Okay, he wasn't LDS anymore— the world said "Mormon," but Mormons said "Latter-Day Saints," "LDS"—not since he and his parents had kind of lapsed so he wouldn't have to go on the two-year missionary tour of duty. Then later, in order to get married in peace with Dorrie's parents, he'd joined Dorrie's church, which was strict, but it was an LDS carryover that he still didn't swear, drink, gamble, or lie. He didn't even allow himself caffeine. All of which made him unsure whether his bad manners and worse feelings were forgivable under the circumstances. He knew he ought to pray outside the Silverado for once, but he didn't feel as if he had either time or patience to talk with God right now. Rigidly he stood beside the phone, trying to regain control. No, he told himself, no way, he was not going to go snooping in Dorrie's closet to see whether clothing and luggage were missing. There was no reason for him to think she might have left him. None.

Maybe she was at church for some meeting or something.

On Saturday night? Sam knew better, but he called the church office anyway. An answering machine welcomed him to leave a message, but Sam didn't want to talk to it. He hung up, then called Pastor Lewinski at home.

"Hello, Sam, how are you?" Lewinski was a thoroughly nice young guy, kind of weedy-looking in a freckly redheaded way, thin, narrow-jawed, maybe just a trifle light in his loafers. That didn't matter to Sam. Live and let live, and anyway, he liked Lewinski. The pastor's Sunday messages generally spoke of love and joy within the comforting limits of God's embrace. Funny how the same church could include all kinds of people, such as Dorrie's gloom-and-doom parents, when the pastor wasn't that way at all.

"I seem to be missing a wife." Sam tried to make it light. "Any idea where she could be?"

But Pastor Lewinski couldn't help. No, there was nothing involving Dorrie going on at the church. No, the pastor hadn't seen her today. In a wry tone that indicated he realized the unlikeliness of his suggestion, he asked, "Is it at all possible that she's gone to visit her parents?"

Lewinski knew Dorrie's parents, of course, because they were longtime members of the church. Old-school. They, not Dorrie or the pastor, had required Sam to join their church in order to marry their daughter. They, of course, were the first people Sam should have called regarding Dorrie's whereabouts, and the last people on earth he wanted to call. Whenever Sam had to deal with Mother and Father Birch, he ended up shaking his head, wondering how in God's name Dorrie—sweet, tolerant, patient Dorrie—had ever been born of such a narrow, negative woman and man. Dorrie excused them to him by saying they had gotten worse with age.

"Hello." Dorrie's mother. Her voice sounded just as usual: flat and comfortless, like her bosom.

Sam found himself speaking too brightly. "Hello, Mother Birch, this is Sam. How are you?" Feeling like a hypocrite for asking.

"The same."

"By any chance is Dorrie there?"

"Candor? No. Why should she be?"

"Because she isn't here." Instantly Sam wished he'd bitten back the retort. If Dorrie's parents got worried, he'd feel bad. If they didn't get worried, he'd feel even worse.

"I should have expected that." Deep disapproval resonated in Mother Birch's voice.

"What? Why?"

"Because of the power of the devil in her."

The old witch, she didn't sound the least bit concerned, only critical. But Mother Birch often said judgmental things about Dorrie. Up until now Sam had ignored them.

This time he demanded, "How can you say such a thing? What has Dorrie ever done that was so bad?"

He heard a mirthless snort. "Look under her mattress."

"*What?*" The old meat cleaver was nuts.

"Look under her mattress. That's where she hid the filth she read—"

Sam burst into nervous laughter. "Romance novels? Mother Birch, I know all about them." Most evenings, while he watched

TV, Dorrie read a novel—not just romances, sometimes pretty highbrow stuff—and it never ceased to amaze him how she entered into the novel the way she could enter into a Pre-Raphaelite painting, totally in another world, deaf to the voices of the news anchors and the new-car advertisements.

"Filth," repeated the old woman stonily. "Devil only knows what she keeps there now. You look."

Sam had no intention of looking under Dorrie's mattress. He took a deep breath, then asked calmly, "Mother Birch, do you have any idea where Dorrie might have gone?"

"In that automobile you went and got her? To hell. Pray for her soul."

Sam preferred to worry about his wife's physical safety. "You pray for her," he said as gently as he could. "I'm going to call the police and the hospitals to see whether she's been in an accident."

FOUR

Things look very different when you're a couple of decades older, the adult at the steering wheel, not the child in the backseat. When I drove my ruined car into Appletree, nothing seemed familiar. Not that the town had grown; if anything, Appletree seemed to be decaying. It should have been about closing time for the shops on Main Street, but—what shops? I slowed my Kia to a crawl, peering around, trying to make sense of shadows. If there were shops anymore, they closed early. The heart of the town seemed hollow and empty, as if night were somehow much later here than elsewhere. The Victorian-era town clock still stood at the square, but one of its faces read 9:35, another read 10:17, the third read 9:52. . . . I didn't look at the fourth face on the clock's ornate blockhead. Appletree's dark silence combined with my overstressed condition made the three-story buildings of downtown seem to loom déjà vu surreal. I felt a chill, as if Appletree itself were my enemy, a stalker, lying in wait for me, plotting to abduct me.

Stop it, Dorrie, I told myself. *You're wigging out.* Lightheaded. In need of food. And also, I realized at that moment, going into a stress-induced lupus flare. As soon as I paid attention to myself, I could feel the fever skewing my perception. I could feel the fiery red rash popping out on my face, the membranes in my mouth and nose ulcerating. I could feel every joint starting to swell, aching even more than usual.

Still crawling along in the Kia, I fumbled a couple of Tylenol from my purse and gulped them dry, having long since learned to take pills without water, on the go, as casually as most people partook of fast food. As soon as I possibly could, I needed to take my heavy-duty lupus meds, or I'd end up in the hospital.

But not yet. Those pills would knock me out, and I had to be able to function. I had to drive a car. I had to keep going until Juliet was safe.

I had to find a place where I could phone—

Whoa! Was that really a public phone on the next corner?

Sure enough, it was, standing one-legged, like a stunted metal stork. NO PARKING signs stood guard on my side of the street, so I turned in at the cross street—not a street, really, but a side road too narrow to park along. I passed a large brick building, apparently deserted, its windows boarded up with plywood, then pulled into a gravel lot behind it.

And nearly screamed.

The van!

Or for a moment, as my headlights caught on it, I thought it was the van. With its rear end toward the street, it stood by itself in a far corner of the premises, the only vehicle there besides mine. I slammed on my brakes, gawking at it, not so sure now; was it the right color? Hard to tell in the dark, but it seemed to be some light neutral shade, spectral in the glare of my headlights. I eased my Kia closer to it, and yes, the chrome lettering on its back doors read DODGE RAM. Yes, stripes of darker paint ran along its sides. My heart pounded harder—

But then I shook my head, angry at myself. Where was the

ram logo I had seen on the wheel cover? This van had no logo, no wheel cover, and no spare wheel. Moreover, any dunce could see that this van was a derelict with four flat tires and no license plate, a junker left to rust in the weeds that had sprung up in the elbow of the parking lot's rotting plank fence. This heap probably didn't even have an engine in it.

Scolding myself, *Dorrie, you can't go seeing that van everywhere*, I swung my steering wheel all the way around and stepped on the gas. In order to park near the public phone, I scooted the Kia to the other end of the parking lot from the derelict van, close to the abandoned brick building.

And received what may have been the nastiest shock of my life.

Sweeping the concrete foundation of the boarded-up building, my headlights illuminated a sizable sample of graffiti printed in crisp black letters on the pale exterior of the basement. It read:

CANDY GOT LAID HERE

Bless my right foot, it stamped on the brake before I crashed into the wall. In that moment I found out what the word "thunderstruck" meant. A bolt of lightning out of the black sky couldn't have incapacitated me more. None of my other faculties functioned at all as I sat staring.

CANDY GOT LAID HERE

It still said the same thing.

Nothing made sense. I wasn't dead and laid to rest. Nobody except Blake had ever called me Candy. And where was "here"? This building—

Oh, God.

It was the library.

I recognized it now, lopsided old edifice, the way one recognizes a face without being able to describe the exact features. With a jolt like an earthquake's aftershock I viscerally remembered this utilitarian Victorian pile, which had been a cigar factory before it had become the Appletree Public Library.

Where I used to go rather frequently after school.

CANDY GOT LAID HERE

A fist of fire clenched my heart, and my vocabulary comprehension improved again as I found out what the word "mortified" means. It means wanting to die.

God. Who had painted that—that—that slap in the face?

Not Blake. It couldn't have been Blake.

But who else knew?

Grandpa knows all about it.

That was ridiculous. I'd never even met Blake's grandfather.

It must have been that girl, the one who had tried to warn me off. Spying. Jealous. Mean. *She* must have written it.

CANDY GOT LAID HERE

Had my parents seen it, way back then when we lived here? Had Mom maybe gotten Dad to drive her down to the library so she could check on me, see whether I was really going there every day after school? They had parked the car here, and— dear Lord, no wonder they had rushed home, packed their bags, left town for good, and never told me why. They were trying to spare me—

No, wait, was I losing my mind? Letting myself think as if this had all happened yesterday, letting that babyish whimper wind out of my mouth, letting my buttocks clench as if I expected to be spanked. *Get a grip, Dorrie.* That misery was seventeen years ago.

Yet—

CANDY GOT LAID HERE

It should be faded, worn away, nearly gone. But it looked freshly painted. Not spray-painted either. Brush printed. Big angular lettering.

Nothing made sense. Either time had slipped off track or I had gone insane. Either way, this place was to blame. Appletree. Making me crazy. Panic kicked me in the gut; I had to get out of here.

Shaking, I whipped the car around and gunned it toward the old parking lot's single entrance/exit. Jouncing, scraping asphalt, I bolted onto the side street—

Saw the pay phone.

God Almighty. Juliet.

For a few minutes I had completely forgotten about her. I hated me. Every second of time passing put her in worse danger. Where was she? What was happening to her?

I had to get to that phone.

NO PARKING, read the signs.

What I should have done was just stop the car in the middle of the empty street. What I actually did showed how badly that graffito was making me lose it. Muttering, "No Parking, Schmarking, Farking," I aimed my poor Kia at the curb, pushed the gas, whammed my way up onto the sidewalk, and stopped beside the public phone.

There, dammit.

Dammit? Where had that come from? I never swore.

Darn it. I turned off the car and tried to get out.

My body didn't want to function. For all the usual reasons, lupus aches and pains and fatigue, but beyond that, I felt as if I'd just been punched out. I reeled like a drunk from my car to the phone, then had to lean against its Plexiglas housing as I dialed 911. By the light of the corner streetlamp I looked at the palm of my left hand for the license number I'd written there, the magic number that would make the police find and stop the kidnapper, wherever he was.

It wasn't there.

I stared and squinted. Detail was hard to see in the peckish streetlamp light. Hard to see when my eyes stung with weariness and unshed tears, hurting almost as badly as my heart. That license number had to be there.

But no, it wasn't. I'd sweated it off while gripping the steering wheel or I'd worn it off wrestling with my smashed hood or I'd wiped it off in the grass when I had squatted in a benighted bush to relieve myself. Remorselessly all the various forces of entropy had removed it from me. It was gone.

Moreover, I was standing there holding a silent phone to my ear.

No dial tone.

But—but I didn't know what to do if I couldn't call the police.

I hung up and tried again.

Still no dial tone.

With shaking hands I fumbled in the bottom of my purse— whoever had designed that purse ought to be hung by the toes—and I found the car keys, for once, when I wasn't looking for them, and then, finally, some change. I shoved a number of coins into the phone and tried again.

Still nothing.

The telephone's cord had a kink in it. I straightened it. I listened for a dial tone again. None. Quite gently I hung up the phone, drooped against it, and stared into the night.

Now what?

A few hours and a few traumas earlier I would have thought, *Find another way to phone, come on, get moving*, and I suppose I might have done so. But even such a simple alternative no longer seemed sensible or possible. What I wanted now was someone to help me. *Help me.* God, I wished Sam were there. I'd seen him buy meals for homeless people, I'd seen him change flat tires for strangers, I'd known him to help down-on-their-luck employees with personal no-interest loans, no questions asked, no blame and no shame. Somehow Sam had come out of his religion ingrained with kindness. So much the opposite of my parents. With the regretful certainty of hindsight, I knew I should have trusted him with my secret from the start. If I had, maybe he'd know where to find me.

But he didn't know.

And there didn't seem to be anybody else around. I'd seen a few cars passing, but nary a human face in Appletree's decaying core. Appletree had never been a place where Saturday night counted for anything, and now it was so quiet it seemed sinister. I felt like a corpse waiting to be discovered, but no one was likely to trip over me till morning. Too punch-drunk to move or think, hanging on to the otherwise useless phone for support, I gazed blindly into the darkness behind the former library. That lumpen Victorian mass of brick cast a large shadow.

Not quite dark.

Funny pale blue flashing light.

Faint. I wouldn't have noticed it if the parking lot behind the deserted library weren't so black.

Sapphire blue strobe flash, very faint. Blink. Blink.

From inside stupid metal bread loaf.

Derelict van.

Dodge Ram. Pale. Darker stripes along the sides. Looked just like . . .

Sapphire blue strobe flashing.

A lightning-bolt jolt of panicked joy stood me straight on my feet. What adrenaline could do was amazing. I don't even remember lunging into my car and finding the flashlight Sam had put in the glove box for me. Instead, I remember discovering the flashlight in my hand as I ran toward the van, keys jangling as my purse jounced on my arm, that and the *chuff-chuff* sound of my cheap sneakers on gravel loud in my ears. At the same time I must have regained vestiges of good sense, because I slowed to a walk, flicked on the flashlight, and scanned the dark corner I was heading into as if I might trip over a body.

My heart pounded, and I started to shake, suddenly convinced that Juliet lay dead in that van.

I couldn't stand to look.

But I had to do it.

Trying to move silently—as if I hadn't already thundered across the parking lot like a rhinoceros—I walked softly up to the van and aimed the flashlight beam in the side window.

Seats, floor, rubber mats on the carpet. Nothing more.

I breathed out.

I scanned the interior, limped to the passenger-seat window, scanned some more. Nothing. No papers, no plastic shopping bags, none of the usual debris.

No dead leaves either, or mouse turds, or bird nests.

Good upholstery. Good carpeting. Protected by mats.

Abandoned van, my hind foot.

I shone my flashlight on the flat tires. The weeds grew up around them, yes, but some weeds also lay squashed under them.

Huh. He'd let the air out of the tires. Removed the license plate. Removed the spare wheel, stowed it someplace. And now nobody would give the van a second glance. This guy was smart.

I still hadn't seen the source of the blue flashing light.

Flicking off my flashlight, I waited until the darkness seeped back and once more I could see the faint sapphire glow come and go, come and go. From under the driver's seat. I couldn't see what was causing it.

It didn't matter. I knew.

Juliet had been carrying her newly purchased bauble in her hand when the kidnapper had hit her on the head. She'd dropped it when she fell. It had rolled under the driver's seat, where he hadn't noticed it. Its flashing hadn't caught his attention in daylight. By dark its battery was dying. He'd overlooked it.

I knew all this as clearly as if I'd been there and seen.

And at the same time I knew it was crazy. Why would the kidnapper have brought my daughter here, to Appletree, of all places?

But the question caused a door to slam and lock in my mind. *Don't go there.* Quickly I decided the Appletree connection had to be a coincidence. Stranger things had been known to happen.

Sam muttered to himself, "I can't face this."

Yet he knew he had to.

He flung open Dorrie's closet door.

And released his breath almost with a sob. There stood Dorrie's old flower-fabric suitcase, right where it belonged. There hung her big soft dresses and tops and skirts, posy-print calico, peach, pale green, denim blue with daisy trim. Taking mental inventory of the closet, Sam didn't see a thing missing.

He felt certain now that she hadn't left him in any premeditated sense of the word.

Suddenly a bit weak in the knees, Sam sank to a seat on

Dorrie's side of the queen-sized bed. He stared at the clothes in the closet, relieved enough to think maybe the police would listen to him now. So far all he'd gotten was *No. No*, there hadn't been an accident or incident, *No*, his wife hadn't been taken to the hospital, and *No*, they wouldn't consider her a missing person until at least twenty-four hours had passed, unless she was retarded, disabled, or suffering a life-threatening medical condition. Sam had tried to convince them that Dorrie needed to have her lupus medication, but he had never been a good fibber. He knew Dorrie carried her meds in her purse, and he knew her purse was virtually grafted onto her arm, and the police had evinced no concern when he had told them otherwise. Maybe they had heard the lie in his voice. Maybe they were too preoccupied by the Juliet Phillips case to care. Anyway, the answer had been *No*. They weren't even sending an officer to take a report.

Later, Sam told himself, after he'd found Dorrie and when he had time to get righteously outraged, certain people in public office in Fulcrum were going to hear his opinion regarding the FPD. But right now he had to focus on locating his missing wife.

Sam stared at the bedside phone. Sitting around waiting for the confounded thing to ring was—Sam suppressed an urge to invoke the word "hell" in a nonbiblical context. The urge showed how upset he was. Couldn't stand much more of this. He needed to do something. Go looking for Dorrie. But where?

Sam blinked and shook his head. He didn't know. He'd lived with Dorrie and loved her for ten years, yet he felt as if he didn't really know her at all.

"Think," Sam whispered to himself.

But thinking was of no use. Anything could have happened

to her. Accident. Rape. Abduction. Murder. And the body could be anywhere.

"Stop that," Sam told himself fiercely. Imagining such things wouldn't help anything. Much as it hurt, it was better to believe that Dorrie might have gone somewhere on her own, on impulse. But where?

Tonight Sam comprehended as never before how alone in the world Dorrie was. Friends? He'd already phoned all three of them. Relatives? Dorrie's family seldom kept in any kind of contact except Christmas cards. Parents? You'd think they'd be closer; Dorrie was their only child, and they ought to cherish her—but instead the old broomsticks poked at her as if she were a wild animal in a rickety cage, as if they were afraid she might attack. Nutty old Birch rods lived right here in Fulcrum, might as well be on the moon for all the good they did Dorrie. Home? Ha. What kind of a—

Wait a minute. Childhood home?

"Appletree," Sam muttered.

Most people felt the need to return to their childhood home at some time. Dorrie would tell you Appletree was her home-town. She had reminisced with Sam about barefoot summers spent catching crayfish in the brook, or helping her mother make strawberry-rhubarb pie, or flying high, higher in the swing her father had slung from the oak tree for her. She fondly remembered feeding chickadees and juncos in the wintertime, playing "church" with fir cones on the old graves in the cem-etery, finding a puppy her parents actually let her keep. But for some reason she never wanted to go back to Appletree, even though it wasn't too far away. A few times, feeling as if Dorrie could use a break from routine, Sam had suggested a Sunday drive down there so that Dorrie could show him the house where she had been born and raised. He'd thought she might like going back there, but she would only look away and shake her head. And she'd warned Sam never to mention Appletree to her parents. But she wouldn't say why.

Sam started to feel a familiar discomfort, almost as familiar as the fear that Dorrie was unhappy with him. That one he usually suppressed by focusing his energy on the machine shop. This one was maybe not quite as irrational, and sometimes he had allowed it a few moments of consideration. Now, for the first time, he vocalized it.

"Something weird happened in Appletree," he mumbled.

He sat for a moment staring into Dorrie's closet. Her dresses whispered "Dorrie" to him even though she wasn't there. Dresses made of soft fabric in gentle feminine colors. Modest dresses, long by today's standards, styled to cling to her waist and swing from her hips. Dorrie didn't wear slacks, not because of her upbringing, but because of the way lupus had enlarged her butt. Generous skirts allowed her comfort while turning her so-called "affliction" into an asset, at least as far as Sam was concerned. A lot of the dresses Dorrie sewed herself so she could choose the fabrics she loved and trim them the way she liked. Sam considered himself lucky; how many men had wives who almost always wore pretty dresses?

Oh, Dorrie.

Sam didn't like to take risks. He had hesitated to open the closet. But the results had been productive.

Trying not to think about what he was doing, Sam ran his hand down the side of the bed and slipped his fingers between the mattress and the box spring.

The kidnapper's van. I'd found it, and my heart beat hard, harder, because—please, God—Juliet couldn't be far away.

If I could just find a phone, I'd have the cops on the spot within five minutes, even if I had to lie. Say I was holding a gun to my head. No, say I was stabbed by a mugger, dying. Whatever.

Phone. Get to a phone that *worked*.

I ran for my car, perched on the sidewalk at the street corner beside the dud phone. Running on high-test adrenaline, I hopped behind the wheel as if I'd never heard of lupus, started the car, slapped it into gear, and stepped hard on the accelerator.

The engine revved, but the car didn't move. Not an inch.

My heart lurched, turned over, fell like a stone.

Now, hold on, Dorrie. Don't panic.

Even though the emergency brake had never worked properly since I'd owned the Kia, I checked to make sure it was off. Yep.

I pressed the gas again.

With the same result: plenty of engine noise, but no forward progress.

I tried it in reverse.

Ditto with no reverse progress. No, I would not have considered that an oxymoron, not under the circumstances: dire.

Now, of course, I remembered hearing cautionary tales of people breaking tie-rods or axles by taking speed bumps too fast. What had I done to the Kia, jumping it over the curb onto the sidewalk?

A couple more times I attempted to get my car moving, but already I knew it was no use. My adrenaline-induced energy drained away, leaving me with the bleak knowledge that everything was wrong and it was my fault, as usual.

I turned off the Kia.

Now I felt my ankles aching, my knees aching, my back

singing the blues. I got out of the Kia to flex my painful joints while I tried to think what to do.

Help. Once again I felt as if I could barely stand upright, let alone deal with an abductor. *I need someone to help me.*

Half-panicky, barely able to focus, I looked all around, searching for any sign of life in Appletree. But the town appeared dead. I saw not even a stray cat moving. Nothing but shadows.

But light came from somewhere to cast the shadows.

Finally it occurred to me to glance upward.

I breathed out, and only then noticed that I'd been holding my breath.

No, I didn't see anyone who might help me. Yet. But a few third-story windows of the downtown buildings showed illumination, wan lightbulb yellow or glacial blue TV glow. As a kid I'd noticed only the shops on ground level—shoe repair, maternity clothing, locksmith—but it would appear that there were apartments upstairs, with people in them.

Okay, my car was immobilized, but I was not; I could walk. I could ring doorbells. I would eventually find help, capital-H Help. Someone—I found myself envisioning a man just like Sam—someone strong, kind, capable, a Good Samaritan.

With a viable telephone.

Meanwhile, what would the kidnapper do?

At the thought of him I stepped closer to the Kia, wanting to dive back into the otherwise useless car and hide from him. Illogically, a spidery sense that he was watching me crawled along my shoulders. I seemed to feel his hostile stare from one of the boarded-up, lifeless windows ranked in first-floor and second-floor rows along my side of the empty library. Dumb, I told myself sternly, because why would he be in the library, and even if he were, how could he see through plywood? *Stop it,*

Dorrie. Stop dithering, being paranoid, paying attention to—to nothing, just a creepy feeling.

Still, it made sense to think the kidnapper could be someplace close by. Maybe even in one of those apartment buildings. He might have heard me pull in or seen me snooping around. Now, in order to go for help, I'd have to turn my back on the van, and the kidnapper might take Juliet and get away. All he needed to do was put air in the tires and drive off.

I had to keep that from happening.

I took a deep breath, released it, and tried to square my sagging shoulders. Forget phoning the police for just a few minutes longer. First, I had to disable that van.

FIVE

S am rolled up the sleeves of his white dress shirt and knelt by Dorrie's side of the bed. Hoisting the mattress with one hand, he probed under it with the other. His fingertips encountered paper, and gripped.

He pulled out two items, one stacked on top of the other. The first was a nine-by-twelve manila business envelope that looked as if it had been around for a while, its corners worn floppy, its mustard-colored paper as soft and nappy as a baby's well-loved flannel blanket. The other item, about the same size, looked almost new: a bright paper folder made of crisp pebble-textured card stock, Easter egg pink.

Being psychologically allergic to the color pink, Sam opened the manila envelope first. Sitting on the bed, he pinched the wire fastener, lifted the flap, and pulled out a rather messy stack of notebook paper.

Messy, because edges had been torn off to shape the papers into crude squares, and the squares had been folded and refolded at angles that made no sense. Picking one up and smoothing it out, Sam scanned large printed pencil lettering that said, "My Candy so sweet, now I've found you at last, every minute I stay away from you is torcher. I'm starving for—"

Sam thrust the note away, muttering, "None of my

business." So Dorrie had kept the love letters some boy had sent her; so what? He couldn't expect Dorrie to have been faithful to him before she even knew him. When were these things written? Sam didn't want to read anymore; he felt queasy even touching the letters, but hastily he scanned the rest of the notes to see if he could find a date on any of them. No, but it didn't matter. Everything about them spelled high school. Notebook paper. With some age to it. Yellowing. And the callow content, occasionally misspelled, and the boy's big childish printing—even his signature, "Blake," was printed, in letters that tried to topple off the edge of the paper.

Funny, Sam thought, that Dorrie had never mentioned this Blake boy to him. You'd think she—

"She doesn't have to tell me anything she doesn't want to," Sam said aloud, fiercely contradicting his earlier prayers regarding the silence, the space, he sensed between Dorrie and him. Sam laid the notebook-paper letters aside, resenting them because Dorrie had saved them and hidden them from him and there had to be something. . . . *No. Don't go there.* Quickly, before he could think anything else stupid, he picked up the pink folder and opened it.

Except it wasn't just a folder full of papers, he saw at once. Rather, this was a lovingly handmade book. Or scrapbook, its pastel pink fabric-textured pages bordered with a dainty rosebud-and-apple-blossom print. The background paper was of such fine quality that it made the computer printouts carefully arranged on it look all too much like, well, computer printouts. Of news articles.

And photographs. Computer printouts, again, from the local newspaper or maybe from school yearbooks.

All of them photos of the same teenage girl.

At first sight of that girl, Sam knew who it was. Why, he

wondered, flipping through the pages, would Dorrie be hiding a scrapbook about herself as a teenager?

But at second glance, starting over and focusing on a single color copy of a photograph, he felt his eyes widen. It wasn't Dorrie.

There was something just a little different about—not the lovely large eyes themselves, but their expression. More sure, more sophisticated. And the poise. The smile, not shy like Dorrie's smile.

Under the picture, in sky blue ink, Dorrie's careful round handwriting labeled it "Juliet, 10th Grade."

Sam passed over pictures of Juliet in ninth, eighth, and seventh grades to scan a computer printout of a newspaper clipping about a debutante affair at the Fulcrum Country Club. The caption told him that the gowned girl second from the right was Juliet Phillips.

Phillips?

It took Sam a minute to connect. Phillips. District attorney. News. Daughter. Abducted.

His gut tightened and lurched as if he were going to be seasick.

Now, don't go jumping to confusions, he ordered himself. Maybe there was more than one Phillips girl. Maybe it was a different girl who had gone missing. Maybe the missing girl had nothing whatsoever to do with his missing wife.

But why in the world would Dorrie be keeping a very pink, very flowery scrapbook about *any* Phillips girl under her mattress?

Sam stood up and wheeled to attack. Seizing the mattress, he wrenched it upward and flung it clear off the bed to see whether anything else was hidden under there.

Nothing was.

He stood panting, leaving the mattress where it leaned against the edge of the box spring with the bedclothes slipping down its sides like frosting melting off a cake. It didn't matter, because he wasn't going to bed anytime soon. Grimly Sam accepted that he was not likely to get any sleep tonight.

He took a deep breath, put his brain into business mode, and considered his options.

Option one: Continue pacing and wanting to puke and waiting for the phone to ring. Counterproductive. Reactive rather than proactive. Also torturous. He couldn't stand much more of it.

Option two: Call the police. Possibly productive. But also risky. They were likely to think Dorrie was mixed up with the Phillips abduction somehow.

Option three: Get in the car and go looking for Dorrie himself. Problem: He wouldn't be home if she called. Tentative solution: Take his cell phone with him and hope she'd call that one too. Go to Appletree—

But it would take him three, maybe four hours to get there. And meanwhile he couldn't be anywhere else. Whereas the police could be looking for Dorrie and her car all over Ohio within minutes.

Okay, maybe they'd go looking for the wrong reason, thinking she'd done something illegal. But what did it matter, as long as they found her safe?

Also, face it—maybe Dorrie *had* done something. . . . Trying to figure out what was going on was like trying to look at one of those pictures Dorrie used to like back in Appreciation of Modern Art, one of those eye-blinker things by whatsisname, Escher, the ones that looked like puzzles where the shapes changed and a checkerboard tablecloth turned into black and white toads. Sam admitted to himself that, having no idea what was going on, he could not rule out the possibility that Dorrie had done something, well, unwise.

But if Dorrie had gotten herself mixed up in anything fishy, it would be because of her naïveté. Dorrie was an innocent.

If Dorrie had done something stupid, he'd stand by her.

First and foremost he had to ensure that she was okay.

Sam's LDS upbringing had made him function out of a bone-deep belief in rules, laws, and justice. He didn't know how not to be a law-abiding man. Now, as he reached for the bedside phone to call the police, he chewed his lower lip, hoping he was right to believe the system worked, praying that he was helping Dorrie, not hurting her.

With my mind made up—like a bed, I suppose, which I now had to lie upon—I got moving.

I found myself looking over my shoulder as I walked to the parking lot this time, and treading quietly, with my flashlight off. Meanwhile, I tried to think how to disable the van. What would my imaginary big, strong, kind Good Samaritan do?

What would Sam do?

Thinking of Sam, I felt a lonely longing for him wash over me. I wished he were here with me to help. . . . Wait. He was helping. I vaguely recalled that he had once told me a story about a high school prank involving a potato rammed up some vehicle's tailpipe.

Standing behind the driver's side of the van, away from the library, I began to fumble in my bag. Although I was hardly likely to find a potato in there, maybe I could improvise.

The best I could come up with was a plump Kleenex pack, brand-new.

I rolled it, compressing it as tightly as I could. Crouching in the shadow of the van, beside its left rear wheel, I groped for the tailpipe, then rammed my plug of tissue into it as hard as I could.

There.

I struggled to my feet to make my escape—

No. Not yet.

What I had done with the Kleenex did not feel adequate.

I doubted it would work. It seemed too simple. Maybe the potato story had been one of Sam's straight-faced jokes. He amused himself that way occasionally, telling me whoppers, knowing I was so gullible and serious-minded that I would believe almost anything.

I needed to be absolutely certain I'd put this van out of action.

I could loosen the bastard's hood latch, the way he had loosened mine. But—risk a crash in which Juliet might be hurt? No. Absolutely not.

My next, more sensible thought was to open the bastard's hood, yes, but then vandalize his engine. I'd never in my life so much as touched a car engine, but I felt sure I could yank out wires and hoses, maybe even unscrew nameless metal parts and fling them into the night.

At the thought I felt a dark, vengeful energy lending me strength. *Good. Do it.*

First I needed to pull the hood lever, which is usually located somewhere below and to the left of the steering wheel.

Flicking my flashlight on but keeping it down behind the van, I slipped a few silent steps forward to try the driver's-side door.

Locked.

Already having decided on a course of destruction, I did not hesitate. The flashlight with which Sam had equipped me was of studly masculine dimensions, with a heft to it. Flicking it off, I raised it, swung as if I were trying to kill a man-sized cockroach, and smashed the window glass.

BLAAT, blasted the van's horn, startling me so badly I squeaked. *BLAAT.* "Dammit!" Dumb, dumb, dumb, but the way the van looked junked, *BLAAT,* somehow I hadn't thought there would be a security system.

As if the noise had hit me a physical blow, almost falling, I staggered back.

From somewhere in the darkness behind the library, on the far side of the van from me, came a metallic kind of slam, as if from a garage door going down. Then I heard the crunch of footsteps on the gravel. Rapid, but heavy and hard. A man wearing boots. Running toward me.

Was it the kidnapper? He hadn't been wearing boots before.

But there was no time to dither about details. *BLAAT. BLAAT. BLAAT.* Ongoing.

Without knowing what I was doing, afraid to turn my back, I stumbled away until I bumped against the splintering plank fence.

Trapped.

There was nowhere to hide.

Except in the thick darkness and remnants of last year's weeds. Camouflaged only by my old brown car coat and the long skirt of my denim blue corduroy dress, I flattened myself on the ground beside the fence, behind the weeds. I froze like a supersized bunny just as the booted man dashed around the back of the van. Trying not to think about what kinds of insects, garbage, or other biting or stinky stuff might be there in the weeds with me, I lay completely still.

BLAAT, BLAAT, yet I found myself holding my breath to listen as the man scrabbled with his keys to get the van unlocked. Then the door clicked open and the dome light came on. I kept my head down, shamelessly praying he wouldn't see me, but I also kept my eyes open. Couldn't see much from my grass-roots angle, but I caught glimpses of motion as he reached inside the van to thrust a key into the ignition.

The noise stopped.

The silence felt almost more frightening than the clamor had been. I cringed. He could probably have heard my breathing if he had listened; I was panting now, and couldn't help it. Couldn't stop myself. But he didn't listen. He swore, I heard a glassy crash, and the dome light stopped shining. My breathing quieted. Darker felt better. I could still hear the booted man cursing the van, its horn, its dome light, its broken window, and whoever had inflicted that iniquity upon it—

He broke off.

Then said more softly but even more fervidly, "What the *hell*? That *can't* be the same goddamn Kia."

Yes, he was the kidnapper.

He stood rigidly staring away from me, silhouetted against the faint ambient light of Appletree. All I could tell about him for certain was that he had darkish hair, his appearance was consistent with that of the all-too-average man I'd seen at the Exxon, and he'd changed clothes. He wore what looked like an all-black outfit now, maybe to blend into the night.

Or maybe to look even scarier than he already was.

Peering toward the corner where the pay phone stood useless and my car likewise, he muttered, "I can't *believe* that fat interfering bitch!" With admirable control he shut the van door quietly, after which I could hear him sprinting toward the library.

Now was my chance to get away, but it was as if my body had taken a blow of some sort that my mind refused to acknowledge. Without understanding why, I felt weak, shaky, unsteady, and not just from the aches and fever of a severe lupus flare. If I tried to get up, I knew, I would struggle for balance, and I wouldn't be able to move fast enough.

I had to try anyway.

But wait. What about Juliet? Was running away to find a phone the best I could do to help her?

I had to help her.

I stayed where I was.

Once again I heard that noise, sounded like some kind of metal door, reverberate in the night.

Then I heard him coming back. The man in boots.

Along with someone else. Someone whose lighter footsteps dragged and scuffled in the gravel.

He ordered, "Get in."

His was a voice of such mastery, such command, such nearly hypnotic authority, that my whole body jerked, wanting to jump up and obey him. Even though he wasn't speaking to me.

I expected to hear the van door opening. Instead, I heard a girl say in gentle, reasonable tones, "But I don't want to."

I breathed out almost with a sob. It had to be Juliet. She was alive. My daughter was alive, at least. And oh, God, she had a sweet, soft alto voice. I'd been longing to hear her voice, but not like this. Not at midnight, in a lonely dark parking lot, in the company of a kidnapper.

He told her again, "Get *in*."

"Why don't you just let me go?" Except for a slight tremor, she was in perfect control of her voice. Just asking, her tone said, not whining, not defying. "What do you want me for? I'm not pretty. I—"

"Yes, you are. More than pretty. You're beautiful."

"No, my head's too small and my neck's too long. That's what they call me at school, Neck. Or Gooseneck. I'm not—"

"Shut up. You're beautiful. You're Candy." His voice didn't rise; rather it reverberated with a note of tent-revival hysteria. "You're the only kind of candy I like, and I've just started to taste you. You can't tell me you don't like the way I kiss."

"I hate it." Now her low tone held defiance. She had spirit. Good. My daughter was not passive, the way I had been at her age.

"You like it! You love it!"

"I hate it and I hate you."

"You are going to love it and you are going to *get in the van*." I heard a scrape of gravel as he shoved or dragged her toward the door. "You are going to do what I say and I am going to taste everything about you and you are never going to leave me. Nobody gets to leave me ever again. Never."

She whispered, "I'm not trying to leave you. I just want to go home and—"

"Nobody gets to take you away. You're coming with me. I am going to taste everything about you. Everything. Including your blood."

I heard a muffled scraping sound.

"Put the knife away. Please." Poor child, she couldn't control her voice anymore. It shook badly.

"Call her by name. Show respect, like I told you."

"Please put Pandora back in the sheath." She sounded close to tears.

"First you get in the van."

I heard the passenger's-side door open. Flattening myself as if I were the one being threatened, I heard her climb into the seat.

"Buckle yourself in. There. Now you're Candy. Now you're sweet, sweet Candy." Softer, his voice seemed even more compelling. "Don't you see, silly Candy girl? It will be perfect. Everything one step at a time."

I heard the kidnapper slam the passenger door. Heard his hard-booted footsteps crunch to the rear of the van. Heard him open it.

No, he wasn't a kidnapper. Time to face it: This had nothing to do with ransom money. It was about sexual perversion. He was an abductor.

And what he intended to do to Juliet—

But I couldn't yet face it all.

I lay in the benighted weeds hurting all over, feeling sick, sick, sick. Every part of me comprehended utterly. Except my mind.

There, in my brain, where it might have helped, I flatly refused to recognize, realize, know. Instead, I assured myself that "candy" was a common metaphor. The man's voice had been deep, probably too deep, nothing similar there except intensity. The writing on the library wall was recent, not left over from years ago.

Coincidence. Odd coincidences did happen.

Some kind of weed I was lying in smelled so foul I wanted to vomit. Fighting down my gag reflex and the noise it would make, I heard the abductor's footsteps taking their time to the driver's door, then the click as it opened. A rhythmic chugging sound began. What the—

Air pump. I'd forgotten about the flat tires.

I had a little time to do something.

Now that there was ambient noise to cover any sound I might make, I no longer felt so queasy. I eased my head up for a look, and sure enough, I could make out a sort of mound in the gloom. Him, hunkered over his left front tire with his back to me, operating one of those tire pumps that plug into the cigarette lighter, very similar to the one I'd used to tie down my hood. Audible, but not noisy. Not loud enough to wake up the neighbors and make them call the cops.

But maybe loud enough so that he wouldn't hear me if I moved.

Do something, Dorrie!

But I felt as if I couldn't get up off the ground. Shaky hungry. Dead tired. Flattened. Sick at heart. Black T-shirt, black jeans, black combat boots, like someone I used to know—

Don't think. Act.

The tire pump quit. I felt so far gone that even the sudden silence didn't scare me, didn't make me flex a muscle. Dully I listened—okay, he was moving to the rear tire. Pump noise started up again.

Next he'd move around to Juliet's side, and—

Juliet.

My daughter.

Tired crying self be damned. I had to save Juliet. Nothing else mattered.

Had to do something *now*. This minute. While his back was to me. Before he moved on.

Staggering to my feet, I stood swaying for a moment as I focused on the vague form, a darker thing in the darkness, of the man crouching by the van's rear tire. I located the back of his head and concentrated on it. I put one foot forward, then the other. Advancing. Didn't need to try to sneak up on him. He couldn't hear me, didn't turn to see me. I wobbled up behind him, hefted my flashlight, and clubbed him as hard as I could, right at the base of his skull, just like the tough guys did on TV.

It worked. He slumped to the gravel.

I screamed over the noise of the air pump, "Juliet, *run!*"

Opening the front door, Sam said reluctantly, "Um, come on in." He hadn't expected the police would want to be so thorough. He'd thought he would just explain that his wife was missing and he had reason to believe there was a connection to the Phillips case, he'd give a description of Dorrie's car, and hi-ho Silver, a posse would form.

But they had sent someone to his house to take a report, a uniformed officer who, to Sam's tired surprise, was a skinny black girl—okay, young woman, but her soft caramel-colored face looked about sixteen years old, and her police tunic and slacks seemed too big for her. Stepping into his living room, she scanned slowly almost full circle, as if her head were a video cam recording the place, and he felt a disconcerting sense of keen intelligence at work. She wasn't just gawking. She would remember details of what she saw, and they would have meaning for her.

"Kittens with butterfly wings?" she inquired of some of Dorrie's more unusual statuettes.

"Um, yes, they're Flutterkitties."

The officer carefully picked one up, looked at the bottom, and set it down again. "Signed originals. She knows the artist?"

"Just online." Feeling an irrational need to apologize for signed originals, which implied a level of wealth and culture to which he did not aspire, Sam said, "It's her only hobby. Collecting art."

The policewoman took her time checking out Dorrie's display of winged horses—clay, carved wood, ceramic, glass—then moved on to the fireplace mantelpiece, home to another collection of porcelain bells upon which perched realistically painted songbirds by way of handles. Gently she lifted one of the bells and tried it out; the tinkling sound of its porcelain clapper could not have been more musical. The officer put the bell back exactly where it belonged. "She has good taste. No kitsch."

"I met Dorrie in art class at college." Sam's throat tightened. He didn't quite know where that had come from. He had meant to say that Dorrie had minored in art history.

"She likes the, um, is it Impressionists?" The young woman had stopped in front a Redon print of winged horses pulling a sun chariot.

"I'm not sure." Dorrie's art collection took up most of the wall space, but somehow did not make the house feel like a museum, Sam thought with dawning appreciation of his wife's skill as a homemaker; it coexisted comfortably with soft moss green sofas, fern-print drapes, lightweight golden oak tables.

"*Angel*, by Moreau," the unlikely cop murmured, pausing in front of another print. "Symbolist?"

"You'd have to ask Dorrie." Pride in his wife combined oddly with Sam's painful worry.

"She's partial to subjects with wings."

"Yes. Anything with wings. Except airplanes."

"I guess maybe airplanes are a guy thing. When women dream of just flying away, it's more organic."

If the young cop had pulled her gun on him, it could not have startled and discomfited Sam much worse. Too loudly he said, "Dorrie didn't run away!"

The young woman swiveled to stare at him with wide loam-colored eyes. "I didn't mean to imply that she did, Mr. White. It's not at all unusual for women to dream of a fairy-tale kind of freedom. I'm sorry if—"

"Look, miss, I just want to find my wife."

"My name is Officer Chappell. Sorry, I should have introduced myself when I came in. What was it you wanted to show me?"

Sam took a deep breath, pressed his lips together, and led the way upstairs to the bedroom. Flicking on the light, he said wearily, "In here." He had thought they would be done before now. He bet Officer Chappell was a rookie, the way she wanted to go over everything one step at a time in slow motion, or so it seemed to Sam. Indicating a location on the box spring of the disheveled bed, he told her, "I found it here." He picked up the pink folder from a bedside table and handed it to her.

Officer Chappell paged through it in complete silence, then tucked it under her arm and made a note on her spiral-bound stenographic pad. "How long has this been going on?"

"I don't know."

"Does your wife have a PC?"

"Laptop."

"If that's what she used, I can find a history on it."

What this had to do with finding Dorrie Sam could not imagine, but he said, "She keeps it in her sewing room." Sam started to show the way out, but the young cop did not come with him. She was swiveling her head again, running her mental camcorder all around the bedroom. Her scanning eyes caught on the squares of notebook paper lying on the mattress and the floor like overlarge confetti. "Were those papers hidden under the mattress too?"

"Yes, but they don't have anything to do with—"

"May I see them, please?"

Reluctantly Sam picked up a few of Dorrie's high school flame's love letters and handed them to Officer Chappell.

Scanning them, the young black woman murmured, "Bubba! Hold the phone."

Trying not to show his annoyance—okay, his jealousy of the letters his wife had kept under the mattress—Sam repeated, "Those don't have anything to do with, um, with anything."

Officer Chappell said, "I hope not. Whoever wrote these is a very unstable, potentially violent individual."

Having seen nothing but sweetness and sexual heat in the content of the notes, Sam blinked. "Where do you get that from?"

"Very revealing handwriting." The young woman appeared unflinchingly serious. She believed in handwriting analysis? Sam restrained an impulse to roll his eyes.

"Even though the subject uses printing instead of cursive, because printing reveals less," she elaborated. "But still, any individual who prints this large has to be egotistic, if not a megalomaniac. And look at the way he ignores the lines, like saying rules don't apply to him. No margins for this guy. He squeezes words to the very edge. No foresight, no impulse control. But what's really concerning—"

Sam interrupted, "Officer, um, Chappell, does this have anything to do with finding my wife?"

"I'll put out a BOLO on your wife and her vehicle right away." Slipping the squares of notebook paper into the pink folder under her arm, the police officer stood with pen and steno pad poised. "Make, model, color, license?"

Sam recited the information. Probably Dorrie didn't know her own license plate number, but he did. He reeled it off.

"Do you know what your wife was wearing?"

"Um, almost certainly a dress like one of those in the closet."

"Description of your wife?"

"Um, she has beautiful eyes—"

"Height? Weight? Identifying marks or scars?"

Sam sighed. "Five foot five, about a hundred ninety pounds. She has what they call a malar or butterfly rash on her face."

"I beg your pardon?"

"Butterfly rash. They call it that because it makes a pattern kind of like butterfly wings on her face. She has lupus. She had to take steroids, and they gave her puffy cheeks. And fatty deposits on her midsection."

"Lupus?"

And so on. Eventually the young policewoman put her notes away and inquired again about Dorrie's computer. When Sam led her to it, she immediately packed it into its case, included the squares of notebook paper and the pink folder, and asked in a perfunctory way, "May I take these with me?"

Now all of a sudden things were moving too fast, and Sam found himself wishing Officer Chappell would revert to her earlier plodding pace. He felt his voice rise as he said, "Those are private things of Dorrie's. I'd rather you didn't."

The young woman replied with an earnest look, "I think they're important. If I have to get a warrant and return for them, it will waste time I could spend trying to find your wife."

Having been raised never to swear left Sam with very little recourse to vent his feelings. Not trusting himself to speak, he raised his hands in a frustrated gesture that the rookie policewoman rightly interpreted as capitulation.

"I'll get on this right away." Swinging the computer case the way an excited child swung a book bag, she added, "One more thing. Could I have a recent photograph of your wife?"

"Um . . ."

Officer Chappell stared at him, puzzled, as if it should have been the easiest thing in the world for him to produce a photo of Dorrie.

"Um, I guess she's kind of camera shy," Sam said slowly, trying to explain to her as well as to himself why there weren't any recent photos of Dorrie in the house. "And we aren't the kind to go snapping away with cell phones." Neither of them had a cell phone that did anything except phone. "I might be able to get a photo of her from somebody else."

"Please do. As soon as possible." After frowning at him for a moment, either in thought or disapproval, Officer Chappell ran downstairs and out the door.

Sam flicked off the upstairs lights, descended the stairs more slowly, sat on the edge of the sofa, and cradled his head in his hands for a moment before reaching for the phone.

SIX

"Run!" I screamed again. "Juliet, *run*! Get away!"

She'd flung the van door open but seemed to be struggling to get out of her seat.

Flicking my flashlight on, I hustled around there to see what was the problem.

At my first sight of her sweating, straining face, her frightened eyes . . . But there was no time for anything I was feeling.

"He's got the seat belt rigged to lock." Like a wounded deer she looked up at me, hair coming undone and hanging in her face, the whites of her eyes flashing. "I can't get out."

"Oh, God . . ." I handed her the flashlight, groped for my purse, and yes, it was still there hanging from my arm; it had come along with me like an appendage of an appendage. I ripped it open and started rooting like a bear, hoping for something, anything, a nail file maybe, that could cut through a seat belt. Wallet, tube of sunscreen, address book, appointment book, checkbook, Tylenol, paste foundation to tone down the rash on my face, lupus meds, ballpoint pens, coupon folder, roll of Tums, loose change—why did I have to be so asininely afraid of knives that I kept "losing" the cute little penknives Sam kept giving me? Damn, there had to be *something*—

Silence fell like a guillotine as the tire pump stopped.

And in the silence I could hear someone moving on the other side of the van. Him.

Boots scuffed in gravel. Through the windows of the van I saw him struggling to his feet. I'd hit him as hard as I could, but it hadn't been hard enough.

"You go," Juliet whispered to me frantically. "Go, run, hurry, get help."

I shook my head. "No way am I leaving you." I took the flashlight back and wrenched open the sliding side door of the van, looking for the heavy wooden cane with which the abductor had clubbed Juliet over the head, but I saw no sign of it.

Footsteps crunched toward me.

I heaved myself into the van.

Lurching onto the rear seat, I didn't stop there; it would be too easy for him to reach in and dislodge me. I slid on over, then down, to the floor, stuffing my large self sideward behind the driver's seat, with my back against the van's wall. I turned the flashlight off and hid it behind my butt. Darkness would be better; I did not want him to see me trembling.

Nor did I want to see him. Ever. Never again. Quivering, I folded my arms over my purse, clutching it to my heart like a shield.

I looked up.

He stood, a shadowy presence, at the van's side door, the wicked sheen of a knife in his hand. All I could see was that blade hovering bright in the darkness like a Cheshire cat's grin. Every detail. Shining steel, maybe eight inches, honed to a razor edge on its curved side. The groove defining its gray spine—not just a pocketknife's fingernail groove; this was a blood groove. Evil, that blade, meant to stab, slash, kill. Even the edge that did not cut, its back, seemed wicked and evil, concave to give a stiletto point to the tip.

The sight of that knife froze me in nightmare terror. In that moment I comprehended, irrationally but right to the marrow of my bones, that I wasn't merely frightened of knives in general; I was terrified of *that* knife.

But . . . but I'd never seen such a knife before.

Had I?

A queasy sense of déjà vu squirmed in my gut. It had to do with—the dark form behind the knife, the man; thank God I couldn't see his face, only the nasty curves of that knife and the sinewy hand and arm that wielded it.

I thought I saw him shifting slightly, as if he was swaying, maybe a bit dazed by my blow. Then—he still had the tire pump gadget, remember, complete with light? He flicked on the light and shone it straight at me, making me blink as well as shake.

With harsh force he demanded, "Who the hell are you?"

He didn't know me.

Relief lifted my heart. This man, this pervert, this abductor, was a stranger to me.

Unless . . . he just didn't recognize me. . . .

Stop it, Dorrie. Let it be.

Just the same . . . Years ago, my voice had been soft, like Juliet's. Now I made myself use the forceful voice I'd learned from teaching school. Yet at the same time I knew I'd better be very careful what I said. I badly wanted to tell him I was the fat, interfering bitch in the Kia, but instead I answered, "I am worried about this girl."

"You fat, interfering bitch." He said it for me. Without looking at Juliet, he slammed her door closed, hand swinging as if he had slapped her across the face, while he cursed at me. "You ugly slut. Get out of my van."

The power of command in his voice was strong enough to

make my whole body isometrically strain to levitate off his floor. Luckily, I was tired. Very, very tired. And inertia had taken hold. I didn't move.

"No." Then, because I'd heard someplace that offense is the best defense, I accused, "You tried to kill me."

"I still can." Raising his knife, the shadowed man took a threatening step toward me—threatening, but unsteady, presumably from his having been conked on the head. I felt chillingly convinced that otherwise he would have cut my throat right then and there.

He ordered, "Out. Now. Get out of my van." He put venom into his commanding voice, and teeth.

I hugged my purse tighter against my chest. "No."

"Stupid bitch, are you *crazy?*"

With what I hoped was matronly dignity I declared, "I would hope that if someone saw *my* daughter being abducted from the parking lot of a shopping mall, she would try to do something about it."

He stood there, maybe thinking, maybe realizing that he didn't really want me out of his van or I'd go straight to the police. Maybe pondering what use he could make of me, or deciding how best to get rid of me. I couldn't see his face, so I had no idea what was going on in his mind. He could see me clearly, but still, I hoped he had no idea what was going on in mine.

Gesturing with the knife, he told me very softly, "Fine. Stay and go to hell. I'll kill you too." With a *wham* that made me wince, he slammed the van's sliding door.

Juliet turned in her seat to stare at me wide-eyed.

I told her the first, utterly inane, very likely untrue thing that came to my mind: "It's going to be all right."

She didn't answer.

My eyes had gotten so thoroughly accustomed to the dark that I could see her hugging her bare shoulders with her hands and shivering, colder than ever now in her skimpy little top. Chilled by fear, I thought. But she looked not quite as panicked as a few moments before. The gallows look in her face was gone now that somebody, a Mom type, had joined her in the van.

God help us, I *had* to save her.

I leaned forward and started struggling out of my car coat. Our eyes met at closer range. Our gazes locked and communicated, each of us saying wordlessly to the other: *We're in this together. Maybe we can get out of this together. Be strong. Be smart. There's no time for us to cry, vent, chitchat. Whatever we say to each other must be important and He must not hear us.*

That was how I conceptualized our captor. He. Him. Like a deity. A being with the power of life and death over us.

The chugging of the air pump began. Instantly Juliet asked me, "Are you with the police?"

"No."

Her dark eyebrows arched. "Who *are* you, then? Where did you come from?"

Oh, God, my heart yearned and burned to tell her, *I'm your mother, you're my daughter,* but a melodramatic revelation was the last thing she needed right now. I wanted to help her, not shock her silly. I babbled, "Me, um, I'm nobody."

"But you know my name!"

Having already mentioned an imaginary daughter, I invoked her again. "My daughter goes to school with you."

"Who is it? What's *your* name?"

I hesitated, and tried to cover my hesitation by dragging my car coat out from behind my back. I didn't want to tell her a false name to which I might fail to respond if she called. Yet

I didn't want to tell her my real name because I didn't want Him to find it out. Instead of answering her question, I tossed my coat to her. "Put that over you."

"Thanks." She snuggled under the coat, which was quite large enough to serve as a blanket for her upper body.

Sitting back with my arms crossed over my purse, I realized that all He had to do to identify me was take it from me, look at my driver's license, and then He would know where I lived. Hastily I shoved the purse behind me along with the flashlight. I shuddered.

Juliet was watching me. "Are you all right?"

"I'm fine. My blubber keeps me warm."

"No, I mean like, seriously, when he had the light on you, you looked, um, infected. I mean, feverish." Nice girl. Tactful, didn't want to mention the rash growing like red mold all over my face. And concerned; she'd put aside her unanswered questions, focusing on me. "Do you have, like, measles or something?"

"Or something."

Silence—He was moving the air pump to the last tire. With a glance that cautioned me to secrecy, Juliet squirmed, reached into her jeans pocket, and handed me a fistful of candies. She gave me an inquiring look; will those help? I nodded back; yes, thank you. Yes, I needed to eat something, even if it was only a hard candy. I unwrapped one and stuck it in my mouth.

Cherry flavor.

I felt the taste run through me like a physical memory, one that made me feel sick. But cherry candy—so what? I told myself. The symbolism of the cherry was universal among predatory males, although when I had been Juliet's age, I hadn't been aware of it. And I hoped she wasn't either.

Maybe He hadn't even given her the candies. Maybe she'd bought them at the mall.

Don't ask.

The air pump started up again. At once Juliet asked, "You really followed me all the way from the mall? Did you call the police?"

"Yes, and yes, but I didn't have the license number."

"It doesn't matter. He has different license plates he sticks on with magnets."

This guy—He—had stalking and abduction down to a science, evidently. "How does He unlock that seat belt?"

"I don't know. He must have a control somewhere but I can't figure out where."

Lord. How many girls had He snatched, molested, raped, then—

Don't go there.

I asked Juliet, "Could you lean your seat back and slip out from under it that way?"

The way she shook her head told me she'd already tried. "I'm strapped in like this is the electric chair," she said. "Why are you sitting on the floor?"

"Partly to be difficult and partly to hide your little blue flasher light."

Her eyes widened. "I forgot all about it! Where is it?"

"Under the—"

Silence silenced us. Juliet turned around to face front, pulling my jacket tight around her shoulders. I heard Him open the van's rear door and toss the air pump in. Heard Him smack a license plate into place. Heard the door slam. Next moment the driver's-side door opened.

"You in back," He ordered as He climbed in, "get your fat ugly ass off the floor and sit where I can see you."

Struggling to obey, I slipped one hand under the driver's seat and palmed a small cylinder lying there.

"In the middle of the back," He commanded, and I meekly positioned myself behind the rearview mirror. From there I scanned the front, noticing a lumpy square of black tape stuck to the dash. Oh, my gosh. Electrician's tape, hiding the little red light that flashed when His security system was turned on. A clever wad of slime He was.

He slammed His door closed. Swiveling in His seat so that He approximately faced me, He thrust His knife toward my face. He told me, "This is Pandora."

Fixated on that blade, a chill silver flame in the gloom, I couldn't move or speak.

He commanded, "Say it."

I whispered, "Pandora."

"Right. Pandora goes wherever I go. Pandora is the queen of all castrating bitches. You stay where you are and don't move or Pandora will slit your fricking throat."

No seat belt? No need. The tone of complete conviction in His threat froze me in place. You couldn't have moved me with a forklift.

He stuck the knife into a sheath He wore at His belt. I heard a jangle of keys. Jamming one into the ignition, starting the van, He ordered Juliet, "Take that thing off you."

"But I'm cold." She used a quiet, reasonable tone.

"Oh, my poor Candy," He said with such melting compassion that for that moment I could have sworn He was a Hallmark made-for-TV movie hero. "Poor darling, you're cold." His voice purred along with the well-tuned motor of the van; I heard in it not a hint of anything except heartfelt sympathy. "But I'll soon get you all warmed up again, sweet, sweet Candy—"

"My name is not Candy," she interrupted with a hint of edge. I stiffened, silently begging her, *Be careful.*

He said just as tenderly, "Of course not, sweetheart. You're Juliet."

How did He know her name? From ID she carried on her, maybe? Or had He coerced her to tell Him?

"And I'm Romeo. We're fated to die together."

I froze, feeling as if an icicle had shot up my spine.

His voice took on the prophetic fervor of certainty. "But in the cosmic sense you're all Candies, all you sweet girls who look like her. You especially. You look more like her than any of the other ones did. You look *just* like her, sweet Candy." As if operated by a toggle switch His tone flipped to brutal. "I want to look at you. Take that thing off."

"All right," she said, but then she added, "In a minute. Let me get warm first."

"I said take it off!" He reached over to rip it away from her. She hung on as if my old brown coat were part of her now. Trying to get that coat from her was like trying to skin an armadillo. He couldn't rip it off one-handed. He would have had to get out of the driver's seat and out of the van and go around to her side to wrestle it away from her. I sat up straight, hoping He would be stupid enough to do just that. I would grab the seat, the wheel, the keys—

"Goddamn tight-ass slut! Take it off!" He tried to hit Juliet in the face. She jerked sideward away from Him, and His knuckles angled off her cheek.

She said quite calmly, "No."

Oh, God, if He drew that knife—

But He cursed her briefly, then put the van in gear. He said, "You know it's coming off once we get out of here." A pit bull could not have sounded more threatening. He backed up to turn the van around and drove out of the parking lot.

• • •

Sam tried phoning his in-laws one more time.

"What do you mean calling so late, Sam?" the old man complained. "We were sleeping."

Only manners drilled in bone deep kept Sam from demanding how they could go to sleep when their daughter was missing. Instead, he blurted like a child, "Dorrie's still not back."

"Not where she belongs? Then she's gone to the devil again. We'll pray for her. Good night."

"No, wait! Don't hang up." Sam took a deep breath and tried to speak calmly. "Do you happen to have a recent photograph of her?" He knew the chances were remote. His in-laws, who felt to him more like out-laws, were no more camera-prone than he was.

"No reason why we should," Father Birch said. "After what she brought upon herself, we did our duty for her and not a bit more. Good—"

"Don't hang up! Please, I don't understand. Why do you say such things about Dorrie? What has she ever done that is so unforgivable?"

Silence except for the whispering of the telephone wire.

Sam tried again. "Father Birch, I really, really need to know. What happened in Appletree?"

"We don't talk about that." The old man's tone sounded frostily final. "Not to anyone. Now, I want to get some sleep. Good—"

Sam demanded, "Did it have anything to do with Don Phillips? The district attorney?"

"I told you, we don't talk about it!" The old man slammed the phone down. Sam stood for a moment listening to the whispers in the phone line and in his mind.

"Huh," he muttered, replacing the receiver quite gently in its cradle.

After a moment's thought, he picked up the phone again and called Pastor Lewinski.

He answered on the second ring, "Hello, can I help you?" as cordially as if he had not just been awakened from righteous slumber.

"It's Sam White again," Sam said perhaps unnecessarily, but then again, perhaps the bedroom phone was old and lacked caller ID.

Lewinski didn't miss a beat. "Dorrie's still not home?"

"No. I managed to get the police to take an interest, and they want a recent photo of her, but I, um, I don't have any." Sam was going to explain how Dorrie treated cameras on a duck-and-cover basis, but apparently Lewinski needed no explanation.

"We'll find one," he declared. "Meet me at the church office, okay?"

"Um, okay." Sam hung up, feeling a bit dazed. He was used to telling his employees what to do, unaccustomed to being a follower, but he needed leadership right now, and he accepted it.

Habitually thrifty, Sam started to turn off the lights before leaving, but then he changed his mind and kept them all on, just about every light in the house, sending up a mute prayer for Dorrie to come home.

Backing the pickup out of the driveway, Sam acknowledged himself to be tired. Very tired and upset. He hadn't been this upset in many years, since the day his sister had taken a bad fall off a horse and everybody had thought she was going to be paralyzed. Now she was fine, of course, and living in Paris, France. Happy ending. With that in mind, Sam ordered him-

self to pay conscious attention to his driving. It wouldn't help
Dorrie any if he got in an accident.

He took the short drive slowly to find that Pastor Lewinski
had reached the church before him. The light through the office windows felt like a warm embrace to Sam, making him
fervidly hope Lewinski wouldn't actually try to hug him; Sam
felt afraid he might break down, embarrassing himself.

Being on emotional edge prevented him from saying anything as he walked in. Even if he could have talked about what
was on his mind, it would have been no use to ask Lewinski
whether he knew what had happened to Dorrie and her parents
in Appletree; the pastor didn't go back that far. He'd come to
this pulpit a few years ago straight out of seminary. Sitting at
the computer in his pajamas and slippers, his red hair wildly
disheveled, bringing up a screen of photos, Lewinski looked
like a teenager. To Sam's relief, he didn't even glance up, just
waved, then gestured toward a nearby chair. "I'm trying the
most recent covered-dish supper first," he said, intent on Pho-
toshop, "and right there with you in the food line, confronted
by a dozen kinds of macaroni and cheese, is your lovely wife.
Now if I can just get her facing the camera . . . okay, there's
one. There's another."

As Sam watched with more anxiety than interest, Lewinski
clicked the mouse on several photos, selected "Edit" from a
menu, then started cropping and enlarging the modified images until several reasonably helpful photos of Dorrie emerged,
some of just her face but some also showing her distinctive
figure and dress style. In none of them was she aware of the
camera. Most of them caught her either talking or eating. To
Sam she looked wonderful in all of them.

As Lewinski printed them out on card stock, he ventured,
"I suppose you spoke with Dorrie's parents."

"Yes," said Sam, at the same time shaking his head as if he hadn't. Or wished he hadn't. He blurted, "They complained because I called after bedtime and woke them up."

"Ow. Ouch," said the pastor softly. "Really?"

"Yes, really. When their daughter is missing. I—I don't understand them."

"Neither do I," admitted Lewinski, handing Sam the improvised photos and waving his thanks away. "Usually I can manage insight into people whether they're pleasant or not, but—this has to stay between you and me, Sam—Dorrie's parents baffle me."

The earnest young man made Sam smile despite the weight on his heart. "That makes two of us. Maybe three, counting Dorrie."

"I hope you find her soon. Sam, do you want me to pray with you?"

Sam definitely did not. "I know you mean well, Pastor, but—"

"Not a problem. I want to help, not intrude. Would you like me to come with you to the police station?"

Sam's smile widened a little. "Pastor, I like your pajamas." They were tropical blue with little white sailboats all over them. "Did someone give them to you?"

"Yes. My mother." Pastor Lewinski returned Sam's smile ruefully, accepting the unspoken hint that he'd better go home and go back to bed. He and Sam shook hands.

"I can't thank you enough." Sam felt himself choking up just because someone was willing to help him.

"Not a big deal. Please call me if you need me or just want to talk. Anytime, night or day." He shook Sam's hand again and let him go.

Walking to his Silverado alone, photos of Dorrie in hand,

Sam assumed at first that he was on his way to the police station. Then he thought of what might be a better plan.

Sam White did not like to jump into things. Settling into the driver's seat, he gave his mind a minute to change. It didn't. His second thoughts remained the same as his first.

"Okay," he said aloud as he revved the pickup. "I know who else isn't sleeping tonight."

It might have been more courteous to make the initial contact via telephone, but Sam decided against it. From his experience of the past several hours he could imagine how the Phillipses felt every time the phone rang, and he didn't want to add to their misery. Anyway, this can of worms, snakes, anacondas, whatever it might turn out to be, required face-to-face. He didn't know the exact address, but figured that once he reached the neighborhood, it wouldn't be hard to find. Just look for cop cars.

Again, Sam reminded himself that he was tired and distraught and needed to drive carefully.

Several cautious moments later, steering his truck into Plover Heights, Sam realized truly how badly he was functioning. If he'd been able to think, he'd have remembered that Plover Heights (actually neither higher nor lower than anywhere else in Fulcrum) was one of those gated communities. Now, facing the man at the guardhouse, he felt dumb, inane, desperate just for being there at this uncivilized hour.

Habitual politeness kept his voice level. "I need to visit the Phillips residence."

The guard's nonexpression hardened slightly. "They are accepting no visitors."

"But it's important. It might have something to do with the disappearance of their daughter."

The man frankly scowled. "Your name?"

"Sam White."

So the Phillipses ended up getting a phone call anyway, while Sam waited at the gate.

It took quite a while, and he did not even think to turn off the truck to save gas. It was still idling when a police cruiser appeared out of Plover Heights and pulled up nose to nose with him. A cop got out, the same skinny baby-faced black police-woman he'd spoken with earlier—what was her name? Officer Chappell.

She looked at him through the windshield, nodded, and came around to his window to talk with him. "They sent me to verify your identity," she explained. "You'd be amazed what news reporters will say trying to get in. Why don't you park here and come with me."

He handed over the computer-printout photographs of Dorrie first. Officer Chappell accepted them as if it was only natural that he should be able to procure pictures of his wife. Somehow her attitude seemed surreal.

Everything felt surreal. Sitting in the back of Officer Chappell's cruiser, Sam felt his sense of reality bowing under the weight of recent events. He knew he wasn't a criminal, but he felt he had been captured and taken for a ride and he didn't know where he was going. Trying to remember that this visit was his idea, he asked Officer Chappell, "Do you have that pink book with you?"

"Yes. I mean, it's at the Phillips residence."

"You showed it to them?"

"Yes."

"And?" Sam leaned forward, trying to get a glimpse of the young woman's face.

No answer. Quietly the cruiser slipped between large homes set on large lots with much landscaping and security lighting.

Sam spelled it out. "What did they say? Do they know of some connection between their daughter and my wife?"

"I can't divulge that, sir." The baby-faced policewoman pulled the cruiser to the side of the street, stopped there, and shut down the engine. "Perhaps they'd care to tell you themselves. I don't know." She got out of the car.

Sam followed, at first not understanding; why hadn't they parked in a driveway? Oh. Because there was no room for another car. The Phillips house would be the one with the U-shaped drive packed with Beemers and Mercedes-Benzes and police cruisers.

Sam tried not to contrast this scene too resentfully with his own empty driveway. His missing wife was an adult who might have gone someplace of her own free will, whereas the district attorney's missing daughter was a minor who had been reported abducted, her vehicle left behind in the mall parking lot. Naturally more attention was being paid to her case.

Lights blazed outdoors and inside, beating back the night. Sam walked as if in daylight under a portico to the front door, automatically observing its bevel glass inserts, its fanlight, noting that the Phillipses' money had been invested not just in real estate but in elegance. His escort did not knock or ring a doorbell, but simply opened the door and walked in. Sam followed, realizing that he was expected.

Very much so. Every head turned as he followed the young policewoman into a large family room; Sam felt multiple stares upon him. Trying not to stare back, he glimpsed several kinds of uniformed authorities, and some men and women who might be servants, and others who might be family members on standby.

Again, Sam tried not to compare this scene with his own empty living room. If he had called his parents, they would be on their way this minute, rushing from Colorado to be with him. It was his own doing that he had decided not to call them until morning, to let them sleep. Lord willing, Dorrie would come home before—

Hope hurt almost worse than doubt. Sam quashed the thought and made himself focus on the people he had driven over here to talk with. They were not hard to spot: a middle-aged couple sitting close together on a camelback sofa. Sam recognized the man's face from news photos. And he recognized the pink scrapbook lying open in the woman's lap.

Sam strode over to them. The man, Don Phillips, stood up and extended his hand, scanning Sam with a quiet, serious look. *Giving me the once-over,* Sam thought, making his own assessment of the other while they shook hands. He liked this man's firm grip and steady eyes. The district attorney was making him feel as if they were colleagues in a very serious case. Which, in a way, they were.

"I'm Don Phillips," the big man introduced himself humbly but unnecessarily, "and this is my wife, Pearl."

Sam turned to Mrs. Phillips and offered his hand. But instead of shaking it, she reached up from where she sat and clasped his hand in both of hers. Sam saw tears in her eyes.

"This was made with love," she said, releasing his hand to gesture at the pink scrapbook in her lap. "It was put together with so much love and care. If my daughter is with your wife, she's in very loving hands. I feel absolutely certain of that."

It took Sam's breath away, the way the woman spoke straight to the emotional heart of the matter, brushing aside preliminaries and practicalities. Dorrie did that sometimes, and it always had the same effect on him. He stood speechless.

"Mr. White, won't you sit down?" Pearl Phillips's voice, heavily burdened, nevertheless held steady. "Would you like a cup of coffee?"

Sam had never drunk coffee in his life. Having been raised Church of Latter-Day Saints, he still avoided caffeine in any form. But he heard himself saying, "Yes, thank you. I'd like that very much."

Some woman behind him said, "I'll get it."

"Thank you. Mr. White, please make yourself comfortable."

These people had manners the way he did, the way some people had bad habits. Sam sat in a wingback chair facing Don Phillips, who had resumed his seat close beside his wife. Glancing at the book in Pearl Phillips's lap, Sam suddenly knew. He just knew.

He knew what shameful secret had happened in Appletree.

But Sam seldom if ever spoke on impulse. Success required caution before courage. Sam asked, "Could I take another look at that?"

Pearl passed him the Juliet book with both hands, as if putting a baby into his arms. Sam opened the scrapbook again to the most recent photo of Juliet Phillips.

Once again it was as if a young Dorrie, younger even than the Dorrie he remembered from college, smiled at him from the flowered pastel page.

This girl was Dorrie's daughter. Had to be. Sam knew it the way he knew floor under his feet.

Not that he didn't feel floor, earth, et cetera, quaking a bit, having had no idea Dorrie had ever borne a child. He barely heard a woman's voice asking him something. Repeating. A question, whether he wanted cream and sugar in his coffee, and never having drunk coffee, he didn't know the answer. He couldn't think what to say.

He looked up to find Pearl holding his coffee. He said, "Thank you," took it carefully by the saucer, lifted the cup to his mouth, and drank. The dark stuff was unpleasantly hot and tasted bitter. Like medicine. Sam couldn't imagine how anyone enjoyed drinking this stuff, yet he swallowed it down, almost emptying the cup before he set it aside and looked at Don and Pearl Phillips.

Both watching him. But also, he thought, to some extent watching over him. In them Sam sensed both caution and sympathy.

Sam said, "Dorrie never told me she had a baby."

Pearl said earnestly, "We're very grateful to her for giving us Juliet. Or not giving *us*, exactly, because she didn't know us—"

"And she wasn't ever supposed to know," Don Phillips interrupted with some edge. "Mr. and Mrs. Birch were supposed to tell her the baby had been put up for adoption. Period."

"She was very young," Pearl murmured. "The mother, I mean. Dorrie."

"We assumed she'd go off to college the way most kids do, marry some guy from California or someplace, move out of state." Now Don Phillips spoke softly, as if others in the room—family, servants, police standing by to trace telephone calls—were not supposed to hear. "We never figured she'd end up living right here in Fulcrum."

Struggling with an increasing sense of unreality, his comprehension lagging, Sam said nothing.

Don Phillips asked him, "Do you know how she found out?"

Sam shook his head.

"Or when? How long ago? Did her behavior change?"

Sam cleared his throat, then said rather hoarsely, "You think she took off with your daughter."

"The police are checking out that possibility, yes."

Sam clutched the arms of his chair. He just barely managed to keep from lunging to his feet, or shouting, or otherwise reacting on impulse. Instead he shook his head. "No," he said almost calmly as he kept shaking his head no, no, no. "No, Dorrie wouldn't do that."

"We're not accusing her." Pearl Phillips reached toward him. "We have every sympathy for her."

"Thank you. But you don't know her. Dorrie is a churchgoing, law-abiding, good . . ." Good woman who had a secret past? Sam fell silent, wondering how well he himself knew his wife.

"Sam, we just want Juliet back," Pearl Phillips said, her soft voice clotted with emotion. "We won't care who did what—"

Sam interrupted. "You're wrong about Dorrie."

"I'm just going with a gut feeling," Don Phillips said, leaning toward him, "and my feeling is, you and us, we're in this together." The guy was starting to sound like a politician. "You just want your wife back, and we just want our daughter back safe and unharmed—"

"Dorrie would never hurt anyone!" Realizing that he was beginning to yell, Sam stood up. "I'd better leave."

"No, please." Don Phillips stood also, with a hand out to stop him. "I understand how you feel, but—"

Someone tapped Sam on the elbow. He turned.

There stood the baby-faced black policewoman. "Word just came in on your wife's car, sir," the young officer blurted with unprofessional excitement. "A caller reports the Kia apparently abandoned in a damaged condition. The odd circumstance—"

"Where?" Sam demanded.

"On the sidewalk, sir, not the street, that's what's peculiar—"

"Where!" Sam nearly shouted. "Fulcrum?"

"Oh. No, sir. Quite a ways from here, actually. Little town called Appletree."

SEVEN

Sitting on the backseat of the van, I sucked another cherry candy, feeling ill, while I clutched Juliet's little blue blinking doodad in one hand to hide it from the man—Him, the one I could scarcely bear to think about—in the driver's seat. To avoid looking at Him, I studied the side of Juliet's head. My beautiful daughter. He'd hit her on the cheek. I didn't see a bruise. If she ever got lupus, she'd bruise easily.

I hoped she'd never get lupus.

I hoped she'd live long enough to never get lupus.

He had *hit* her. And He planned to do worse than that to her. To both of us.

He and Pandora.

Shifting the van into first gear, He began to turn it around.

Simultaneously, as if we had just sashayed into an automotive square dance, around a corner and onto Main Street slewed another vehicle, this one flashing a blue light a good bit brighter than the one I hid in my hand. I turned to look: A police car was pulling up by my Kia. And just before the van swung into the shadow of the library, I glimpsed the silhouetted form of a woman standing on that corner. An actual human being, far too late.

Where did this madman at the wheel of the van plan to take us?

His U-turn completed, He gunned it toward the street.

But before He got there, the van stalled.

Cursing, He turned the key to start it again.

The starter cranked, but the engine didn't respond. My heart revved instead, racing with hope for—something, a stay of execution, a spanner in the abductor's plans, maybe even a rescue—as the van drifted to a stop behind the erstwhile library. In the shadow of the building. Out of sight of the people on the corner.

Three more times, swearing, He tried to get the van started. No go.

He pounded the steering wheel with His fist. Then He swiveled in His seat to confront me, His face a looming mask of shadows in the night. "You!" His left hand shot toward me. "Bitch, what did you do to my van?"

My entire oversized body somehow relocated out of His reach without my consciously moving. I squeaked, "Nothing!"

"You tell me or I'll kill you."

"I didn't do a thing!" I cried quite sincerely. We were talking about engine trouble, and I hadn't touched His engine. Certainly, I had meant to, but His alarm system had stopped me. Bless my muddled mind, I had completely forgotten about the wad of Kleenex I'd stuffed up His tailpipe.

He must have accepted my genuine stupidity in this regard, because He slewed away from me, cursing, and slammed out of the van.

A few long strides took Him around the hood. I stayed where I was, not about to go anywhere without Juliet. There wasn't time to say anything to her, but the instant He opened my door, I decided, I would scream like a steam whistle. If the cop was still at the corner, he couldn't see the van back here, but with any luck he, or the woman who had been standing by my car, might hear—

As if He had heard me thinking, He opened Juliet's door instead, and with a lurch in my gut I saw the glint of steel as He pressed that fearsome knife to her neck.

"Not a sound from either of you," He warned in a low but very convincing voice from the shadows, "or I'll slice her head off."

With His left hand He slid my door open. Then He yanked my coat off Juliet, but she kept hold of it with her fingertips as He hauled her out of the van.

Sometime, somehow, He'd released her seat belt. With a remote control in His pocket, maybe. He jostled her into the captive position, her back to Him and His knife poised to slit her throat. She stood there very still with my coat trailing from both hands. From my seat I could see it dragging on the dark ground like a shroud.

I heard Him say, "You, freak face, get out."

Presumably He was talking to me. Quite slowly I began to bestir my large self to obey. The more time I took, the longer I stretched out the faint possibility of a rescue.

"Move, Goddamn you!"

Obligingly I scooted toward Him, having made a quick but very counterinstinctive decision: I left my purse where it was, on the floor in the shadow of the seat. He seemed not to have noticed it there or realized its significance, but I felt most of my mind clamoring: leave my *purse*? Leave behind my money, my keys, my pills, my charge cards, my driver's license, my identity, my selfhood?

That was the point, of course; I didn't want Him to find out who I was. Yet what if there was something in the purse I needed, or Juliet needed . . .

"Move!" He visibly tightened His grip on Juliet, nudging the razor-edged knife blade closer to her throat. I couldn't seem to see anything farther away from me than her pale face. That other face—His—half-hidden by her frightened head, was just a pair of wild eyes glaring from shadow.

Limping, aching in my joints and muscles almost as much as in my heart, I clambered out of the van and turned to close the door as loudly as I could.

With His left hand He thrust me sprawling onto the gravel. If I lived to see daylight, I was going to find some truly impressive bruises on several parts of me. He slid the van door shut quite softly, closed the passenger door the same way.

His voice issued dark out of the night: "You think you're smart, don't you, bitch? Get up."

I got up.

"Stay in front of me where I can see you. Walk."

I walked. Slowly. Feeling my way with my sneakered feet on the gravel. How, in this gloom, could He see me? Or anything else? Was the man human, or some sort of jaguar black hunting cat?

I could only dimly sense the old library, a huge looming shadow at my left shoulder. I couldn't see the black letters spelling "CANDY GOT LAID HERE," but I knew the stinging words were there. I knew I was walking close by them.

There was a metallic wrenching sound, the garage-door sound I'd heard twice before. Then He, our captor, said, "Down here."

I opened my left hand, letting a little metal cylinder fall to the gravel, covering the sound with words. "Down where?" I couldn't see a thing.

He pushed me, and I fell hard and kept falling, down something that felt painfully like concrete steps. At the bottom, blackness awaited me.

Sam followed the young policewoman across the Phillipses' expansive foyer to a formal dining room where men in suits sat around a table strewn with papers and what appeared to be communications equipment. Extension wires ran across thick cream-colored carpeting to the fax, the computer, and some high-tech components Sam couldn't identify.

Among the suits sat a single bulky uniform. Sam strode to it and marginally introduced himself. "Sam White." He felt conscious of his scruffy appearance, no tie, no shave, his shirt collar getting limp and sweaty, yet he found himself holding his head up straight and his shoulders hard. He realized his manners were getting shorter by the minute, and dictated himself a cautionary mental memo: *Stay cool.*

The bulky man in uniform nodded without standing up or offering to shake hands. "Bud Angstrom here."

Sam knew the name: Fulcrum chief of police. Big shot. Sam told him, "I want to see my wife's car."

"And these other gentlemen are from the FBI," said Bud Angstrom as if he hadn't heard him.

Sam gave them a glance and a nod. FBI meant nothing to him. The FBI was looking for the Phillips girl, not for Dorrie. "I want to see my wife's car," he repeated.

"It's in Appletree. Out of my jurisdiction. But there's no reason the Appletree PD wouldn't let you check it out." Angstrom swiveled in his chair to face Sam with a sort of public-relations affability, light catching on his bald head fit to give him a halo. "Maybe you'll spot something they missed."

Humoring me, Sam thought. He didn't like it. But knowing himself to be not in the very best of moods, he said only, "You'll inform the Appletree police I'm on my way?"

"Sure. No problem." The chief became expansive. "They tell us they found a shopping bag in the vehicle," he said agreeably, "with a credit-card receipt that places your wife at the Fulcrum mall on the day of, and near the time of, the Juliet Phillips abduction."

Sam made himself take a long breath before replying. "Of course she was at the mall. She said she was going to the mall."

"Yes, but now we can prove that she was there. We also have a witness who spoke with your wife at the mall and says she was acting nervous, making inappropriate conversation, looking around like she was watching for someone, asking the time for no reason."

"Maybe she just wanted to know what time it was."

"Just the same, it's an additional indication."

"Indication of what?"

"That your wife, who had motive and opportunity, may have kidnapped the Phillips girl."

Sam breathed in, held it, and mentally counted to ten. Then, after exhaling, he said almost calmly, "Wait a minute. I thought I heard on the news you guys had a description of an SUV or a van or something."

"Oh, yeah. That." Lazily the chief turned away from Sam and shifted his focus to the rookie cop. "Play it for him, Sissy."

Sissy?

Without comment the young black officer walked around the table and pressed a button on one of the more obscure items of electrical equipment. Sam heard a rapid, stressed female voice saying, *Juliet Phillips has been abducted from the mall parking lot by a man in a van.*

"But that's Dorrie's voice!" Sam blurted.

Leaning back in his chair, the chief of police nodded without bothering to look at him. "We thought as much," he said placidly.

. . . Caucasian, maybe in his thirties or forties, not fat or anything, kind of average . . .

Sam demanded, "Where'd she call from?"

"Cell phone. We could only trace it to a tower not far from the mall."

"That's it! She saw the girl being snatched and she took off after them!"

The chief looked at Sam once more, and his voice turned pitying. "You really think your wife would do that, sir?"

Sam yelped, "Well, what do you think?"

"We think she made the call to put us on the wrong track. She doesn't give any make or model or license number—"

. . . kind of beige, or silver. A light silver brown. Kind of taupe. Actually, it's the color of a Weimaraner.

"Dorrie's not observant of numbers," Sam explained.

Studying his own stubby spatulate fingernails, the chief drawled, "Well, she seems god-awful observant of other details."

. . . a wheel cover on back with a design that looks kind of like one of those diagrams in a doctor's office of the female reproductive tract, you know, the ovaries and the uterus and—and stuff.

Sam felt his eyes start to tear up at the sound of his wife's earnest voice, and he had to blink hard. It was just like Dorrie to go after the exact color, the unique comparison.

"She could have called back if she was really in pursuit," Chief Angstrom pointed out without bothering to look up, "but we didn't hear from her again."

Sam had to count to twenty this time before he spoke. "You

won't consider the possibility that she would take off after a criminal," he argued slowly and clearly, "yet you will readily accept that she would plot and carry out a kidnapping?"

"Quite a coincidence, isn't it, that the missing girl is her illegitimate daughter?"

Sam clenched his fists. Took a deep breath. Let it out again. Then asked, "What did she buy?"

Chief Angstrom alerted sufficiently to raise his bald head and give Sam a puzzled glance. "Huh?"

"My wife," Sam said, one measured word at a time. "You said she bought something at the mall. What was it?"

"Oh. Um, I've got that in a report here somewhere. . . ." Pawing at papers and manila folders on the table, the chief called, "Sissy . . ."

Still standing, Officer Chappell supplied, "Wire mesh desk baskets and a packet of graph paper, sir."

Sam felt emotion grasp his throat and squeeze, making it difficult for him to speak a few words. "For my office."

From his chair, the chief of police frowned up at him from underneath eyebrows like scrub brushes. No hair loss there. "Graph paper means something to you, Mr. White?"

Not the graph paper; it was the wire mesh baskets that had choked Sam up. But he passed over that point to make a far more important one. "Do you really think my wife would have bought office supplies for me if she was planning to kidnap the Phillips girl?"

An unexpected voice spoke in support. Sissy Chappell. "Sir," she addressed her chief, "Mrs. White's computer shows that she has been aware of Juliet Phillips for more than a year without making any attempt at contact. Why would she suddenly approach her now?"

Chief Angstrom silenced Officer Chappell with a scowl,

then peered at Sam to make his pronouncement, which took the form of a kind of verbal shrug. "The preponderance of the evidence points toward your wife's involvement in the disappearance of Juliet Phillips," he told Sam blandly, "and that is the paradigm we're proceeding under at this point in time."

If I was knocked out, it was only for a moment. I felt Juliet stumble over me, heard again the metallic clashing sound, and wondered momentarily whether I had been knocked blind; the darkness was so total. Then I felt a hard hand grasp my arm and lift. The guy was strong. Acted like He was going to pick me up by the arm. I don't think He could have, but I floundered to my feet so He wouldn't dislocate my shoulder. He pushed me in a direction, I stumbled forward so I wouldn't fall again, and then He shoved me again, this way, that way, hauled me around a corner, and I heard a door shut behind me.

Oh. No. Juliet. Where? Separated from me?

Electric light blazed on.

I blinked, barely able to see. I breathed out. With my coat wrapped around her like a mantle, Juliet stood in the room, dungeon, wherever we were, beside me.

Then I gasped and struggled to breathe again, catching sight of—Him.

He stood glaring at us both in the plain light of a 75-watt overhead bulb, and there was no way I could deny away the pain any longer.

He—I still couldn't bring myself to think of Him by name—the love of my life hadn't changed much. He still affected the same black army boots, tight black jeans, tight black T-shirt showing off His narrow body, the gothic sort of clothing most people leave behind after adolescence. His face—life

had added a few scars, as if He'd been in a fight or two. Somebody's fist had flattened His nose and knocked it a bit crooked.
Time had grayed His skin. But He was still average, ordinary
looking, nothing to attract anyone's attention—except when
He spoke. Then, no one could ignore the authority of His
voice and the vehemence of His stare.

Or Pandora. No one, I think, could have ignored that wick-
edly curvaceous hunting knife in His hand. As for me, the sight
of it nearly paralyzed me.

Looking at the knife, then looking into His predatory, stony
eyes, I knew. He was insane. He'd been crazy even back then,
when we were kids, but I'd been too lonely and naive to realize.
I had mistaken His predation for attraction, His irrationality
for ardor, and now—years had passed, and He'd aged a little,
yet He seemed not to have grown. Or grown up. At all.

Except that He'd grown even more psycho.

I stood gasping, sobbing, and I felt Juliet's hand on my arm,
her touch asking me to look at her, but I couldn't—I didn't—it
was as if all my life I had been gazing at visions of angels, angels, angels, but now I was living an Escher, suddenly seeing
that the angels were only empty white spaces between devils,
devils, dark dark devils. Very real devils, while the angels had
been white holes like the gaps in my daydreams. An illusion. A
fantasy way to escape from the dismal reality of living with my
parents. And after that, a dream of romance during my boring
marriage to Sam—

Poor ever-so-careful Sam. I wondered what he was doing
right now. Worried about me. Frantic, probably. Unable to
sleep. Pacing the floor with no idea what to do, as innocent as
a newborn angel when it came to this kind of danger.

While I stood there facing my very real, very personal devil
incarnate.

"You call the cops?" He demanded with cattle-prod voltage in His voice.

I jumped as if I'd been hit. Crying too hard to speak, I shook my head.

"Don't lie to me, bitch!" *Flick*, a blur like a rattlesnake striking, and I found myself blinking cross-eyed at the wicked tip of His knife poised maybe two inches from my face. "That's your car by the phone on the—"

"It doesn't work!" Wincing away from the knife, I babbled between sobs, "The phone is—dead, so—I couldn't call."

"Phone's *dead*, huh?"

The way He said it tightened a noose around my throat. I couldn't respond.

"So you tried to steal my van instead." An inch from my nose, Pandora quivered with rage. Light shimmered off the honed edge of her blade.

I closed my eyes.

"If either of you moves an inch, I'll carve you both." I heard booted footsteps heading someplace rapidly.

I opened my eyes in time to see Him standing with His face to the room's paneled outside wall. His back to us.

But only for a second. As I watched, unmoving, uncomprehending, He turned and strode back to us.

His mood seemed to have eased marginally. Thumbing the edge of His wicked knife, glaring at me, He barked out a flinty laugh. "Fat crying ugly woman," He said. "I hate fat women."

When I was young, He had compared my eyes to the great limpid eyes of deer, to pools of deep water, to morning dew—but now He did not notice the same eyes dwarfed amid my blotched, puffy face.

He barked, "I hate crying women. And most of all I hate

ugly women. I'm going to enjoy killing you, bitch, as soon as I decide how."

I had loved Him. Loved Him. Dreamed of Him for years. And He didn't even know me. He saw only a fat ugly crying woman, make that bitch. Didn't recognize who I was. Or care. He had—

Made love to me?

No. Made use of me.

Helped Himself to my virginity.

In this very room.

I knew. I just knew, even before I turned my head to look around. Yes, it was that same place. That high-ceilinged square room in the basement of the library, taller than it was wide or long. The same wormwork of pipes overhead, painted gray like the plaster. The same dark, cheaply paneled walls, the same ugly green and white checkerboard linoleum, the same dank subterranean smell, and—no, that couldn't be the very same Kmart art on the wall over the sofa. But He had placed a similar mass-produced still life with pink peonies there.

Just as He had arranged a similar sofa in the same position by the inner wall.

Presumably for the same purpose.

Remembering what had happened on a sofa in this room, I dried up instantly. Things were getting too bad for weeping; it was a waste of precious energy. All that mattered now was to save Juliet from Him.

I blinked away my tears and turned to her. "You okay?" I asked her just to let her know I was still with her.

"Shut up," He snarled before she could answer. Then to Juliet He said tenderly, "Take your coat off, sweet sugar Candy, and sit down." Even when His tone flipped like that, like a light switch, His flat eyes didn't change at all. Neither did the wooden expression on His face. "Make yourself at home," He told Juliet. "Candy. The sweetest Candy I've tasted yet. Welcome once again to my humble hideaway."

Shivering, she stood where she was and, if anything, she clutched my coat more tightly around her.

He lifted His knife expressively. "Pandora says sit."

She backed a step away from Him.

"Don't be stupid. Whatever Pandora says, you do."

She didn't move.

"Sit *down*. Do it, or I'll kill . . . you." I think He had almost said "myself."

I interposed to distract Him. Once my tear glands had shut down, my mind had started to work again, thank God. In firm teacherly tones I inquired, "Who was Pandora?"

He turned on me so sharply, knife trembling in air, that I thought He would slice me to pieces right there and then, neatly severing my joints like my mother cutting up a chicken. I felt my back tighten and my spine freeze in terror. But the question had done what it was supposed to. It had distracted His focus from Juliet and riveted it on me.

He barked, "I already told you. Pandora's my knife. Pandora's my twenty-four-hours-a-day sweetheart, only girlfriend I can count on, only real woman I ever met, my wife knife, and you shut up."

I could barely keep my mouth moving, but I had to. Had to keep His attention. Lips fumbling for the words, I asked, "All right, then, who was Candy?"

He went white. White. Hoarsely He demanded, "What the hell are you talking about?"

"I saw writing on the building, something about Candy, um, somebody named Candy." I had to be careful not to know too much. "Now you keep calling this girl Candy, when I happen to know that her name is Juliet. Who was Candy?"

"Shut up! You don't get to say her name." The blade of His uplifted knife shook and shimmered like a chill silver flame. "I can say Candy, Candy, Candy whenever I want, but you shut up. Shut up about her! I hate her! I hate her!" His wooden face cracked like a mask, showing some raw, red feeling both hurtful and ugly. Gripping His knife hard, He lunged and stabbed some ghost in the room. "I hate the dumb fuck!" His voice panted, ragged. "She didn't give me a souvenir. Nothing! Not even a curly hair left behind. And I didn't get to do everything I wanted. No goddamn Candy gets to leave me before I'm done with her."

"Oh." Like Juliet, I took a step back, shaking. But forget terror; my job was to keep His attention away from her. I managed to say, "She, um, Candy, she left?"

"She fucking disappeared."

She was disappeared by her parents, I thought, and for years afterward her—my—favorite folk ballad had been a sad song: "I wish I were a tiny sparrow, and I had wings and I could fly; I'd fly away to my own true lover—"

This monster?

"—and all he'd ask, I would deny."

I had never understood that vicious little thrust of anger at the end of the sweet lyric, but I had kept singing it; I had liked it.

Now I understood why. Without knowing, I had known what He was.

But He must never understand. The tiny sparrow swooped through my mind in the time it took for my mouth to fumble out, "She, um, Candy, maybe something happened to her."

He sneered at me. "You don't know a thing about it, asshole.

Dogface bitch." He lowered His head, bearlike, and lurched toward me, in my face, close enough so I could feel His hot breath as He ranted, "Christ, I've never seen such an ugly slut. What is that crap all over your face, pimples with pus on them? What kind of crud you got, bitch, AIDS?"

The rash was ulcerating and oozing, evidently. How nice. I wanted to tell Him that my crud was worse than AIDS and He was likely to die just because He'd breathed on me, but I didn't. I couldn't, because I knew what I might have to do any moment now.

Backing away another step, I said, "It's nothing. A skin condition. Just something that happened. The way something might have happened to Candy," I added, directing Him back on task, as my Ed Psych teachers would have said, but carefully keeping my tone gentle. "Something she couldn't help." I eased one hand over to Juliet, touching her rigid shoulder. She stood with both arms clenched around herself, wrapped in my coat as if in Kevlar. I gave her only a quick glance; had to keep my eyes on our captor. "Um, maybe somebody made Candy go away," I ventured, thinking of my parents, who had—I realized for the first time in my life—rescued me from Him. Bless their narrow-minded heads, they had saved my life, however blindly and harshly, by removing me from Appletree. Remembering that hegira, I said, "Maybe somebody took her away from you."

He, of course, attributed to the suggestion a very different meaning from the one I had intended. "Shut up! She wasn't that kind. Not Candy. There wasn't nobody else for her." He glowered at me, so vehement that I flinched, thinking He would hit me or, much worse, stab me—

But then His knife hand sagged. "See, all the other girls I had up till then were just slut du jour. . . ." Pandora tilted uncertainly. "They were ordinary, they'd done it before, they dished it out or not, they said, 'Okay, but you got to wear a condom,' or they'd say, 'No, I don't want to get warts,' or crabs, whatever, or first they'd say, 'Sure, whatever you want,' and then they'd change their dumb-ass minds and say go jack off. But Candy . . ." He glared at me. "Candy was different. She thought different. She even looked different. She was smart and yet she was sweet and pure. She'd never been there before. She didn't know a thing. *I* took her. I took her every step of the way. One thing at a time. And she loved it. Nobody can say she didn't love it. And it was her first time. It was like holy rape. Like rapturing the Virgin Mary."

Dear God. How much horror had my parents saved me from?

I babbled, "But I thought you hadn't gotten to, um . . ." Playing my part. I knew all too well what He had done. I knew. . . . I knew . . . something I'd whitewashed over in my bowdlerization of my personal fairy tale, couldn't remember. . . . But it didn't matter, because I was playing a role. Had to remember that. Stupid fat ugly interfering bitch, especially the stupid part. I prattled, "I thought you hadn't consummated the relationship?"

"Con-sum-mated the re-la-tion-ship?" Mimicking my voice, He started to laugh again, the yapping laughter of a vicious dog. Then *flick* went the mood switch. Two steps and He stood inches from me, glowering, knife poised. "You dumb fuck," He whispered fiercely, "of course I screwed her. I screwed her plenty. What I didn't get to do was join with her in blood. What I didn't get to do was slit her wrists."

EIGHT

Knowing that Chief Angstrom wouldn't give her an inch of slack when other cops were watching, Officer Sistine "Sissy" Chappell waited for an opportunity to speak with her boss alone. Normally she would have tapped on his office door at the Fulcrum PD, but he (like her, and all the others) was still at the Phillips home waiting for a possible ransom call. Maybe an hour went by before he noticed her and called, "Sissy, ain't your shift up? Go home. Get some rest."

Crap. She had to do it. Walking over to stand by Angstrom's chair, she asked, "Chief, could I have a word with you?"

"Sure. Shoot."

It wasn't just sheer laziness that kept him from moving his ass from that chair, Sissy intuited. He was testing her. She had no choice except to unzip Dorrie White's laptop computer case and pull from it a rather messy wad of notebook paper, which she placed on the Phillipses' dining room table in front of her boss. "Those were hidden along with the pink notebook under Dorrie White's mattress. They're notes from her high school boyfriend, and his handwriting strongly suggests that he might be a psychopath. I think—"

By speaking rapid-fire, she managed to get this far, but no further, before Chief Angstrom stopped her with a snort of disgust. What she wanted to say she thought was that instead of calling this the Phillips case, with Dorrie White as the perpetrator, somebody ought to consider that it might be the Dorrie White case with some unknown subject, maybe this high school boyfriend, as the perp. But right now Chief Angstrom was interested only in bawling her out. "Sissy, I told you before, don't go talking nonsense to me about handwriting. There isn't a speck of proof—"

With unusual daring she interrupted. "Handwriting analysis is not a science *yet* because there haven't been enough studies made. But there *have* been extensive studies of the handwriting of the prison population, which enables me to say with certainty that this"—she pointed to Blake's love notes—"is the handwriting of a dangerous felon."

"You say," Angstrom shot back. "So what? You're nothing but a green rookie, and even if you were a so-called expert on handwriting, that kind of testimony is not admissible in court."

"Polygraph test results aren't admissible in court either, but we still use them as an investigative tool—"

With lessening patience he overspoke her. "Have you read these?" He jabbed at the pancake stack of yellowing notebook paper with one expressively offended finger.

"Yes, of course."

"And is there anything in them that says the boy is criminally inclined?"

"His handwriting—"

"Screw his handwriting! You want to check him out on the basis of nothing but his handwriting?"

"Yes, sir."

"Well, forget about it. You're off duty. I'd suggest you go home and get some rest."

"Yes, sir."

• • •

Sissy considered that a suggestion wasn't an order.

She drove to Fulcrum PD headquarters and, rubbing her eyes, settled her weary body at one of the computers there. What she did on her own time was her own business. Using a departmental computer on her off time might not be considered her own business, but if Chief Angstrom said she was a green rookie, okay, she would be a green rookie who didn't know any better.

Waking up the computer—which was doing what she should have been doing, sleeping—Sissy keyboarded her shield ID number plus a departmental password to log on.

While she waited for the computer to do its thing, she couldn't help remembering how definitively Chief Angstrom had shut her up. Maybe a half hour had gone by since, but it still stung. She sighed. Not so much angry as philosophical, she wondered when, if ever, she could expect respect as a police officer. So far she got none from anyone, not her fellow officers and especially not her own family. Her mother opposed her choice of career because it was too dangerous, while her father seemed to think it wasn't dangerous enough; he wanted her to go into the military and maybe follow in his footsteps as a fighter pilot. Her sisters thought she was trying to be a hotshot, her brother in the marines sided with her father, and her other brother, the family underachiever, warned her she'd better find a job far from him and his street gang. Not wanting to shoot him any more than he wanted to shoot her, she had complied, graduating from her local police academy back in New Jersey, but then finding her first job in another city across state lines.

Which took her away from her family, but unfortunately also took her away from all her old friends. And Fulcrum was proving to be not an easy place to find new ones outside of a church.

Her gangsta brother, now, he got respect in the old neighborhood, and Sissy rolled her eyes at the thought; her brother's criminal friends had his back, but who had hers? Neighbors? She hardly knew them except as apartment numbers in her building. Fellow officers? Maybe, but nobody really wanted to connect with her, the greenest of rookies, until after they had seen her in action for a while.

The computer gave a kind of satiated burp that meant it was ready, and Sissy began, as protocol demanded, with a background check on Candor Birch White even though she felt certain Dorrie was cleaner than a detergent commercial. Partly Sistine believed this because she'd seen Dorrie White's home, Dorrie's choice of harmonious and soothing colors, and her many big pillows and soft surfaces, comfortable sofas and easy chairs and recliners made even more welcoming by pastel lap robes Dorrie had probably crocheted herself.

Sissy's intense interest in handwriting analysis was just part of her study of the larger field of graphology: personality as revealed in unconscious doodling or conscious creativity, choice of colors, choices in the different ways of filling space. Sistine could not imagine that anybody who collected Flutterkitties could ever plan and execute a violent crime. She had seen a peaceable but yearning soul in Dorrie's collections of figurines and art as well as in the daisy and butterfly and rainbow magnets on her fridge. She had noticed that Dorrie White kept liquid hand soap in flowered dispensers beside all the sinks, preferred rounded corners to sharp ones in just about every context, used ruffled pillow shams on the beds. To Sissy's eyes, a hundred details in the White house revealed Dorrie to be a homebody who put others above herself and probably contributed to charities alleviating the suffering of hungry children or stray animals.

Even more important, Sistine had seen Dorrie White's handwriting in that pink Juliet Phillips scrapbook. Smallish handwriting, very round, slanted a bit toward the right, with short ascenders and a small midzone but ample descenders, garlands, and end strokes. In other words, Dorrie White was timid, very kindhearted, and warm but lacking in self-esteem. She was unhappy in her daily life but had no ambition to do anything about it; she was probably a romantic dreamer.

And she was generous. Very generous.

While thinking all of this, Sissy checked wants and warrants in her region, then statewide, even nationwide, before she finished off by Googling "Candor White" to see whether she had ever made headlines of any kind. All the results were negative, meaning good. Dorrie White could not have been more clean.

In Officer Chappell's opinion, presumption of innocence in regard to Dorrie White deserved a lot more attention than it was getting in the Fulcrum Police Department right now.

Not for the first time, Sissy mentally questioned the competency of Chief Angstrom. Not because he was maybe racist and almost surely sexist; those all-too-common attitudes she could deal with. But she simply could not understand how Chief Angstrom could be so stupid as to discredit handwriting analysis. How could he, a law enforcement official, not understand that the entire legal system he upheld was based on signed documents simply because each person's handwritten signature is as individual as a fingerprint? And nobody disputed that experts could match handwriting, that each person wrote differently despite the public school system's best efforts to teach all children to write alike. So how could anybody say that the differences were not due to variations in personality?

"Get over it," Sissy muttered to herself. The chief was her CO. He hadn't even bothered to look at the love notes signed "Blake." She was through trying to educate him.

Rookie cop Chappell used another departmental password to access NCIC, moved the mouse to the search box, and typed into it a single name: "Blake."

She pushed "GO," then rubbed her eyes again and leaned back in her comfortless plastic chair to wait. This was a long shot and it was going to take a long time.

As the computer hummed and chirped to itself, compiling a list of every "Blake" in the NCIC, Sissy Chappell took another look at the handwriting samples she had found in Dorrie White's bedroom.

Oh, yeah. Throughout his scrawls, "Blake" exhibited the "felon's claw," an unmistakable kink of the descenders. Sissy had never seen it so pronounced in any other real-life handwriting sample she had studied; this guy's handwriting provided a textbook example for the studies that had been conducted of the handwriting of criminals, very different from that of the overall populace. A hint of the felon's claw in someone's handwriting usually indicated a liar, especially an adulterer. But when it appeared as blatantly as it did in the samples she held, it was thought to be characteristic of rapists.

Not that any one trait meant a whole lot in handwriting. Like a medical diagnostician, Sistine depended on experience, intuition, and an overall impression for her conclusions. But that was just it: Taken all together, the grandiosity and swagger of this man's handwriting, its instability, its toppling impetuosity, and especially those final *d*'s, bloated, protuberant, shaped like a clenched fist giving the finger to the world—

The computer ceased its mutterings and gave an electronic "Ta da!"

Sissy looked: 79,462 hits for "Blake."

With a sigh, she bent over the computer, beginning the process of sorting and discarding. Eliminate missing children and teenage runaways. Then try "Blake" as first name or aka, not surname. Establish "Blake" as around Dorrie White's age, say, between the ages of twenty-eight to thirty-eight. Make it twenty-five to forty. Cross-reference "Blake" plus "Fulcrum, Ohio." "Blake" plus "Ohio" . . .

"Take me instead," I said.

I couldn't manage to sound flirtatious or provocative. Nothing in my upbringing had taught me how to act sexually alluring, and the present circumstances seemed unlikely to encourage any latent talent. But I was desperately sincere in the offer, and I suppose He could tell. He gawked at me.

"Let this girl go," I repeated, facing Him steadily, willing myself not to step back, even though He had imposed Himself far too close to me, looming only inches from me. "She has her whole life ahead of her." I heard a choked sound from Juliet, a whimper, a sob, but I couldn't turn to her. I kept my gaze fixed on our captor. "Take me instead. Do whatever you like to me. It's all the same in the end. You want blood, I've got blood. You—"

He burst into yelps of laughter. I could feel His spit flying into my face. "You crazy fat cow!" He cried, laughing so hard He bent over and had to step back from me to avoid placing His head upon my bosom. "You think I'd touch you with a rabies pole? Dumb ass, you're either a retard or a psycho!"

I breathed out, relieved not because He had refused me but because the energy in the room had lightened, shifted. I had amused Him. Fine. Keep Him laughing. Straight-faced, I inquired, "You don't appreciate what an older woman has to offer?"

"This is not about your *age*, you—What the hell is your name, anyway?"

I shot back the first female name that came to mind. "Maria Montessori."

Peripherally I saw Juliet turn her head to give me a startled look. Perhaps her parents had sent her to Fulcrum's Montessori preschool.

Our captor, however, didn't blink. "Well, Marie, honey, you are not only physically repulsive but you are also the goofiest broad I've ever met."

"Thank you. I imagine you've known lots of women?" And insulted them, I thought, and mispronounced their names?

"Oh, yeah."

"How interesting." Maintaining steady eye contact and nonjudgmental active-listening posture and all the sincere artifice they'd taught me in educational psychology, I casually sat on the sofa where He'd wanted Juliet to position herself. Not looking at her. I didn't want Him to look at her. I wanted Him to focus on me and keep talking. And I remembered that He liked to talk Himself up.

I burbled, "Mostly younger women?"

"*All* younger women, Ma-rie ba-by," He bragged. He could call me "Ma-rie" all He liked as long as He wasn't calling Juliet anything. "Hundreds of them. White, black, yellow, brown—I take them all, and the younger, the better."

I'd sized up His ego rightly. Or more than ego, really: His was an absolute sense of entitlement. His father had been a cripple, He had told me once—that was the word He had used, not handicapped, not disabled, but "a cripple"—and both His mother and father were dead. In an automobile accident? A tragic house fire? He had never divulged. He had worn an air of mystery the way He wore black clothing. He was an orphan, shuffled from foster home to foster home. He had suffered an unhappy childhood and now He deserved—

Oh, my God.

Something in me recognized something in Him. I had been a Cinderella once. He still was a sick male Cinderella, a hungry self centered on bottomless need. Physically, in my breasts and belly, I remembered the starving-baby sensation of His feeding on me.

I whispered, "What did they do to you when you were little?"

Luckily, He didn't hear me. He had turned away, swaggering to the far wall again, arms bowed like a bodybuilder's, knife at the ready, His belligerent back sending a message clearer than words: Don't Even Think about Trying Anything with Me. He peered at that same place on the wall—oh. A peephole. Now, from my seat on the sofa, I could make out a small black metal circle let into the paneling. But it was well below ground level. How could He see anything through that?

Yet evidently He could. "No pigs yet," He remarked, wheeling and striding back to Juliet and me.

My cognitive processes not at their very best, I couldn't think what He was talking about: pigs? My focus had once again fixated on the knife.

"You don't like Pandora?" He inquired, tilting the blade toward me like a teacher with a pointer.

My social conditioning enabled me to respond politely if automatically, "Um, I've got nothing against her personally. She's okay."

"Damn straight she's okay. She's the best fuck ever was. She taught me everything I know. I don't mess with no *boys* or *children*"—upholding standards of morality, He punctuated the air with Pandora for emphasis—"but girls, oh, yeah, all I gotta do is whistle. As soon as they're ready to bleed, they come running to me."

Ready to bleed? Was He referring to menstruation?

I was a coward. No way was I going to ask what He meant by that. My mind thrashed like a drowning person in dark water, grasping for the right question to keep Him talking.

I blurted, "Have you kept track of your, um, your conquests?"

"Oh, yes. I mean not every single piece of tail, hell no, but the Candies, you bet I keep track of the Candies."

I'd known. Somehow I'd known He would want to keep a scrapbook or something. Something deep and dark in me knew far too much about Him.

"Blake plus Appletree, Ohio . . ."

Slumped over the computer keyboard, Fulcrum Borough police officer Sissy Chappell straightened to attention as NCIC spit back a response.

UNLAWFUL FLIGHT TO AVOID CONFINEMENT—RAPE, CRIMINAL HOMICIDE, AGGRAVATED STALKING

BLAKE RANDALL ROMAN

ALIASES

Randall Romano, Roman Black, Romeo Black, Troy R. Black, Troy R. Blakely, "Blake the Knife"

DESCRIPTION

Date of Birth: June 26, 1976

Hair: Brown

Place of Birth: Cassandra, NC

Eyes: Brown

Height: 5'10"

Complexion: Light

Weight: 180 pounds

Sex: Male

Build: Medium

Race: White

Distinguishing Scars or Marks: Tattoo upper left arm, "CANDY" on heart in open mouth as signified by parted lips. Multiple knife scars inner arms and wrists. Nose shows disalignment of having been broken.

Remarks: Habitually wears black, carries and displays a large hunting knife. Attracted to people with physical disabilities, may seek employment at physical therapy facilities. Has resided in Ohio, Indiana, Michigan, Wisconsin, Minnesota.

CAUTION

BLAKE RANDALL ROMAN IS WANTED FOR QUESTIONING IN CONNECTION WITH THE ABDUCTION, RAPE, MUTILATION, AND MURDER OF A 16-YEAR-OLD GIRL IN 2008 IN SOUTH BEND, INDIANA

CONSIDERED ARMED AND EXTREMELY DANGEROUS

Too bad the NCIC didn't supply handwriting samples, but the "CANDY" tattoo made Sissy feel almost certain she had found her man: the one who had written the love notes that Dorrie White had kept hidden under her mattress. She wanted to yell "Wahoo!" but she was just too tired.

"Blake Roman," she murmured.

Average height, average weight, average build. Clicking on the link for more info, Sissy discovered that he had served time in Wisconsin for statutory rape, in Michigan for stalking and sexual assault, and in both states plus Ohio for aggravated assault. He was wanted in all three states for parole violations as well as being a suspect in the South Bend rape/homicide. When in prison he had not been a troublemaker, and he didn't seem to associate with career criminals. But "on the outside" he broke parole at once simply by disappearing, moving on. He appeared to be a drifter and a loner.

Maybe his parents had been some sort of drifters too. Born in North Carolina, how had Blake Roman landed in Appletree, Ohio? Sissy didn't know, but she saw he had attended public school there, and also that he had been in Ohio foster care starting at age fifteen.

Foster care meant that something had gone seriously wrong at home.

But that didn't have to mean a criminal rap sheet.

Blake Roman. A could-have-been-nice middle-American boy from the small town—a very small town indeed—where Dorrie White's car had been found.

Blake Roman. A guy with a history of sexual predation.

There had to be a connection with Juliet Phillips and Dorrie White. There just had to. This Blake Roman had to be the Factor X, the unknown subject, the abductor Dorrie White had seen at the mall. . . .

But officially, the Fulcrum PD did not believe Dorrie White had actually seen an abductor at the mall. Nor did the FBI, apparently. Or anyone except Dorrie's devoted husband.

Sissy blinked at the computer screen, self-doubt trying to set in because she was so, so tired and should have been asleep hours ago. But the next moment she mentally kicked both doubt and weariness aside. Both reasoning and gut instinct told her that Dorrie White was no perp. Dorrie deserved a voice in the wilderness crying that she had told the truth. There was an abductor. Blake Roman might be the one. At the very least he needed to be recognized as a piece of the puzzle.

Sitting up straight and flexing her shoulders, Sissy pulled up a blank document in order to start writing a report.

Our cordial host/captor reached behind Him and opened a refrigerator. The original library lounge had included a fridge, so I suppose He needed to have one, but He wasn't using it to refrigerate. Rather, it seemed to be for closeting things, or maybe concealing them. I saw a few items of clothing in there, and some shoe boxes, and—were those guns?

Black handguns in a rank like soldiers where brown-bag lunches were supposed to go.

I felt Juliet slump trembling on the sofa beside me, but I couldn't comfort her or even look at her. I didn't dare to look away as He—

Scornfully turning His back on us again, He pulled a shoe box from the fridge and set it on the table. The librarians' lounge had featured an oval wooden table, so there had to be one, I suppose, although this table was somebody's kitchen reject, rectangular, aluminum and laminate with aluminum-and-vinyl chairs.

He sat at the table with the shoe box in front of Him, facing us across the table's unlovely width. His wooden expression lightened marginally as He opened the shoe box and tossed the lid aside. Still cradling His knife, aka Pandora, in His right hand, He explored the shoe box with His left, then pulled out something red and held it up. It hung limp from His fingers like an animal He'd shot.

"Atlantic City," He announced, His tone eager, almost happy. "Saw her on the beach. That was back before I started hunting on the Internet. It was just dumb luck, and right away, like hitting hot on the slots, I knew she was a Candy. She just had that look, like a gazelle. I followed her. Turned out she worked at one of the casinos."

The limp red thing, I realized, was a thong panty. My stomach lurched.

"I caught up to her after work," He went on. "I showed her possibilities she never knew before. We did everything. Everything. I ain't telling you where I hid the body." He sounded so normal, His tone so light I wanted to believe He was joking about hiding a corpse. Denial is our protection against extreme shock, and I still couldn't believe . . . I mean, He sounded like an emcee, or somebody hosting a party.

I felt Juliet pressing against me from shoulders to hips, quivering, but I kept my eyes on our host.

He dipped into the box again and held up a delicate gold bracelet. "Oh, yeah. Grand Rapids. A *nice* Candy. Hey, you want something to eat?" He sounded almost affable, and serious in the offer. "I could get you a peanut butter and jelly sandwich. Candy?" His tone turned sugar sweet as He spoke to Juliet. "Something to eat?"

I felt her trembling stop suddenly, ominously, and I joggled her with my elbow before she could say anything. "Yes, thank you," I replied brightly. "Peanut butter and jelly sandwiches would be wonderful." I had never felt less like eating.

He opened a rusty old Coca-Cola machine—yes, there had been a Coke machine in the old librarians' lounge, so there had to be one now. He pulled bread and peanut butter and grape jelly out of it. Apparently He enjoyed using things for the wrong purposes, guns in the fridge, bread in the vending machine. And beer. He grabbed two cans of beer, tossing them to us left-handed from across the room. "Catch!"

It was as He lobbed the beers that I noticed the scars.

Not the scars on His face. Those were just from fighting. But now I saw significant scars on His wrist. Knife scars.

On both wrists.

More than once He had attempted suicide and failed.

I watched, sickened and fascinated, as He made the PB&Js with His vicious-looking knife, flourishing it with evident pleasure. "Pandora always loved peanut butter and jelly."

Because I was looking for scars now, I saw more. A crooked latticework of scars ran up the inside of both arms.

Not a fighter's scars. From self-mutilation?

Pandora scars?

Finished making sandwiches, He wiped the knife on His T-shirt, first one side of the blade, then the other, as if He were caressing Himself with Pandora. He tossed the sandwiches to us, or at us, the way He had thrown the beer cans. Both of us managed to catch the PB&Js before they fell into gooey sections, and He showed His teeth in a grin of sorts. "Eat up."

I forced down a bite of PB&J. Juliet held hers in both slack hands.

"I said, eat up!"

"This girl in Grand Rapids," I prompted, "you located her by using the Internet?"

"Yeah, that was after I got smart. I never had my own computer, but you can always use one in a public library. And I've always liked public libraries." I pretended I saw no innuendo in His chilly grin. "Even so, even on Facebook, Candies are hard to find, like unicorns, you know? But I check the Girl Scouts too, and the high school Web pages. Juliet, here, the most perfect Candy I've found so far, I traced her Facebook links to her high school band and her daddy's political campaign. Then I busted my ass to Fulcrum all the way from Wyoming—"

And He had been stalking Juliet at the same time I was— unbearable, to think of myself as a stalker. I cringed almost as much as I felt Juliet cringing. "The Grand Rapids one," I cut in to divert Him from Fulcrum. "The Grand Rapids Candy came first."

"Oh. Yeah, she was tasty." He sat at His table with His own PB&J, a beer, and His box of souvenirs, telling us about the Grand Rapids "Candy" graphically and at some length. I felt faint, then sick, then numb, as I smiled and nodded and occasionally managed to swallow a bite of sandwich, knowing I would need it for strength. The beer I only pretended to sip. Covertly I spilled some of it down the sofa. I was thirsty, but I had never tried beer or any drink with alcohol in it, and I wasn't sure how it would affect me on top of a severe lupus flare, and an empty stomach, and skipped medicine. I longed for a glass of water, but didn't dare to ask for one.

Talking, gesturing with both hands, our captor had laid His knife on the table. As I was thinking about the glass of water, He gave the knife one of His wooden looks, then poured a little beer on the blade. "Drink up, Pandora." He nodded at me robotically. "Pandora gets thirsty."

"I'm sure she does."

"Now, here's something interesting." He reached into the

shoe box again. "This ring. See the two silver hands clasped over the little gold heart? Very romantic. I got it off an Irish Candy in, let's see, bunghole town in Wyoming—Ten Sleep. Weird Indian name. Ten Sleep. And that's what I did. I slept with her exactly ten times. . . ."

He kept talking more and more eagerly, almost compulsively. I barely needed to murmur encouragement at intervals as He relived His adventures almost minute by minute, showing us His souvenirs—a black lace bra, a pink plastic rosary, a coin purse in the shape of a goldfish, a coil of braided brunette hair. . . . All that mattered was to let Him talk, not hurt us. From time to time He would get up, give us a warning glare, and stalk to the peephole for a moment, keeping an eye out for pigs. My exhausted mind envisioned herds of marauding peccaries in the parking lot. But none materialized. Sitting down, He would once again preside as if hosting a dinner party, laying His knife on the table to gesture with both hands. Words spewed out of Him, telling us the things He'd done. He needed to tell His story. We all did. And I doubt He had ever told His before. He'd never encountered anyone so willing to listen before. Interested, nonjudgmental. Female, fat, middle-aged, nonthreatening. Utterly safe, actually, since He would dispose of me when He was finished off-loading His burdensome memories on me. First, seductions. Later, rapes.

And more recently, murder.

Murder. Three girls, two of whom had never been found.

As He told us all about it except exact locations, Juliet slipped her untouched sandwich and her unopened beer into the pockets of my old tan coat, still wrapped around her. Pulling it close, she leaned against me. After a while she laid her head on my shoulder. From time to time I felt her relax and heard her breathing slow down as she dozed. Exhausted. And wise, to shut away tonight's terror with sleep, even if only for a few moments.

Our host seemed not to notice. After His sandwich and His second beer, He said, "Come on, Pandora," took the knife, stood up, turned His back to me, opened the fridge, pulled out one of the vegetable crisper drawers, and urinated in it. That is to say, I heard Him unzip, saw the back of His straddle stance, and heard Him whiz. Then He shook the drops off His favorite body part, zipped up, slid the crisper drawer back into place, and closed the fridge. He got Himself another beer out of the cola machine, sat down at the table again, laid down His knife, returned His focus to me, and kept talking. I smiled. I nodded. Inwardly I screamed and screamed, promising myself globs of chocolate ice cream and psychotherapy when this was all over, if I lived through it.

After His third beer, our captor's tone had turned downright affable, although His expression remained as flat as ever. "So that's ten, eleven, twelve Candies so far," He was saying as He sorted through the pile of baubles, lingerie, and miscellaneous show-and-tell on the table. "An even dozen."

Evidently the shoe box was empty. But I had to keep Him talking. "Um, and you brought them all here?"

"I didn't say that."

"But this is where you live, isn't it?" I thought of Sam, the way he'd make complimentary small talk whenever he entered anyone's home. He was good at that, observant, friendly, genuinely interested. A good salesman, a good businessman, a good manager, and even a good husband in his way, just not . . . exciting. Poor Sam. I wondered whether he'd called the police yet. I wondered whether he was getting any sleep. I wished I had told him I loved him very much, as I suddenly realized I did.

But I couldn't start wishing I'd said things and regretting I hadn't, or I wouldn't be able to focus on what I was doing. Wrenching my mind away from Sam, I told this other, nightmare man, "Very nice." I scanned the basement room, nodding seriously. "Very nice indeed. You have electricity—"

"I spliced into the neighbor's line." He leaned back in His chair, mellow, bragging. "They'll never know why their bill's so high. They don't even know I'm here. Nobody knows. I made sure the room's lightproof." For no apparent reason He reached out and picked up His knife. Pandora. Her stiletto tip, pointed toward the ceiling, glinted sharp and nasty, like evil in someone's eyes, as our host asked, "Are you scared of the dark, Marie baby?"

Apparently it was a rhetorical question, because He didn't wait for me to answer. The light went out.

I could see nothing but blackness. That room was as dark as my mother's heart. I gasped, just barely holding back a scream. Juliet, drowsing on my shoulder, squeaked as she woke up.

Before I could think, move, take advantage, the light blazed back on.

I sat blinking like emergency flashers. He sat at the table. He hadn't touched the light switch by the door, about eight feet away from Him. Come to think of it, He hadn't used the light switch when we'd walked in here either. The light had come on as we had all stood in the center of the room.

"Sounded like somebody's scared of the dark," He remarked, and the light went out again.

Darkness tangible coffined us. My heart pounded; I felt as if I'd been buried alive. I heard His chair scrape back as He stood up. I heard His footsteps. In the utter blackness, I felt Juliet grab for my hand. I squeezed hers, and her need for me made me react almost calmly. "How'd you do that?"

I heard Him give a kind of low bark, almost a laugh, and zap, the light was back, making my eyes wince. He stood at the peephole, but facing us.

"I'll be damned," He remarked. "It's morning. Daylight."

"How can you tell?" I pretended stupidity, wanting to know how that peephole worked.

Instead of answering, He tossed His knife toward the ceiling. It spun in the air. He caught it by the handle, flung it upward again, caught it, did it again. And again. I watched Him, my mind so blurred with fatigue that I felt hypnotized.

"Psychokinesis," He said.

"Huh?"

"Psychokinesis." Holding the knife, He sat at the table again. "You didn't think I knew any big words, did you, bitch?"

Actually, I knew all too well how intelligent He was. "You're smart," I said humbly. "Did you go to college?"

"Hell, no. I never finished high school."

"Then how did you learn to do all these thing? Lightproofing, electric heat, and"—I tried not to look as if I needed to know—"I wouldn't be surprised if you have running water in here too."

He remained unsuspicious. "Sure. No problem. Cistern on the roof. People forget these old buildings have cisterns built in."

"What was this building originally?" I asked. "Some kind of factory?"

I was just making conversation, stalling for time. But His face flattened, and His stony eyes went extra cold. "Dumb-ass slut, you think I'm stupid? You think I'm gonna tell you where you are?"

"No, I just wondered—"

"Shut up." As if someone had flipped a toggle in His head,

His mood had switched, and He was done talking to me. He had used me and now He was finished with me. "I don't know why the hell I'm bothering with you when I could be halfway there with number thirteen." He nodded at Juliet.

He had not raised His voice, only changed His tone. Yet I felt Juliet's whole body jerk upright, rigid.

Knife in hand, He stood up, shoving the table out of His way. Swaggering to the middle of the room, He loomed over us. "You, Candy, get your wrappers off," He ordered, thumbing the edge of Pandora's blade. "Start with that coat."

NINE

After catching the scantiest of naps on a sofa outside the department building's restrooms, Sissy was awakened by the arrival of the early shift.

Once on her feet, she shuffled to the front desk. "Boss here?" she asked the harried woman who worked Sunday mornings.

"Just came in. Been all night at the Phillips place."

"Anything new on the missing girl?"

"Nope." The woman was not friendly, not unfriendly. Like most of the department employees, she had worked there for over a decade, and would not begin to regard Sissy as significant until Sissy had lasted at least a year.

"How's the chief holding up?"

Expressively the woman arched one eyebrow.

"That bad, huh?"

"No sleep, DA's daughter's missing? If Chief Angstrom was a terror threat, I'd color him red."

"Hoo boy. Thanks." Sissy walked off, no longer shuffling. It wasn't as if she didn't know what she had to do anyway. After just a minute in the women's room to wash her face with cold water and consult the mirror to straighten herself up, Sissy tapped on Chief Angstrom's office door.

"Enter." The roar from within sounded neither louder nor softer than usual.

Sissy entered. Stood in front of his desk. Said, "Sir," instead of "Good morning, sir," because she felt the latter might be inappropriate under the circumstances.

He peered up at her from his chair, and she was startled to notice that one of his heavy, scowling eyebrows was parting company slightly with his forehead. The boss wore false eyebrows? Eyebrow *toupees*?

"Well, what is it?" he barked.

Fake scary eyebrows. What a hoot. Sissy wondered if everyone in the department knew except her. With remarkable ease because she could not be intimidated while trying not to laugh, she said, "Sir, I have something new on the Dorrie White case."

"If you mean the Juliet Phillips abduction case, you've wasted your time, not to speak of making improper use of department computers." He aimed a scowl her way to impress upon her that of course he knew what she had done. "We don't have jurisdiction at this point in time. It's Appletree's case now."

"And the Dorrie White missing persons case?" Sissy volleyed without an eyeblink's hesitation. The warning scowl, meaning Bud Angstrom Knows All, had failed to intimidate her when she was hoping that one of the beetling eyebrows might fall off.

But a snort of unfunny laughter from the boss stiffened her spine, reminding her she was still a rookie. "What missing persons case? You know they'll find Dorrie White when they find Juliet Phillips."

Very likely true, Sissy knew, although not in the way Angstrom meant it. In his mind he had already convicted Dorrie of abduction.

In her hand Sissy held a report on an alternate suspect: Blake Roman. Although there was not a word about handwriting in it, Sissy did not really want her boss to see it anymore. In her most sure-'nuff tone she said, "I guess I'll just fax this to Appletree PD, then."

But Angstrom was alerted at once. "Fax what?"

She did not allow herself to sigh in resignation to her fate. "Blake Roman," she summarized her document, "wanted fugitive, raised in Appletree, a couple years older than Dorrie White. Went to school with her when she was Dorrie Birch. Served time for sexual assault, wanted for parole violation and for questioning in the abduction, rape, and murder of a teenage girl. I found pictures of the girl. She bears a marked resemblance to Juliet Phillips, who looks almost exactly like Mrs. White did when she was young."

"From the photos of what she looks like now, that's hard to believe," said Angstrom acidly.

But at least he showed some interest. Good. A man capable of understanding and exploiting the psychological nuances of bristly eyebrows perhaps deserved more credit for smarts than she'd been giving him, Sissy reflected.

"Based on?" he asked.

"When I was at her house, I saw her wedding photos. Do I need to get a copy of one?"

"You need other things a lot worse. What else have you got?"

"Just to sum up, the love letters Dorrie White hid under her mattress were from someone named Blake," she said. "Maybe it was Blake Roman. Maybe, like a lot of rapists, he was hung up on somebody he couldn't have, and that somebody was Dorrie. Maybe he abducted Juliet because she looks like her biological mother."

"And maybe instead of just plain balls you've got crystal

balls," Angstrom said. "All this based on his effing *hand-writing*?"

"There's not a word in the report about handwriting."

"Huh," he grunted, apparently involuntarily.

Sissy pressed her case. "Just the facts. Which fit."

Angstrom chewed his lower lip and gave her the peer from under his eyebrows again.

"All I'm saying is heads up, this man exists," Sissy told him.

"All right, if you found him in NCIC, he exists, and I suppose the Appletree PD ought to know. Did you send them copies of the White woman's photos yet?"

"No, sir." How could she, when she'd just learned of the jurisdictional change? Angstrom liked to take advantage of any excuse to bark.

"Well, get on it!"

"Yes, sir. Is that all, sir?"

"Damn right it is! Go the freak home and get some effing sleep!"

"Yes, sir. Good morning, sir."

Sissy did not allow herself to smile until she had closed the chief's office door behind her and headed toward the fax machine.

Sam exceeded the speed limit considerably on his drive to Appletree and pulled in around dawn on Sunday morning, twelve hours and a sleepless night since he'd come home to find Dorrie missing.

Maybe it was his lack of sleep, or his mood, or the gray light or the crepuscular time of day, but Appletree seemed ominous to him, like a movie set, like the sort of small town where bad things happen and are hushed up. He noticed there was hardly anybody on the street, as if people were either afraid to venture out or else waiting for their cues. Rolling at sixty miles per hour right through the middle of what seemed like a ghost town, Sam saw the blue sign he'd been told to watch for and pulled in at the Appletree Municipal Building/Fire Hall/Police Station.

Driving around back to park, under sulfurous security lights he saw a yellow rollback emergency road-service truck.

And on the truck, Dorrie's Kia.

Abandoning his Silverado in mid–parking lot, Sam ran to the rollback and climbed onto the truck bed. "Dorrie?" he called as if she might be asleep in the car.

God, the front of the car was a mess. All rumpled up. Windshield smashed. Didn't look like any normal kind of accident Sam had ever seen. An attack?

From below and behind him a deep voice demanded, "What the hell you think you're doing?"

Sam turned, saw a muscular man in a police uniform, and counterdemanded, "Did you look in the back?"

"Get down off there before I—"

A second, softer, gravelly voice said, "Now hold on, Walker."

A second cop stood there, a craggy, crater-faced man approaching retirement age. He asked Sam, "You Mr. White?"

"Yes!" Sam's head ached from clenching his jaw, his eyes burned, his mind swam with fatigue, and all his manners seemed to have deserted him. "Did you look in the back! Somebody might have stuffed her into the back!"

"Yes, we looked. No, we didn't find anything." The old cop's voice managed to be gritty and gentle at the same time.

"You're tampering with evidence, Mr. White." The burly cop spoke more quietly, but his resentment sounded barely restrained.

"We been over that car with a fine-tooth comb," said the old cop. "Let him look. Mr. White, we found no bloodstains in the car and no damage in the occupancy area. The car has a messed-up axle, and you can see it's got extensive damage to the hood and the windshield, but there's no indication that anyone was hurt."

"What the—" Sam stopped just in time. Good Lord, he'd be swearing next. Then he'd sound like a bum as well as looking like one. Tightening his control on his voice and himself, he tried again. "What is the air pump doing hanging on front?"

"Looks like somebody secured the hood with it. Funny way of going about it."

Sam found himself breathing easier, beginning to feel intimations of hope. The old man had said no one was hurt. And yes, Sam began to believe, Dorrie had survived the accident, because Dorrie had tied that air pump there. It was just the sort of thing Dorrie would do.

"So the hood flew up and smashed the windshield and then she tied the hood down. . . ." Speaking somewhat more calmly, Sam moved around to the side and yanked open the passenger door to peer into the car. "No purse or anything."

"We figure she walked away from the accident, whatever kind of accident it was, and she took it with her."

"Then why wouldn't she use her cell phone? She always carried it with her."

"We don't know."

"Why would she tie the hood down, then walk away?"

"We don't know that either."

"You shouldn't be messing around in there," said the other cop in resigned, rote tones, "but since you already are, you notice anything else unusual?"

Sam looked. "Tools in the backseat. They should be stowed with the spare tire."

"Any sign she had a passenger in the car?"

"*No.*" Sam couldn't seem to get the edge out of his voice. Leaning into the car, he flipped open the glove box. Kia manual, insurance forms, registration, all the usual items were still there. Except one. "The flashlight's missing."

"Flashlight, huh?"

"Yes."

"Well, I guess it would be natural for her to take a flashlight with her in the nighttime. You come down off of there before the high pooh-bah of FBI arrives and I have to put handcuffs on you."

Sam jumped down. As his feet hit the ground, he demanded, "What have you been doing to find her?"

The younger cop scowled. "Waiting for the FBI. The way I figure, they've got a lot more resources than we do. And when they find the Phillips girl, they'll find your wife." He yawned, showing some fillings in his molars.

Sam could not imagine how anyone could just assume Dorrie had taken off with the Phillips girl. And he especially could not imagine how anyone could yawn when Dorrie had not yet been found. Tightening his lips, he fought back several unwise comments, saying only, "So you don't have any new information to go on? Anything at all?"

"Not that I know of. Bert? I thought I heard the fax machine printing out something."

"Just the usual morning junk."

"BOLOs from California?"

"As if anybody from California would ever show up here," the older man explained to Sam. Then he turned back to his apparent boss. "Yep. That kind of thing."

"I thought I heard the paper shredder going too."

"Right." The craggy old cop turned to Sam again and asked, "Would you like a cup of coffee?"

The old guy's voice was kind. Suddenly unable to speak, Sam nodded, telling himself he was accepting the coffee for the sake of caffeine, to stay awake.

"Cream and sugar?"

Nod. The bitter concoction had to be more bearable with cream and sugar.

"Inside," said the surly younger police officer, leading the way.

Following him and the old cop into the station, Sam found his eyes stinging, going blind with tears. He blinked fiercely. No matter how tough things got, and no matter how exhausted he felt, he couldn't let himself get emotional. He had to stay calm. He had to find Dorrie.

"I told you, get that coat off!"

Sitting rigid next to me on the sofa, Juliet did not obey. Maybe defiant. Maybe too terrified to move. He had His knife. He towered over us.

Loudly and firmly I intervened. "I have to go to the bathroom."

This was absolutely true. I'd been saving up to have to go to the bathroom at some crucial point.

"So do I!" Juliet gasped. "I have to go to the bathroom too!"

His wooden face went balsa pale. The color of a skull. Death. He lifted the knife to lunge.

He was going to kill us.

Juliet screamed.

I shoved her toward the far end of the sofa as I leapt up to

fling myself between Him and her. Or tried to leap. I staggered, lurched, wobbled to my feet. Damn lupus. Damn stiff
legs and barely functional back. Hitching forward to stop Him,
I realized I'd already succeeded, although not in the way I had
intended. Frozen a couple of steps from the sofa with His knife
in the air, He stood gawking at me.

When I was a little girl playing on my uncle's farm, I had
seen how the hen pheasant flounders and flutters, pretending
her wing is broken, to lure danger away from her chicks. And
even knowing this, whenever I had nearly stepped on a flapping
hen in the weedy meadow, I had still chased after her.

Now I was the frantic, playacting hen luring the predator
away from my chick. Pretending to ignore Him, limping heavily,
I floundered to the door and tried the handle. It was locked, of
course.

He demanded, "Stupid slut, what you think you're doing?"

Somehow my voice still came out strong. "I need to go to
the *bathroom.*"

"You saw where it is." He motioned toward the fridge. "Help
yourself."

Unwisely I turned on Him. "I'll empty it on your head
first."

And maybe following my lead, Juliet flared, "Throw some
on precious Pandora too!"

We'd gone too far. Snake-quick, He coiled to strike her,
knife hand raised. I couldn't see His face, but I saw the look on
hers as she closed her eyes so she wouldn't see death coming.
Before I had time to scream or hurl myself toward—

He said, "Candy need to go pee-pee?" Just like that, His
tone had flipped to the sickeningly sweet extreme. He tossed
His knife into the air and caught it by the handle almost play-
fully. "Tell you what, sugar Candy, I'll let you and pukeface

Marie both go potty in the ladies' room down the hall if you give her ugly coat back to her."

I limped over there, signaling Juliet with my eyes, *Do it.* She stood up, letting my thick quilted coat slip from her thin shoulders. I took it from her, holding it over one arm. In her skimpy top and jeans, she stood trembling like a deer.

"Now you're sweet sweet Candy," He pattered like a carnival barker. "See how nice I can be when you're my good sugar Candy? Come on, babies, Pandora and I will take you to the potty." Waving His knife like a signal flag, He directed us both toward the door.

I expected Him to step ahead of us and unlock it, His back to us. I hoped maybe I'd be able to throw myself on Him, knock Him down.

Instead, from behind us He ordered, "Go."

I said, "Unlock it."

"Already did."

I tried the handle. It turned. He had it rigged up somehow, like the ceiling light and like the seat belt in the van. Pulling on the door—it opened inward—I felt all too much the way I used to when my father hogged the TV remote: helpless and furious. Seething, I stepped out into a basement corridor, all too aware that our captor could flick off the light at any moment and trap us in total blackness. The only illumination came from the room we were leaving, and even with it, that passageway seemed dim as a tunnel. Especially with that awful dark paneling, that mottled brown indoor-outdoor carpeting . . . the same mud-toned carpeting I remembered from seventeen years before, although it lay in threadbare patches now.

I knew where this hallway went.

"Stop there," ordered the voice from behind me. That strange, familiar voice. Daydream voice. Nightmare voice, now.

I halted outside a door that looked as elderly as the building, tall and solid, probably oak, with rectangular insets but no glass except—what was that glass door over the top of the door called? A transom. I suppose, back before there had been either air-conditioning or electric light, they'd needed it up there for ventilation and some illumination of the hallway. Now the transom's wavy old glass showed only darkness.

Juliet stood close beside me, skinny arms wrapped across her chest, hugging herself.

"One at a time," our escort directed. "Light switch is inside on the right. You'll notice the lock is on *this* side." He flourished His knife toward a substantial bolt on the outside of the doorframe.

Oh, no remote control device on this door? "Kind of low-tech," I remarked.

And wished instantly that I hadn't. The look He gave me froze my blood. "But very effective," He retorted too softly. "Don't try anything stupid or I'll leave you in there to die and rot." His stony eyes shifted in thought. "Might be the way to do it, Marie," He added, almost friendly. "I don't want any of your weird-ass freaking blood on me or Pandora." He gestured with the knife. "You say you gotta go, all right, go."

He terrified me. I didn't want to go into that room. Not at all.

Only my pride and a desperate plan made me do it.

I clenched my jaw, straightened my shoulders, and stepped into the bathroom. Flicking the light on, I closed the heavy oak door behind me. And from the other side I heard the bolt snick.

Oh, God, I'd left Juliet alone with Him. What if He took her and—

Don't dither. Act.

I blundered into one of the two tall old wooden stalls. This must have been a private bathroom for the librarians, smaller than the upstairs restroom I remembered using as a child, although every bit as ugly: the same bilious green paint, and no window except a tiny one at the very top of the wall, boarded over from outside. Way out of my reach anyhow. Why had they made the ceilings so darn high in these old buildings, even in the basement?

This room, like the other one, must have been lightproof. Or else He figured that nobody would notice a little light seeping around the plywood covering the window, not in the daylight. If it really was daylight. If He hadn't been lying to us, playing mind games with us.

No wonder I felt surreal, like I was swimming in a fever dream, half-crazy, not knowing whether it was day or night or what time it was. I wished I had my wristwatch.

I wished . . . so many things I wished. I wished I'd lived more and worried less. I wished I'd been able to have children. I wished I'd gotten to know my husband better. Sam was a truly good guy. I wished I'd told him more, trusted him more. What had seemed like "sparing him" at the time now looked like cowardice. If he found out things about me after I died, he was going to be terribly hurt.

Sam, I'm sorry. . . .

Once again I made myself stop thinking of him, because I had to keep my mind on staying alive, and keeping Juliet alive, one minute at a time. Sitting on the toilet, I made myself hurry up and use it, all the time listening for—I don't know. Voices cursing, or shouting, or screaming.

But I heard nothing.

I stood up, adjusted my clothing, flushed. Out of the stall, I turned on the water at the sink so it would sound like I was washing my hands. Actually, I was sticking my face under the spigot to gulp a hasty drink. And at the same time I was emptying the pockets of the coat Juliet had handed back to me: a peanut butter and jelly sandwich, a can of beer, some wads of Kleenex. Good.

Finished with my drink, I stepped back into the stall, took Juliet's PB&J first and used the beer can to ram it down the toilet, then followed up with the aforementioned can and the wads of Kleenex. Plugging things, such as the van's tailpipe, seemed to be my new forte. Adding a generous handful of toilet paper, I plugged that toilet very quickly and, I hoped, very well.

"What the hell is taking you so long?" demanded a harsh voice outside the door.

Good. Good, He was right there, not back in that horrible room, not—not doing anything to Juliet.

I called, "Coming."

"Get your filthy ass moving."

I tucked the ends of the wet TP out of sight in the bowels of the toilet, then stood up and took one more look. Nothing showed. Good job. I didn't want this toilet to look like a mess. I wanted Juliet to use it.

The knife-edged voice outside the door shouted, "*Move, bitch, or I'm coming in!*"

There wasn't time to mess up the other stall.

But what if Juliet used the wrong toilet?

I left my coat draped over the stall door of the one I'd tampered with. I felt sure Juliet would notice. She would head for that stall to get the coat back. But whether she would sense a signal, I had no way of knowing.

Turning off the sink faucet, drying my hands on my skirt for lack of a better option, I reached the door just as it banged open and, knife raised, the abductor scowled in at me.

I let my gaze slide right over His glare to focus on Juliet instead.

"Next," I told her, looking her intently in the face, trying to tell her without words, *Use the stall with the coat.*

He closed the door behind her and bolted it, all the time keeping His knife at the ready and His eyes stonily on me. I could see Him all too well now that electric light poured out over top of the bathroom door, through the transom.

"What took you so long in there?" He demanded.

"It takes women longer," I informed Him in teacherly tones, "especially after we get to a certain age." Mentally I prayed, *Juliet, the one with the coat, and hurry.*

"Bullshit. You were up to something. I can see it in your ugly face." He balanced His knife on its thick black handle in the palm of His hand. There it stood with its blade up like a silver flame of hell. Even in my worst paranoia—and I'd been entertaining a morbid phobia of knives for a long time—even in my worst nightmares, I never would have imagined there were so many ways to scare a person with a knife. This man and His dear Pandora had threatened me a dozen times a dozen different ways and each one intimidated me more. Or maybe it was His stony-flat crazy glare, or the way He lowered His head like a stallion closing in on a filly. I started to sweat.

He said, "I want to know what you—"

I heard the watery whoosh of a toilet flushing, and then Juliet shrieked. And bless her, she flushed it again, and kept screaming hysterically. "Let me out! It's going everywhere. It's going to get on me. Let me *out!*" I heard her throw herself against the inside of the door, pounding with her fists, so frenzied she scared me, and I had been expecting something of the sort.

"What the—" Our captor lunged for the bolt.

With His back to me.

He flung open the door. With my coat clutched around her, Juliet darted out of the bathroom like a cat spritzed by a sprinkler.

And as He peered in there to see what the problem was, I shoved Him from behind as hard as I could.

Sitting on a cold folding metal chair in the bulky cop's cubicle, Sam informed him that Appletree was Dorrie's hometown. He couldn't believe the big, obnoxious jerk—what was his name? He couldn't believe Walker hadn't known. Only then did Sam realize that probably the Fulcrum police hadn't informed the FBI of the significance of Appletree either, or hadn't known themselves, and he wished somebody had taught him how to swear.

Instead, he answered too many questions he'd already been asked before. Additionally, he gave a description of the missing flashlight. The craggy old cop, who apparently functioned as a gofer, brought coffee. Sam drank his. Yeah, the brew tasted not quite as gruesome when loaded with cream and sugar, but it didn't cut through his fatigue as much as he'd hoped. He still felt as if he were trying to conduct business underwater.

He told the Walker cop—one of those people too legendary in their own mind to use a first name—"I want to see where you found Dorrie's car."

"This isn't Fulcrum, Mr. White. The Appletree police department consists pretty much of me, myself, and I, and now the FBI is going to be all over me like flies on a rump roast—"

"I'm not asking you to take me." Sam tried to keep his voice under control. "I just—"

"What I'm saying is, I have to stay put waiting until the FBI gets here, and I can't spare *anyone* to take you."

"So just tell me where it is and how I get there!"

"It's a crime scene. Restricted access. Sorry."

A gravelly voice said, "I'll take him." The venerable cop who had brought the coffee still stood in the doorway.

"Bert, now, think," Walker complained before Sam could say thanks. "In what vehicle? I don't have a vehicle to spare any more than I have a man to spare."

"You can spare me. I'm just deadweight left over from the previous administration. You can't wait till I retire. Anyway, I'm on my six-in-the-morning lunch break." Bert turned to Sam with twinkling eyes that didn't look sleepy at all. "We'll have to go in your truck."

"That's fine! Thank you, um . . ." Sam glanced at his name tag, wanting to thank the nice old guy by his proper name and title. But the plastic pseudo-metal tag was so worn and faded he couldn't read it. It had probably been on the job as long as this cop. Definitely it was ready to retire.

"No, it's not fine," snapped Walker. "It isn't regulation."

"Well, we're going anyway."

Walker growled something worth ignoring. As Sam mentally counted to ten, the old officer escorted him out of the station.

Crossing the parking lot, Sam handed him the keys. "You drive."

"You sure?"

"Positive. You don't want me driving. I've been up all night."

As the old cop chauffeured him through Appletree, Sam leaned back and closed his burning eyes, feeling nerves firing and muscles jumping in his legs.

"I been trying to remember your wife," said the old cop. "Her maiden name was Birch? I recall a Douglas Birch, used to run a used-car lot—"

Sam shook his head. "No relation." Sam felt too tired to explain that Dorrie's family, like other members of their religious sect, had kept very much to themselves, even to the point of ordering their household goods wholesale and growing their own meat and vegetables.

"Not Catholic, huh?" Receiving no response, the old man added, "Was her mother a Miller? I seem to recall one of the Miller girls married some guy from out of state, might have been Birch—"

"No." Sam's mind and mouth felt too sluggish to vouchsafe Dorrie's mother's maiden name, but he did manage to open his eyes. "Thank you."

The old man gave him a puzzled glance. "Thank me for what?"

The reason seemed obvious to Sam at the time. "For trying to remember her."

The old cop shrugged. "I got a good memory for people. It bothers me that I can't place her."

If Dorrie was dead, who was going to remember her? *Me. Three friends. And her parents. Barely.*

Sam turned and stared out his window so the old man would not see his blinking eyes.

The car stopped in the roadway and Bert said, "Here's the FBI's so-called crime scene."

Sam looked where Bert was pointing, out the driver's side window at the corner across the street. The "restricted area" was just an expanse of disintegrating concrete sidewalk cordoned off with yellow police tape—inconveniently for pedestrians, who had to walk in the street to get past. A couple of old men were doing just that, shuffling along the asphalt, eyeing the empty sidewalk. A massive, bored-looking woman in a police uniform stood guard with her back against the corner building, which still read WILSON UMBRELLA REPAIR in faded gold paint on the window. How long had it been since anybody repaired umbrellas?

"Car was right up on the sidewalk by the phone booth," Bert said, rolling down his window and waving at a vehicle behind him to drive past.

Sam saw the pay phone, though he wouldn't have called that box on a post a booth. He saw a newspaper vending machine. He saw the old guys walking past. He saw the guard. None of this helped him.

He admitted, "I don't know what I expected to accomplish here."

"Well, let's have a closer look." Bert flicked the left blinker on, waited for a break in traffic, then turned into the narrow side street that ran beside the public phone. Past the first building he swung right into a gravel parking lot, where he stopped the Silverado. Turning it off, he got out.

Sam trudged after him, only marginally aware of the few other vehicles parked in the gravel lot, then the derelict building to his left as he headed diagonally across the street. Abandoned buildings made him feel depressed, the mess people made of them, breaking windows so they had to be boarded up with plywood, scrawling graffiti. . . . Sure enough, he saw graffiti printed on the concrete basement wall of this structure, but he turned his bleary gaze away.

He and Bert stepped up the curb and stopped at the yellow POLICE LINE DO NOT CROSS tape. "Hey, Paula," Bert said to the guard.

"Hey, Bert." She barely looked at him.

"This is Mr. White."

"Niceta meetcha." She barely looked at Sam either. Sam took this as permission to pretend she wasn't there.

So did Bert, apparently, turning back to Sam. "Your wife's car was thereabouts," he told him, sketching the positioning of the Kia with both hands swinging in air. "Like so, pointed thataway."

"How the heck did it get up here on the sidewalk?"

"We don't know."

Three times now Sam had heard Bert's gravelly voice say those words. He didn't like them. But he did like Bert's honesty. With mixed feelings he grumbled, "Well, at least you'll admit it."

"First thing I learned as a cop. Know when you don't know."

Sam stared at the cracks in the sidewalk. They told him nothing. He asked, "Is there anything we *do* know?"

"We know your wife's car was here. We presume she left it. But nobody's seen her that we've talked to. We knocked on doors for a block in every direction last night. Now the FBI's come in, they'll probably do it again."

"They're here?"

"Heard it on the radio a little while back."

"Where are they? What are they doing?"

He noticed that the impassive guard actually rolled her eyes, although she still didn't look at him.

The craggy old cop replied without expression, "They didn't consult me, but I can imagine. They're checking the bus station. Trying to get hold of the management of the local so-called airport and the guy who runs the taxi. Checking reports of stolen cars. Trying to figure where she went with the girl when her car failed."

Sam burst out, "Dorrie is not a kidnapper! Why can't they get that through their heads?"

"They got hold of this thing by that end and—"

"But that's asinine! How did her car get so messed up? And why would she drive it over the curb and leave it on the corner?"

The old cop's scratchy voice kept getting lower. "Gotta admit it doesn't make much sense to me either." Bert paused, then added gently, "Unless maybe somebody forced her off the road."

Oh, God. Sam's breath stopped.

God, that was it. He'd grabbed her. The real kidnapper. The guy who had abducted the Phillips girl. The guy Dorrie was pursuing.

"No!" Explosively, Sam regained his breath. "No, that can't be it." Shaking his head doggedly, Sam faced the gray-haired cop. "I mean, yes, it's a possibility, but there has to be some other . . ." Sam's frantic gaze caught on the pay phone. "Something happened to her phone. Maybe she wanted to use this one."

"She could have just parked across the way like we did."

Amazingly, the woman standing guard spoke. "That phone don't work. Hasn't worked for months."

"Oh, for the love of mercy . . ." Scanning desperately, Sam focused on the boarded-up building across the street. He pointed. "Have you looked for her in there?"

"The old library?" Bert eyed it, chewing on his lower lip. "You'd practically need dynamite to get in there, they've got the old place sealed up so tight. The guys checked around, saw no signs of forcible entry."

"So nobody could have gotten in there."

"Nope. There's no access."

TEN

Yelling at Juliet, "Get the door!" I shoved our captor with all my might into the bathroom.

All my might doesn't amount to much, because lupus sabotages muscle tissue and also because, heck, I never had much upper-body strength to start with. Plus, this—this evil man whose name I knew but couldn't bear to acknowledge—He was solid. I didn't send Him flying. He took only one stumbling step inside the bathroom doorway before He turned on me with the knife, the white-hot fury in His face so incandescent it immobilized me. His uplifted knife might as well have been a sword of fire. Silver fire with a name. Pandora. Mother of all evil. In a moment I would die—

"Bitch!" He screamed, lunging to stab me.

And He slipped in the water under His feet.

He fell.

Whump. With a splash, on His face in the water running over the floor. His knife flew into a corner. I heard His head hit the tile with a goodly whack.

And Juliet slammed the door just as I regained my wits and started to reach for it. I jammed the heavy bolt into place.

Juliet flung herself onto me, sobbing, arms around me in a tight hug.

My daughter. Hugging me.

Nothing had ever felt so good. And nothing had ever given me so much strength. In that moment I could have done anything. Anything. And would have, for her.

I patted her heaving shoulders. "We're not out of here yet, sweetie. Come on." Already I heard Him stirring, swearing, floundering on the other side of the bolted door.

She heard too, and turned me loose. Grabbing her hand, I ran up the hallway to the back stairwell.

Her clunky shoes thunked, my sneakers thudded, echoes flew like bats in the darkness. We could see only dimly as we left the light from the bathroom transom behind us. We actually slammed into the barrier before we saw it.

"Ow!"

A wall rose where the doorway to the stairwell should have been.

A crude wall made of scrap lumber solidly screwed or nailed in place.

In that moment I knew we were still trapped.

We had to find a way out.

"About-face," I tried to joke. We ran back past the bathroom, braving a nightmare clamor of pounding fists and barely human shouts. It was like dodging past the faceless monster in a very bad dream. Wincing, flinching, we ran away from threats distorted almost beyond understanding by rage.

"Should have knocked Him out," I panted as we darted to the other end of the hallway.

Should have kicked Him unconscious, was what I should have done. Kicked Him in the chin. Or better yet, grabbed the heavy cover off a toilet tank and clobbered Him. Why had I lacked the good sense to beat His evil head in?

". . . way we came in," Juliet gasped over her shoulder,

veering right as we came to the door of the room in which we'd been imprisoned.

Another dark, shabby hallway ran that way for maybe ten feet.

"It doesn't . . ." I was just about to say it didn't go anywhere when Juliet thudded around a corner into darkness.

"Damn!" she wailed as she banged up against another barrier. "Where's the knob?"

A door. Right. We'd come in this way. Through a door.

But it didn't feel like a door. It felt like a wall. A steely cold metal wall, impermeable, impregnable. I ran my hands all over it, standing on tiptoe, then crouching to the ground, and felt nothing except Juliet's searching hands bumping against mine. That, and the stark smooth metal under our fingertips, our palms.

In the bathroom, not nearly far enough away, our enemy's clamor changed shape, hardened like a flexed muscle, and focused into a single percussive blow. Rigid, I listened. There was a gathering silence, then another even harder *WHAM*, like a cannon firing.

"He's trying to kick the door down! Come on." Clutching at Juliet, I ran back into the hateful room we'd started from. I slammed the door behind me and leaned against it, blinking in the blaze of the electric light. Thank God He hadn't turned it off. Maybe too enraged to think of it. Or maybe the control was somewhere here in this room?

"Lock it!" Juliet cried. "Lock the door!"

"I don't know how. He's got it on some kind of remote control." I limped a few steps and grabbed one end of the sofa. "Help me wedge this in front of it."

Instantly she ran to the other end, put her shoulder to the sofa and heaved for all she was worth. She shoved that heavy thing in front of the door almost entirely by herself. My daughter. So quick, so strong.

Not like me. My strength had lasted only a moment. Now I felt as weak as the third cup of tea.

With the sofa in place, we stood panting and listening. Silence. Not a nice silence. Then *WHAM* down the hallway, and I heard the sound of shattering glass.

"He broke the transom!"

"The what?"

"The window thing over the—"

My flailing, drowning mind grabbed hold of something, I couldn't yet tell what, and I stood there with my mouth open.

"The bathroom *window*?" Juliet cried. "It's boarded over, and anyhow it's *way* too high to get out. Why did they have to make everything so *tall*?"

Window.

That was the mental flotsam I was trying to grab.

I lurched into action, ordering, "Table. Quick!"

"Huh?"

"Table over there. Hurry." I pointed toward the wall opposite the door, then found some strength again; I shoved the table there myself without waiting for her to help. I rammed it against the wall beneath the peephole.

I still didn't fully understand, but the peephole had to be connected to the hidden window somehow. I knew there used to be a window. Light in my face, affronting my guilty eyes as I lay on the sofa. Feet passing in the parking lot. I remembered now.

"Up," I told Juliet. "On the table." No way my disabled bulk could climb up there. "Hurry!"

Looking totally bewildered, my daughter climbed onto the

table. As she knelt on top of it, I snatched the clunky shoes off her feet and handed one of them to her.

"Stand up, use that like a hammer—"

"Stinking bitches!" roared a crazed male voice right outside our door. "Dumb sluts! Pandora's going to butcher you!" Something, probably His foot, crashed against the wood. "Pandora's going to cut you bloody wide open and carve the dog parts out of you!"

Juliet went pale. "He's out," she whispered.

"Listen to me," I told her fiercely. "Hammer the paneling up there in the corner."

As I pointed, the room light went out, leaving us in darkness thicker than fudge.

Juliet shrieked, then began to sob.

"Do it, girl!" I ordered, making my voice as commanding as I could. "Reach as high as you can and hit the wall as hard as you can. Now!"

She sure did. I heard that heavy clunky-heeled shoe whack like an ax, and with a stab of hope in my heart I heard wood splinter. The cheap paneling caved in. Daylight poured through the breach.

"Oh!" Juliet cried.

"Break through and get *out*." I limped to the fridge, opened it, and grabbed a gun.

Whack, whack—I heard Juliet striking at the paneling. *Hurry*, my mind prayed, but I couldn't spare time to glance back and see how she was doing. As I lifted the gun, the room's door opened a crack, pressing against the sofa, inching it forward.

With the pistol heavy and alien in my hand I flung my considerable weight against the sofa, trying to force the door closed again.

And I did it. Strength of panic. Safe. Safe for a moment. Door closed, blocked. Panting, I braced myself against the sofa, the gun I had appropriated sagging at my side as I swiveled, trying to face the enemy.

Whack behind me, and a sound like angel bells, beautiful, glorious, the tinkle of glass breaking. Juliet had broken through the window—

Without even a yell or a curse for warning, the top of the door exploded in, shards of wood flying like bomb shrapnel. Over the top of the sofa my dream nightmare man came flying, shoulders first, smashing into me—incidentally, I think, because I happened to be in the way. I landed butt first on my back, my breath knocked out, seeing without quite understanding as He somersaulted to His feet, lunged at Juliet, grabbed her by the ankles, and flung her off the table.

She hit the floor headfirst.

I staggered to my feet and pointed my gun at Him. "Stop it!" I yelled.

He gave me that wooden look. "Dumb fuck," He said, striding toward me, "you don't know how to use that."

He was right, of course. My hand shook so badly I was afraid I'd hit Juliet if I fired at Him. But on TV guns were magic, right? Shoot one and everybody got scared and scuttled away except the police, who came running. I pointed the pistol in a vaguely upward direction, closed my eyes, and squeezed the trigger.

Click. Nothing happened.

I opened my eyes to find His face inches from mine, His glare freezing me witless. He grabbed the pistol by the barrel and wrenched it away from me. In the same swift movement He clobbered me on the head with the handle. Hard. Knocked me out.

• • •

"I'm sorry I dragged you out here," Sam said as he and the craggy old cop walked back toward the parking lot where they'd left the Silverado. "I don't know what I expected to prove."

The old guy gave him a wry look. "Nobody expects you to prove a thing. That's the FBI's job."

"Just the same, I'm wasting your time."

"What else would I be doing, making coffee?"

Sam sensed that the safest response would be not to respond. In silence he and the gray-haired officer crunched across the gravel back to the pickup truck.

Opening the passenger's-side door, Sam got in. Outside the day was turning sunny and fine, but in Sam's mind the weather was a snowing, freezing blank. He couldn't see farther than his next step—the old cop would drive him back to the Appletree police station, and after that, he just wanted to lie down and give in. Escape from this all-too-real nightmare. Sleep and never wake up.

As he sat in the car, blearily gazing at the hulking derelict that had once been a nice solid brick building, his glance caught once again on the graffiti. Too tired and discouraged to turn away, he automatically read:

CANDY GOT LAID HERE

Sam sat bolt upright, all thoughts of stopping, rest, and sleep forgotten. "Officer Bert," he whispered to the man getting into the driver's seat next to him.

"Just call me Bert. I'm no proper cop anymore."

CANDY GOT LAID HERE. That was what it said. Sam's nightmare had just worsened in a way, but in another way things were turning around. He had something solid to grab hold of now.

"Officer Bert," he repeated without taking in a word the other man was saying, "who wrote that?"

"Who wrote what?"

Sam pointed. "Candy got . . ." He couldn't say the rest of it.

"Now, that's interesting." Bert settled behind the steering wheel with the air of a man in no hurry. "That there particular message," he drawled in his gravelly baritone, "has been in place for close to twenty years. The library staff scrubbed it off and within a day somebody painted it back on. They painted over it, painted the whole damn foundation, and within a couple days again somebody wrote it back on. They painted over it again and hired a guard and still somebody wrote it back on. And so it went for five, ten years. The library board won't admit it, but the scuttlebutt around town is that graffiti drove them out of this building."

"But—who—"

"Nobody knows who put it there or who keeps putting it there and nobody has a clue who Candy is or—"

Sam whispered, "My wife."

"—or was—" Bert stopped short, gawking at Sam.

Only marginally aware of the old cop's surprise, Sam found himself stumbling out of the pickup. As if drawn by a skewed gravitational force, he trudged past the few other vehicles parked in the lot, stopping when he reached the looming brick building. Almost close enough to spit on it, he took in the basement wall's message again, letter by letter.

CANDY GOT LAID HERE

Mostly numb, Sam began to feel anger stirring like molten lava in his core. At first he didn't recognize the fiery earthquake feeling, for Sam seldom became angry, and never had he felt such marrow-deep wrath at anyone. Then he comprehended, and focused: What bastard had written this thing?

How could the man be human? How could anyone of human-kind have done this to Dorrie? Okay, he knew now that Dorrie hadn't been a virgin when he'd married her, and he knew that, given some time to chew on the facts and swallow them and digest them, he could accept that some boy had made love to Dorrie and given her a baby. Heck, every boy who'd ever known Dorrie should have fallen in love with her.

Or—suppose it wasn't love. Okay, Sam considered that, again, given time, he could probably even accept—no, not ac-cept really, but understand—if some young Romeo had found Dorrie physically attractive and had persuaded her to have ca-sual sex with him. A teenager, either gender, is pretty much a mess of hormones sneaking around on uncertain feet. Nobody could blame Dorrie for wanting to find out what it was all about. With some boy, okay, Sam could handle that concept.

But this . . . this indecent braggadocio . . .

CANDY GOT LAID HERE

"*What* did you say?" asked a hushed, gravelly voice by Sam's side.

Sam had to shut his eyes for a moment before he managed to voice it again, rather harshly. "I said, my wife."

". . . now my whole freaking day is freaking ruined. It was sup-posed to be perfect, don't you understand, Candy baby. First the sugar and then the strawberries and then the cherry and finally the chocolate and the red red syrup running together, perfect and beautiful and tragic like in a movie, but the silly Candy girl had to go and break my lightproofing and my spy periscope and my window and now the way things are sup-posed to go is just all freaking fucked-up and little baby Candy has to sit in the corner while I get rid of dumb-ass Marie, it's all her fault. My sweet Candy girl wouldn't have done a single bad *thing* to my spy periscope if that ugly bitch hadn't butted her fat nose in. Now, silly Candy girl, just sit back and take a rest, hold still . . ."

I heard His nattering voice, a knife-edge of saccharine near-hysteria in His tone, as I regained consciousness. Without opening my eyes, I lay leaden still, listening. To say I was playing possum would be a lie. I'd given up. Didn't feel as if I could move ever again. Down-and-out, flattened, exhausted, every part of my body moaning in pain and fever from lupus, while my heart and soul were harrowed by misery, and—and what could I do? What could I possibly do? This madman who broke down doors, He would break me in half to have whatever He wanted.

". . . hold still and give me a nice deep juicy sweet kiss the way I taught you."

Without turning my head, I opened my eyes. Even that slight movement hurt. Peripherally I could see that He had Juliet sitting in one of the aluminum chairs. The overhead light remained turned off, but rays of sunshine sifted down from the high window she had mostly uncovered. I saw Him, backlit like an angel and dark as a devil, bending over her. He'd ripped my coat off her; it lay beside her chair like something dead. At first I thought the glinty gray stuff obscuring her wrists was part of the chair; then I saw that He had duct-taped her hands behind her, arms wrenched around the chairback. And He'd duct-taped her feet to the chair legs.

"C'mon, Candy. Give me a kiss and I'll put this on your mouth nice and easy."

Bending over her, He held a rectangle of duct tape in one hand, His ever-loving knife in the other. I couldn't see Juliet's face. She had twisted her head to the side.

"No, silly little girl, don't turn away or Pandora will cut right into your pretty cheek." With His knife hand He forced her to face Him. She looked sick.

With that shiny bright edge in His voice He told her, "See, I'm stronger. The man is supposed to be stronger. That's the poetry of it. Now give me a deep, deep, sweet suck-your-candy kiss."

His mouth locked over hers.

God fry His soul, that pervert would have to kill me before I let Him do that to my daughter. Gathering all the slight strength I had left in me, I lifted my head to start struggling to get up.

At the same time I saw defiance flash in Juliet's eyes. I saw muscle ripple in her jaw.

With a choked scream He jerked away from her. Blood thinned by saliva seeped from His mouth. His face clenched stone white. "Bitch!" He slapped her hard across the face; then in almost the same movement, as if He'd had practice, He smacked the duct tape onto her mouth.

Out of the deepest anger I'd ever experienced, a blast of energy erupted, volcanic, within me to hoist me to my feet.

I knew what I had to do.

I flung myself over the back of the sofa and out through what was left of the door.

"Last I heard, her name was Dorrie Birch White."

"She goes by Dorrie. Her proper name is Candor."

"Candor . . . When she was a kid they called her Candy?"

Only one person that Sam knew of. But at the thought of the love letters he'd found under the mattress—*Dearest Candy, My Very Own Candy, Sweet Sweet Candy*—his teeth clenched so tight he couldn't speak.

"Well," said old Bert gruffly after a pause, "if your wife saw this, it explains what might have made her lose control of her car and run it up over the curb—"

"But where *is* she!" Sam wanted to shout it, but the words came out choked and low.

"Depends on why she came here, I guess."

Why. Why? His brain hazed by worry and lack of sleep and, face it, hurt feelings, Sam couldn't begin to think—

Had to think.

Look. I'm a businessman. All the time I deal with people's motives, people's hidden agendas. Every day I've got to figure someone out.

But he'd never really tried to figure out Dorrie. His own wife.

I've been scared to.

Scared, not knowing why, even though Dorrie was a good woman. Loyal. Honorable.

CANDY GOT LAID HERE

Bert said, "Maybe she's been getting funny feelings the way women do sometimes, and she took a notion to head back home, you know, just to think things over."

Sam broke his gaze away from "CANDY GOT LAID HERE." He shook his head. Clenched his fists. Swung around to face the old cop and almost shouted, "She was at the mall. She saw the Phillips girl get abducted. She phoned in a description of the vehicle. A van—"

Sam found himself looking straight at it.

There it sat. Parked behind the old man.

Speechless for a moment, gawking, Sam pointed.

"Huh?" Bert turned.

Sam found his voice and spoke, although not very cogently. "It's *exactly* the color of a Weimaraner."

• • •

After landing on the hard floor outside that awful room, I couldn't quite get myself standing upright, but crawling was not a good option when there was a long skirt in the way. Somehow, half-standing, hanging on to the wall, a crippled mother hen, I hitched down the hallway.

He would come after me. He would leave Juliet alone to come after me. He had to come after me. He knew by now that He'd have to kill me before He could do a thing to her.

I made it past detritus lying on the threadbare carpet outside the bathroom—shattered glass, shards of wood, a heavy porcelain cover off a toilet tank. Maybe He had used it to shatter the transom. What did it matter? My mind had no time or strength to spare for what had already happened. Every thought had to be focused on what to do now.

I tottered onward to the end of the hallway, as far as possible from Juliet. When I could go no farther, I turned. Back against the wall. Literally. I needed to lean against that crude wooden barrier for support.

As I turned, I saw that, yes, He had followed me. The man of my lifelong dreams and my current nightmare stood halfway down the hallway, watching me struggle. He knew I couldn't go far, and I felt that He was amused, probably, or gloating, although the flat wooden look on His face hadn't changed.

As I watched, He picked up the heavy toilet tank cover, presumably to use as a club with which to bash my head open and splatter my brain. He'd replaced His sacred sacrificial knife in its sheath at His belt. Didn't want to sully Pandora with my ugly blood, evidently. I wondered why He bothered to keep the guns in His fridge at all, He so obviously preferred the more primal weapons.

Balancing His club in both hands, He strode up to me. "Dumb slut," He told me, "you should know by now you can't get away from me."

I didn't bother to tell Him I wasn't trying to get away from Him. All I was trying to do was lure Him as far as possible from Juliet, and not just because I was drawing a predator away from her.

I also had another, new reason: She mustn't hear what I was going to say to Him. She must never know.

Keeping my voice low so it wouldn't reach her, but very clear, I said, "We need to talk, Blake Roman."

I saw those two words, his name, strip him of his authority, stagger him like a rope around his ankles. They shook him so badly that he lost his grip on his heavy white weapon, which fell to the shredded carpeting with a thud. The wooden mask of his face turned to something more like gray clay. His mouth sagged. He tried to speak, but managed only a wordless sound, wet, like the blood from Juliet's bite on his lips.

I told him, "If you have a soul at all, Blake Roman, you will keep your hands off that girl. She's your daughter."

ELEVEN

Sam perceived a gritty, annoying noise trailing along behind him as he strode to the van. Oh. It was Bert, saying, "Wasn't the vehicle your wife described supposed to have a spare wheel with a logo—"

"There it is. Dumped in the back." Already at the van, peering in, Sam flapped one hand toward the tire on its rear floor, then hurried on to the passenger's-side windows. "The driver's window is busted in. There's broken glass on the floor. And some kind of bag . . ." His voice stopped with a squeak. He recognized that handbag, yet felt afraid to recognize it; women and their everlasting purses—they spent hours shopping for just the right one, but who could tell them apart anyway?

Sam grabbed the handle of the van's side door, and it slid open; it was not even locked. Diving into the belly of the van, he grabbed for the darkish, sprawling object he had seen.

"Wait," said Bert in bored tones. "Don't touch anything."

But already Sam stood with the purse open in one hand as he pawed through its contents with the other. "It's Dorrie's!" he cried at the sight of her pills, her checkbook, her wallet.

Bert remarked, "Walker's gonna shit a brick, you messing with evidence like that."

"Walker schmalker," Sam said before he could stop himself. "Bert, Dorrie's in that building."

No question which building. Its shadow hung over them like a gallows.

"Now, don't go off half-cocked. You don't know that." The old cop started groping at the paraphernalia hanging from his belt. "First we got to call in about the van and the purse—"

Beginning to lose patience, Sam said, "No, Bert, first we have to go get Dorrie."

Bert gave him a quelling look. "Can't get a search warrant without some kind of probable cause—"

Now, that was just plain stupid. "Her car is *there*," Sam yelled, pointing. "Her purse is *here*, her name is *there*—" His hand started to shake, aimed like a handgun at the reprehensible message painted on the old building's foundation.

"Doesn't mean she's in there," Bert said.

"Then what the—What does it mean?"

"Darned if I know." Bert succeeded in fumbling a two-way radio out of its case on his belt. "Doesn't seem to make any sense at all."

"How could it make more sense?" Sam knew to the marrow of his bones that Dorrie was trapped, somehow endangered, in that place from out of her past. "Bert, I run a machine shop. When the chips fly here, here, and here"—Sam gestured wildly south, northwest, and northeast—"then the part you're milling is in the middle! It's that simple."

The old man eyed him with what appeared to be honest sympathy, but shook his head. "Walker's regulation minded, as you may have noticed," he remarked. "And I hate to say, but I believe it was him personally who checked the building last night and said it's sealed solid. Plus he's got the FBI riding on

him like fleas on a coonhound. You aren't going to get him to
ask the judge for a warrant—"

"Warrant?" Sam couldn't believe what he was hearing. "But
that's going to take time!"

"It's not going to happen at all," Bert pointed out, "unless
you can come up with some way anybody could have gotten
into that building."

"Juliet. She's your daughter," I repeated, not sure whether
Blake—only desperation could make me acknowledge the
name—whether he had heard me or comprehended. His face
remained lumpen, stunned.

But in a moment his mouth stirred, stretched, shouting,
"Bitch, are you out of your half-assed *mind*? I don't have a—"

Juliet must not hear. Keeping my voice low, I cut him off.
Instinctively I used the only words that could have silenced
him. "Pandora says you do."

And the moment I said it, my heart tried to stop beating and
die, because I realized I hadn't always been terrified of knives.
Not when I was a young girl. The fear had come later.

I had managed to forget it or repress it till now, but I
had made Pandora's razor-edged acquaintance once or twice
before.

No. No! Don't remember.

My invocation of the knife's name stopped Blake's shouting.
I saw it stagger him. *"What?"* His voice cracked like an adolescent boy's.

Keeping my voice very firm, teacherly but low, I told him,
"You *do* have a daughter. Pandora knows it and I know it."

"You lie."

"I'm telling you the truth. That young lady sitting in the other room is your daughter."

"*You* say. Freaking crazy—"

"I happen to know."

Hoarsely he demanded, "How?"

"I know. I was there."

"You were—who the hell *are* you?"

"Me?" I shrugged. "I'm nobody." This wasn't about me. It was about Juliet. I was doing it for the sake of whatever time, whatever hope, whatever change of plans, I could gain for her, even if it was only that he would kill her—and me—more mercifully. Trying for plausibility, I explained, "I went to high school with you. You wouldn't remember. I was one of those chubby girls nobody remembers." Blessedly, where I stood, at the end of the dim hallway, I think he could barely see me. I saw his face only in Escheresque white/black outline, by the canted light that knifed through the shattered bathroom door.

"You liar. I know damn well there wasn't no Marie—"

"Not in your class. I was in Dorrie's class. I knew her."

"Bullshit. She didn't have friends."

"I just said I knew her. My mother went to Bible study with her mother. I heard Dorrie got pregnant and her parents took her away."

That smacked the truculence out of him. Apparently his cognitive processes had not yet progressed from abstract to specific; "That girl is your daughter" had not yet developed into "You got Dorrie knocked up." Gray as clay, he whispered, "Pregnant?"

"Yes."

"But . . . she never told me."

"She didn't know till it was too late. Her parents wouldn't let her tell you. They kept her locked in a room and wouldn't let her ever see you again. It broke her heart. She was crazy in love with you."

I shouldn't have said that.

Trying to pander to his ego, I went too far. Saying those words, I felt my aching, disillusioned heart start pounding, blushing, swelling, yearning for that once-upon-a-time white flame of passion. I had forgotten about the knife, Pandora, and the way in which I had first made her acquaintance. I remembered only the other days, the angel white, cherry red earlier days. I had forgotten to be a fat interfering bitch. My voice had softened. Something must have shown in my eyes.

Or maybe he was remembering too. Maybe my words had opened something in him that had been closed before.

He saw.

Shock of seeing flew between him and me like scarlet lightning.

In that moment he knew who I was, and the knowledge nearly knocked him to his knees. He reeled, eyes wide, everything wooden about him shattering. This man wasn't made of wood or clay either; he was made of raw bloody hurting anger. His mouth stretched as if to scream, but I could barely hear him or understand him. "No! No, you can't be!" He snatched his knife from its sheath.

I'd met that knife—my mind had mostly obliterated that time with a kind of mental perfect fog filled with a rosy glow, I couldn't remember exactly, but—one of those last days before my parents had taken me away, he had held that grinning blade to my throat as we made love.

Just for thrills? Or had he raped me?

A jab of long-belated anger gave me strength to demand, "I can't be *who*?"

"Shut up!"

"Shut up, *who*? What's my name?"

"You're not her!" He raised the knife, its blade shivering cold as my spine. Trembling, he screamed, "You're ugly! No Candy of mine gets fat and ugly! Traitor!"

Traitor? My parents and their hellfire-based religion had inflicted guilt upon me in many forms, but never that one. I whispered, "You think I—I betrayed you?"

Raving, he didn't even hear me, yet echoed the word. "You betrayed me. Fat, ugly, old, you got no right! You were supposed to stay. Stay!"

Softly, reasonably, I said, "I just told you, they took me away."

"Dumb fuck!" He stamped the floor. "You turned into a typical woman." He couldn't have given me a higher compliment, yet he made it sound like a curse. "I can't stand it." His stony eyes remained arid, like pebbles in a desert, yet he sobbed. He staggered. Reeling, he attacked the air with his knife, slashing, stabbing. "Big, fat, mouthy . . ." He gave me a rabid glare. "No Candy of mine gets past eighteen. Candy's supposed to stay sweet and young. Stay."

Oh.

Just as I began to understand, he turned on me, knife raised, to kill me.

I thought of grabbing something to use as a weapon or a shield. But something in me had gone stoical, like doom, and also relentless, like fate.

I didn't move, but I kept fighting.

I demanded, "Blake. Why did you paint me a whore on the wall?"

Not very clearly phrased, that question, but he knew exactly what I meant.

His knife flashed down, but he'd flinched, or I had, or both.

Instead of stabbing me in the chest, the blade glanced off my upper left arm. I felt the slash before the knife struck the make-shift wall behind me.

I wouldn't cry out. Would not clamp my right hand over the bleeding wound. Would. Not. I stood there.

Yanking his knife out of the board it had pierced, Blake stood panting, gasping.

I demanded, "When did you paint that awful thing on the wall?"

"Back . . . then."

"*Why?*"

He met my eyes and cried, "Because you pulled back, you kept trying to chicken out, I could tell you didn't want to do it!"

"So you had to advertise that I'd done it anyway?"

"I ain't talking about getting *laid*, you bag of shit. Stupid slut, I don't know why I ever thought you could understand, and now you've gone and turned into—into—you're Candy's *mother*?"

Juliet's mother, he meant?

Or did he mean that I had turned into my own mother?

Something, the way nothing made sense, a shining knife-edge of hysteria in that word *mother*, gave me an inkling.

A hint of who had made him crazy.

A sense that I had to be crazy too, in order to talk with him.

So, sweetly conversational, I nodded. "I love being a mother," I confided. "Mothers are the nicest people, don't you think, Blake?"

Instantly I knew I'd made a connection that could either save me and Juliet or get us both killed. I knew because every-thing changed in that moment. His face flattened into a mask again. He went profoundly still. His silence sobbed, shouted, screamed.

"Sure," he said tonelessly. "Mothers are very nice."

"Was your mother nice, Blake?"

"My mother is dead."

"I'm sorry," I said as if I hadn't known this before. "I'm very sorry," I said, feeling the blood running down my arm. I knew I couldn't back off. I had to be insistent, obsessive, as psycho as he was. "But when she was still alive," I said, my voice softer yet and pitched higher, "wasn't she a nice person?"

Silence. A pause that seemed to last a minute. He didn't move so much as a hair, but a nerve in his face twitched, and twitched again, and again.

Finally, "She and my father loved each other very much," he said, each word equally inflected, equally expressionless. And as he said it, he drew his knife blade lightly across one scarred wrist.

What had his parents done to him?

"She and your father loved each other," I repeated, expecting that next he would say they had loved him too. And expecting—dreading, actually—that he would caress his wrist with the knife again.

But that wasn't what happened. One flat word at a time he said, "They died together. They slit their wrists together. They did it to each other. They didn't do it to me."

With his size-thirteen feet planted stubbornly on the gravel of the parking lot, Sam stood fuming behind the deserted library.

Bert had "reported in" on his antiquated radio. Bert expected the FBI would want a look at the van. Meanwhile, while waiting for the FBI or Walker or the "lab boys" or whomever, Bert had wandered off to "have another look around the perimeter." Not trusting himself to be civil, Sam stood where he was, glaring.

CANDY GOT LAID HERE

Monstrous. The whole thing was monstrous. What sort of monster would have put that there? In big print letters that practically shouted? The guy had to be sick, sick, sick, some kind of psycho, a—

A very unstable, potentially violent individual.

Sam stiffened, blinking. He looked at the graffito one more time, letter by letter. Then he grabbed his cell phone, and thank technology, yes, the number was still in memory from the night before. He called the Fulcrum Police Department.

"Officer Chappell, please."

"Who?" The receptionist sounded tired and bored. "I'm not familiar with any Officer Chappell."

"Young woman, skinny, black." To heck with political correctness. Sam was in no mood to pussyfoot around.

"Oh, you mean Sissy!" Apparently Officer Chappell got no more respect from the secretarial staff than she did from her chief. "She's off duty—"

Another tired, bored female voice sounded from the background. "She was in here sending a fax about half an hour ago."

"Then I guess she's back on duty already?"

"Ma'am," Sam interrupted between gritted teeth, "I need to *speak* with her."

"Well, um, if she's still in the building, let me see if I can page her."

"*Please.*"

Moseying around the old building, Bert Roman carried almost seventy years of Appletree history with him. Heck, he'd worked

his first job here at this place, back when it was still a cigar factory making all of Appletree smell like apple cider, which was
a heck of a lot nicer than what a paper mill would do. He'd
started in the cigar factory as a floor sweeper, advanced to
being a wrapper, then a machine operator. He remembered the
people he'd worked with. He'd gone to school—elementary,
junior high, high school, it was all in the same building back
then—within a block of here. He remembered people from
school too. He remembered people he'd had dealings with over
the years. Arrested. Rescued. Watched die. He remembered
births, weddings, funerals, scandals—there wasn't much that
went on in Appletree that he didn't know about. He knew more
about this jurisdiction, and more about life in general, and way
more about being a cop, than Walker ever would.

And the son of a bitch treated him like a messenger boy.

Fine. Retirement was coming up in just a few months now.

Taking his time, Bert scanned the old Appletree cigar building from roofline to foundation, took a few steps, scanned some
more. He loved these old factories. They didn't build them generous and solid like this anymore, rows and rows of stately
double-sashed windows giving natural light to rooms twelve
feet high, basement twelve feet deep, access through an outdoor
concrete stairwell with a double metal door—firmly padlocked,
Bert noted—over top of it to keep the rain and dead leaves and
such from puddling at the bottom. Sloping door, nearly horizontal; they didn't make basement entryways like that anymore.
Or basements that rose into a three-foot foundation with real
windows, not just window wells, for illumination—

There was a broken basement window.

Bert frowned, wondering why this window hadn't been
boarded up like the others. Looked like it had been covered

from the *inside* for some reason. Now it looked like somebody had put a rock through it.

Probably had nothing to do with anything, but Bert made a mental note to point it out to Walker when he got here.

Movement on the parking lot caught his eye: Sam White waving at him like he wanted to talk with him. Sam was a nice guy, Bert had decided, but excitable. Required a lot of smoothing down. Bert didn't mind; smoothing people down was one of the things he did best, and anyway, he'd finished his look around. Smiling, he ambled over to the White fellow, who was speaking into a cell phone clutched in one hand and was saying, "You think it's him? Blake Roman?"

Bert lost his smile.

"I know it's not certain, but—" Sam listened for a moment; then in heightened tones he said, "Apparently somebody here overlooked your fax. Look, would you please send it again? I'll make sure Appletree PD pays attention to it. And the FBI. They're supposed to roll in any minute now."

More silence as Sam listened and Bert thought about the fax he had read that morning and then destroyed, for reasons that applied to him and, as far as he knew, nobody else. Good thing those newfangled shredders minced the thing into diamonds so fine that nobody could ever prove what he'd done. If asked, of course he would deny it.

Sam said into the cell phone, "I wish you were here to see for yourself, but to me—well, first of all, it says Candy, and nobody that I know of ever called her that except . . . Yeah. Yeah, and that wild scrawl—this looks the same to me, just kind of rings a bell, but I don't know why. . . . The *y* in 'Candy'? Yes, the tail comes to a point and then hooks back in a big curve that kind of underlines the word."

He paused, listening to—Bert felt himself getting pretty anxious to know who was on the other end of that conversation, but he tried not to let it show. He put on his poker face.

"All it says is 'Candy got laid here.'" Sam White's voice thinned, stretched translucent by stress, saying that. "Yes, the *g* in 'got' has a hook tail like the *y* in 'Candy.'" He listened, then responded, "The *d* on 'laid'? Yes, it looks weird. Kind of toppling off the end of the word. It—what? I—I really can't tell." Stretched even worse, his voice nearly broke.

He took a few deep breaths as if to steady himself, and then perked up, relief showing in his face. "You *will*? You already *did*, while we were talking? Thank you. Thank you so much, Officer. I really appreciate your help."

Clicking off, he told Bert, "She sent the fax again."

This news hit Bert in the gut, but he didn't let his poker face slip. Years as a cop on the beat had given him a lot of practice at hiding his feelings. He said only, "She?"

"Officer from Fulcrum. Chappell. Handwriting expert. Thinks this—" With a grimace, Sam White gestured at the bold black letters painted on the wall. "Thinks it may have been put there by an individual named Blake Roman. Do you know anything about him?"

Bert felt Sam's desperate gaze upon him.

"Blake Roman," he repeated thoughtfully.

"He's a convicted rapist, he's wanted for questioning in connection with the murder of a young woman, and apparently he was raised in Appletree. I have reason to think my wife might have known him when they were both kids in school."

"Blake Roman." Bert was not quite able to meet Sam White's worried eyes. "No, can't say as I ever really knew a Blake Roman."

In a sense this was not a lie.

• • •

Once before, years ago, Blake had told me about his parents.

I had repressed that aspect of my daydream romance completely.

I had done this to myself. But why? How could I have turned this sick, insane, knife-obsessed person into an angel in my mind?

Now, standing against a rough wall with blood running down my arm, I remembered how terrified of him I had been as a girl. And now I had experienced that which I had feared: Pandora's razor edge, Pandora's dagger tip. I had just been stabbed. I knew what a knife wound felt like. And I had survived so far. I was still alive, on my unlovely feet, standing there. The blank of whitewash in my mind ran red, and I remembered.

I am sixteen, lying mostly naked on the sofa in the librarians' lounge, shivering as Blake shows me his most prized possession. It is a knife. Larger and much more frightening than the jackknife he brought out before. This knife is too big for him to hide in his pocket, and if he tried to keep it in his room, his foster mother would find it and confiscate it and probably phone his caseworker. So he keeps it in a rotting leather sheath and stows it under the heavy pediment of the same concrete park bench where he had first kissed me.

Today he retrieved it as we walked to the library. He has made me conceal it in my purse for him. And it would seem he has brought it here for a purpose. He has mostly undressed me, but instead of caressing me as usual, he reaches for the knife. My stare freezes onto its silver curving razor-edged viciously pointed blade.

"It was my father's hunting knife he took with him to the Gulf

War," Blake tells me. "He gave it to me. It's the one I used—I mean, he used it to kill towelheads. Lots of them."

He drops his pants and holds the knife alongside his erection. I cannot wince my glance away from the sight of his penis as I usually do. The knife transfixes my stare there, the flat of its blade pressing against Blake's tender genital skin as if displaying it on a steel plaque.

"Which one's bigger?" Blake challenges me.

I can't answer. I don't dare. Trembling, I stare.

"Here." Blake offers me the knife. "Heft it. Hold it."

I shake my head. I want him to touch me in all the ways he has taught me, yet I want to put my clothes back on and get out of there, yet I am afraid to. I am afraid of—why am I afraid? I shouldn't be afraid of Blake. He is my prince, my hero, my angel, my white—

In a voice as hard as the steel blade, he commands me, "Take it, Candy. Hold it." He thrusts the handle toward me.

I would rather hold a live rattlesnake, yet I take the knife in my shaky hand. The way Blake tells me, like a prophet, I have to. Awkwardly I hold it by the haft, which is made of some disintegrating brownish substance.

"Deer antler," Blake says as if reading my mind. "Falling apart. I'm going to replace it. Customize it." He smiles, yearning, eager. "Go on, move her around." He gestures toward the knife. "Get used to her."

Her?

"Move her around, Candy!" That compelling tone of command again. "Balance her in your hand."

Gingerly I lift the long, heavy thing.

Blake extends his arm toward me, underside up. Something about the gesture reminds me of a puppy rolled over on its back, baring its neck and belly. The underside of Blake's arm looks as petal-soft and creamy pale as the skin of his penis.

"Cut me, Candy," he urges.

I freeze, uncomprehending.

"Just a little cut, like my mother used to give me." He points at a faint scar on his upper arm. "Come on, Candy. Then I'll cut you."

I didn't remember any more. I couldn't. I didn't want to. I didn't need to.

I couldn't remember whether I had obeyed him and cut him. But I knew I hadn't let him cut me.

I knew this partly because of the vengeful writing on the outside of the library basement wall. Evidently I had not performed all that Blake had required of me, so he had painted that message there. In back, where anyone who parked a car would see it, but where I, walking in the front door from school, would not notice at first.

It might have been a day or two later that my parents had taken me away.

I wanted never to remember what had happened during the intervening day or days. But one thing I knew: There were no scars on my arms.

Whereas Blake was standing before me now with dozens of scars sprawling, a white scribble of pain, all the way up his forearms.

Grabbing his cell phone to follow up on Sissy's fax, Sam decided that, under the circumstances, his habitual good manners might be worse than a bad habit; they might be just what Dorrie didn't need right now. He jabbed the Appletree PD number with unnecessary force of finger. When a female voice answered, he demanded without preliminaries, "Walker."

There was nothing Sam could do about the irritating wait

before the cop picked up, nothing except hate the unfortunate hold-the-phone music, yee-hah country music, as he had never hated music before.

Sometime short of forever, the music clicked off and someone picked up. "Walker here."

"Sam White here. Did you receive the fax about Blake Roman?"

"Just came in."

"It came in earlier too, if anybody would have paid any attention. Have you read it?"

"Yes, but I don't see—"

Sam steamrollered over him. "Did you give it to the FBI?"

"No, because—"

"Are they there?" Sam became louder and more terse with each utterance. He had used not a word of profanity, yet he felt a sense of taking command. He had never been in the military, but knew to some small degree what General Patton must have felt like.

"Yes, they're here, but we—"

"Walker, you're not—"

"*Captain* Walker."

"Captain Walker, you're not hearing me. I'd like to speak to the FBI." Sam wished he had paid more attention to the FBI agents when he had seen them at the Phillips house, so he would know which ones were the most likely jackasses, and what he was up against, and whom to ask for by name. "Their top agent, please."

"Mr. White—"

"*Now*, Captain Walker."

Without another word the prick put him on hold. Sam endured yet more down-home music. If anybody had ever put

General Patton on hold, Sam thought, clenching his jaw, Patton would have ordered a nuclear strike.

Somebody picked up. "Hello, Mr. White?" A pleasant enough male voice, neutrally midwestern.

"Sam White, yes."

"I'm Special Agent Frank Gerardo. I've just scanned the Blake Roman report, and I understand your concern that it was overlooked earlier in the day. I know—"

Sam interrupted. "Agent Gerardo, it's what you don't know that worries me. I need you and your men out here an hour ago."

"Out where?"

"Where the abductor's van is. Did Bert by any chance report that my wife's purse is in it?"

"No, I hadn't heard that." Gerardo started to sound genuinely concerned. "You think—"

"I think my wife and the missing girl are inside this abandoned building. I have good reason to believe that the graffiti on it was written by Blake Roman."

"What? Wait a minute, Mr. White. How can you know—"

"Sissy Chappell!" Sam exploded. "The Fulcrum officer who sent the report. Ask her! She's the one who spotted this Blake guy as a felon in the first place from some old love notes we found. She's a handwriting expert."

TWELVE

Bert recalled well enough that there had been a Roman family in Appletree. He particularly remembered Randall Roman, a brilliant young man up till he enlisted, got sent to the Gulf War, and had a losing confrontation with a land mine. He'd gone away a graduate of the high school's "gifted" program, planning to use his GI money for a college education and a career as a theoretical engineer. He'd come back in a wheelchair and messed up in the head as well—flashbacks, drinking problem, couldn't go to school or hold a job. Ended up living on disability in a trailer behind the old foundry.

All of which could have been overcome, Bert considered, if it weren't for Randall's biggest liability: his wife, Pandora, Penny for short, piece of work he'd met at Fort Bragg and brought home like trash stuck to his shoe. And their kid, conceived before Randall had gone off to get his legs and nether parts blown to smithereens. Afterward, there'd been no more kids, just the one son, a boy, totally spoiled and messed up. Presumably there'd been no more kid-procreating action from Randall Roman. It had been common knowledge that Penny supplemented the family income by entertaining gentleman visitors. While Bert had a low opinion of whores, he knew every little town had at least one; it was nothing to get excited about—except this Penny Roman had a kink that brought her company all the way from Akron.

She did it while her husband watched.

She made him watch.

Sometimes she let her son watch too.

The phone rang persistently beside Sissy Chappell's bed. Face-down in her pillow, groping for the source of the noise, she peered at the glaring red numbers on the digital alarm clock with one bleary eye. It was 8:08 a.m. She'd had just about half an hour of sleep.

Approximating the phone to her ear, she mumbled, "'Lo?"

"Officer Chappell?"

"Yes." Sissy sat up, instantly awake. She knew that voice, even though the guy was talking on a staticky cell phone. "Agent Gerardo?" The FBI top gun heading the Phillips case team.

"Right," he said. "Officer Chappell, I'm sorry to call you at home, but it's important. We need you here in Appletree to help sort out Blake Roman's possible involvement with Dorrie White. I'm sending a helicopter for you; it's already on the way. I understand Fulcrum PD has a landing pad on the roof. Can you be there ASAP?"

Sissy replied without hesitation. "I'll be there in ten minutes."

"Good. See you soon. I already spoke with Chief Angstrom, and you're to bring the handwriting evidence with you."

"Bubba!" Sissy whispered after she had hung up the phone. The FBI had spoken to her boss wanting to borrow her to do *handwriting analysis*? Angstrom had to be having eyebrow meltdown.

She got a chance to see for herself about nine minutes later as, hastily dressed in jeans, a sweatshirt, and Adidas, she ran up the steps to the PD. Angstrom was coming out the door.

"Sir." There was no avoiding an encounter and acknowledgment. "Going home to get some sleep?"

"Yes, I am." He sounded a bit wrought, but his glare seemed much as usual, his eyebrow no more unstuck than before. "What you do with your off time is your own business. But if you're not back here for your regular shift, Chappell, you're fired."

"Yes, sir."

"And since when are you a *handwriting expert*? Are you accredited or something?"

"It's not something I need a license for, sir. Excuse me, sir." Even from where she was standing, Sissy could hear the chopper on the roof.

Running upstairs rather than waiting for the elevator, Sissy knew quite well that she was not likely to be back from Appletree in time to go on patrol that afternoon. She knew that she would probably lose her job because of what she needed to do, and possibly even her law enforcement career—yet her feet ran even faster toward the helicopter, and her heart beat even faster, more eager than ever.

With Dorrie White's case folder in hand, Sissy Chappell had been called on a rescue mission. After months of giving out speeding tickets and parking tickets, maybe today she would do something a little more like the cop she wanted to be.

"That wasn't broken by somebody throwing a rock in, Bert!" Sam got down on his hands and knees to take a closer look.

Gravel cut through his ruined suit pants into his leg as he studied the basement window the old cop was showing him. "Somebody was trying to break *out*." His chest tightened so that he could barely talk, but he had to get through to this guy. "Look how the wood and glass are shattered out from the inside."

Bert stood silent, then muttered, "I'm not so sure."

Instead of answering, Sam held his breath, listening. He thought he had heard a sound from behind that broken window. But now that he was paying attention, all he could hear was traffic swishing past on Main Street as the good people of Appletree headed for church.

Which was probably where Dorrie's parents were right now, Sam realized. In church. Praying. He wondered whether they might possibly remember to include their daughter in their prayers.

But it was nonproductive to think of Dorrie's parents right now. Sam dismissed them from his mind.

"Anyway," Bert was saying, gesturing at the broken window, "nothing we can do about it till Walker gets here."

"Shhh."

"Huh?"

Sam knelt with his big hands cupped behind his ears, listening. And yes, he thought he heard it again, just an intimation of a soprano whimpering sound buried in the ambient noise of a small town, the sandy sound of mundane time sifting through its hourglass.

The sound in the boarded-up basement could have been a puppy or a kitten or a child.

Or Dorrie.

Or his own quaking brain disturbing the wax in his ears.

He mumbled, "I thought I heard something."

"Heard what?"

"Somebody crying in there."

Bert hunkered down beside Sam, listened for a moment, then commented gently in his gravelly way, "Now, don't start imagining things on me."

"I heard somebody crying inside." Opposition made Sam more sure. "Bert, we have to go in there." Eyeing the broken window, Sam admitted to himself that there was no way his husky body with its ample belly would fit through it. But he tried to convince himself that Bert's skinny old frame might. "*You* have to go in there," Sam amended.

"Already told you, we can't do a thing till Walker and the FBI guys say so. And a judge gives the warrant."

"*Bert—*"

"I'd have to bust more of that window away," Bert said. "That's illegal."

"Bert, what if she's in there? What if she's in trouble?"

"You think she got in there through that three-inch hole in the window? I keep telling you, there's no way anybody *could* get in there. And when Walker gets here, he'll tell you the same thing."

Sam started getting that unfamiliar fiery molten feeling in his chest again. Anger. Frustration. Having no idea what to do with such emotions, he turned his back on Bert and strode away.

Once in motion, Sam found that he couldn't just stand around waiting for Walker, et cetera, to show their sorry butts. Had to do something. He did what Bert had just done, walked around the building, looking for a way in or any sign that anybody had forced a way in. But except for that broken basement window, which was too small for anything bigger than a rabbit to get through, every orifice of the old factory-cum-library appeared to be boarded up, nailed tight, chained, padlocked, impregnable.

Sam ended where he had begun, in the parking lot, shaking his head.

Bert was right.

Bert couldn't be right.

For no reason except that he could not stand still, Sam started to search the gravel of the parking lot.

Bent over, scanning, he worked his way back the fence, into the weeds at the far end, then out again. At the edge of the gravel he spotted a flashlight he recognized lying on the ground. He stared, swallowed hard, blinked, and didn't touch it or move it. Captain Walker should be proud of him for not messing with the evidence.

"Sam!" Bert yelled from around the street-side corner of the building. "They're here."

Walker and the FBI guys had finally arrived, evidently. Sam turned to go tell them about the flashlight.

"White! Sam White!" Walker bellowed. "C'mon over here."

"Have you ever flown in a small aircraft before?" The copter pilot had to yell in order to be heard above the engine noise.

"No!" Sissy yelled back.

"Well, here." Over his shoulder he handed her something made of gray paper folded flat with a sort of oversized twist tie along the top—a barf bag. Sissy laid it aside without comment, but she knew she wouldn't need it. Nervous Nellies with butterfly bellies didn't go into law enforcement.

"Buckle up! Here we go!"

Sissy felt liftoff almost as if she were in an elevator, then a quirky sort of slue, a slight tilt, and the chopper bumbled toward Appletree. Sissy looked down through a window with delight; despite the seriousness of her situation, it was a revelation to see the Ohio countryside, flat as a billiard table, from low altitude.

"I never knew there were so many mounds!" she exclaimed even though no one could possibly hear her.

The slanting early-day light showed them clearly, earth-works left by prehistoric people before even the Mongolian "Native Americans" had come there, excavations encircling conical hills, or sometimes double mounds resembling peanuts, and one long double serpentine complete with snake head. Over and past them, seemingly without noticing them, ran a modern surveyor's pride of patchwork-quilt property lines. Dairy farms and soybean fields, train tracks and roadways, housing developments and industrial parks, formed a thin overlay upon something that had nothing to do with them, that was ancient, very ancient and primitive.

Sissy watched a freight train, visible from end to end, crawl across the enigma below her like a worm.

Ahead lay what looked like toy blocks and matchboxes clustered around a golf tee—houses, businesses, water tower. Gee, someone had painted a big apple tree on the latter. Mentally Sissy shifted gears to be all police business when the copter sat down on what appeared to be the high school parking lot. Now she got to do the crouch-run head-low-beneath-rotor-blades thing she'd seen so often on TV.

As she did it, a man got out of the back of a waiting police cruiser, left the door open for her, walked around, and got back in on the other side.

Waving to the copter pilot, Sissy bounced in with him. Immediately the uniformed officer in the front seat drove off at what Sissy would classify as a level-orange speed.

The man in the backseat with her shook her hand. "I'm Agent John Harris." He introduced himself with no trace of ego, and he looked more like a slim, fit college professor in a rumpled raincoat, Columbo-style, than an FBI field agent. Maybe he was in forensics.

"Sistine Chappell," Sissy responded, "no relation to the Vatican."

Harris chuckled. "Thank you for reminding me of the advantages of having an ordinary name." Indicating the case file she clutched with both hands, he asked, "Could I have a look at that?"

"Of course." She handed it over, then gazed around at Appletree as the cruiser zipped them through it.

With boarded-up stores, pawnshops, and tattoo parlors, the place looked like an armpit among small towns, one of many. The streets and sidewalks were empty, and Sissy heard no sirens, but she saw quite a conglomeration of flashing lights up ahead. Their car turned into a side street, then stopped.

Harris, Sissy saw, had one of Blake's love notes in his hand as they both got out of the car. "Follow me. We have to get through this crowd."

And quite a crowd it was, dressed-up gawkers who had probably been on their way to church being held back by annoyed-looking police who didn't look very spiffy in comparison. Sissy felt underdressed, especially when a broad-shouldered man in a well-fitting suit took hold of her elbow, smiled at her, and started shoving people aside for her special benefit, kind of like Moses parting the Red Sea, except this guy definitely worked out.

Within a few moments Sissy found herself on the other side of the police cordon, standing along with Agent Harris among more men in suits. One step forward and she had a clear view of the focus of everyone's attention. A three-story brick building with ranks of boarded-up windows, probably a factory from back in the days when they depended on daylight. Between her and it, a van of an odd gray-brown color apparently deserted in its gravel parking lot. And along the building's foundation, boldly painted graffiti.

Sissy's eyes widened, taking in the handwriting, more like brushstroke writing. At the same time her ears tuned in to Agent Harris, by her side, saying to someone, "The probabilities are very high that it was written by the same individual who wrote these notes Dorrie White had in her possession."

Oh, crap. Was that all they had wanted her here for, to bring the notes so that *their* handwriting expert—who did comparison only, never analysis—could look at them in juxtaposition to the graffiti?

Sissy's heart shrank. For this she was sacrificing her job?

"Officer Chappell," said the man to whom Harris had been talking. Sissy looked up just as he turned to her and offered his hand; shaking it, she faced a pair of gray eyes so crystalline that they gave his otherwise standard face cinematic good looks. "Gerardo," he introduced himself unnecessarily; now she remembered having seen him in the Phillips home. Because he had been bent over papers, she had not noticed his remarkable eyes. "Chief Angstrom has told me that you do a kind of profiling from handwriting—"

"*Angstrom* told you that?" Sissy could not hide her surprise.

Gerardo grinned. "Well, not without profanity."

"I bet he didn't call it profiling."

"No. But I do. I would be interested to hear any insights you can offer into our unsub."

"Unsub," she remembered, meant unidentified subject. This man was cautious. All he could be sure of was that Dorrie White long ago had a boyfriend named Blake.

Sissy said, "Discounting the love letters, just looking at

what's written on that wall"—with her chin she pointed toward the painted scrawl—"you can see he's unstable. His slant's all over the place, although predominantly it's toppling to the right. That indicates how emotional and impulsive he is. See the *d* at the end of 'laid,' how it's falling off the word? And how it's kind of bloated to look almost exactly like he's giving you the finger?"

"Son of a—"

"Or not you, exactly," Sissy quickly amended. "The whole world. Attitude."

"That's uncanny. How could I not see that before?" Agent Gerardo studied the offending letter. "Do you think it's conscious on his part?"

"No way of telling. It's a common trait in the handwriting of felons, like the distorted descenders—the hooked tail on the *g* and *y*. Aside from rebelling against the natural flow of handwriting, they're in the lower zone, making them sexually kinky."

Gerardo let this pass, seeming better able to deal with the deformed *d*. "Just from the handwriting, would you say he's dangerous?"

Sissy paused to consider, noticing how all the background noise, all the babble, came from behind her, from the civilians in the crowd and the cops restraining them. Loudest was Walker bellowing for Sam White to come over here: "Get your butt over here!" Sam White, who arguably had the best right of anybody to scream his head off, completely ignored Walker while searching the parking lot for some reason, quite silent. Just as silently the Weimaraner-colored van sat abandoned in the middle of the gravel, while beyond it, on the far side of the lot, the "CANDY GOT LAID HERE" building gave off no fireworks, no gunshots, no fiery explosions, but stood as still and silent as death. Waiting.

Sissy Chappell replied with care. "Yes, I think he's danger-ous. The sick kind of dangerous, if you know what I mean, like this guy probably had a horrific childhood and is terribly screwed up."

"Another common trait among felons."

"True. I don't see any clubbed strokes—that would indicate a brutal sort of cruelty—but there's a disturbing deformity in his writing. It's not only very angular—that's common among aggressive men—but the angularity is habitually recurved to form shapes kind of like the point of a saber. I think this guy might have an affinity for knives."

"Interesting."

"Just a self-educated guess."

"You mean you didn't go to school for this?" Gerardo grinned. "Make me another self-educated guess. Do you think it's Blake Roman's handwriting we're looking at?"

"I personally think so, yes, although there's no proof. Just facts that fit. He's from Appletree. Only a couple of years older than Mrs. White. He could have known her in school. He could be the one who called her Candy. You know her real first name is Candor."

"No, I didn't know that. Stick around, would you?" Gerardo turned away abruptly, looking for someone. "Walker! Where's Captain Walker?"

"Right here." The man walked up to stand directly in front of Sissy but facing Gerardo. Somehow even in obedience he managed to look belligerent. He asked no questions, just stood there.

"Walker, what do you know about anybody surnamed Roman who used to live in Appletree?"

"Somebody by that name does still live here." Walker spit on the ground. "But you'd have to ask Bert."

THIRTEEN

"Bert! Get over here!"

Bert heard, and without looking knew the bellowing voice to be that of Captain Walker, and pretended he hadn't heard. He knew all too well what Walker and the FBI wanted to ask him, and he wasn't ready to answer. Sheltering himself from view behind the van, he tried to feel darkly amused by the whole thing, Sam White snubbing Walker while looking at the gravel as if he hoped to find his wife there.

Bert recalled having a wife once, but she'd been gone so long he barely remembered. . . . Why couldn't he remember his sweet, sensible Lillian nearly as vividly as he recalled his son's slut of a wife, Pandora?

That bitch.

The way Pandora ran things, her regulars got their kicks from screwing her in front of her crippled husband—that was what she called him to his face, *crippled*. She and the client would lift Randall Roman out of his wheelchair, park him wherever they wanted him, tie his hands, do their thing, and enjoy it while he cursed them and cried. The more sadistic johns were likely to give Randall a bloody nose or a split lip if he called them the wrong name. For this, rumor had it, they were charged extra.

Anyway, Randall Roman had killed himself. Slit his wrists. Or that was the common view.

Maybe even true.

What made it hard to figure was that Pandora Roman was found dead in the bed with her husband. Wrists slit. Both of them naked.

It was the kid, their boy, who had found them that way the next morning. Kid was fifteen years old at the time. Found the bodies all bled out, called 911. Dead calm on the digital recording. Kind of wooden. Numb. In shock.

Understandable. Kid couldn't have loved his dad or his mom all that much. There'd been rumors that she had been known to make him watch too.

Or let him watch. Whichever.

So there lay Penny and Randall Roman dead in what looked like a double suicide, like they'd made a pact and done it together, like in their own sick way they'd really loved each other.

Public opinion wouldn't leave it at that, of course. Randall Roman a suicide, sure, people could believe that, but Penny? It had to have been a murder-suicide. Randall had slit her wrists and then his own.

Except why would she just lie there after her wrists were slit, unless someone forced her to? And how would her no-legs no-balls husband force her to?

There'd never been any official verdict. Death under suspicious circumstances, that was all. Could have been suicide-suicide. Could have been murder-suicide, maybe even with Penny as the murderer. Could have been murder-murder by a third party unknown.

To Bert it looked like murder-murder.

By a third party known.

To him.

And to him only.

Because of something he knew that nobody else alive knew. Except the murderer.

Bert hadn't said anything, but he happened to know that Randall Roman didn't go naked. Ever. At all.

The diaper had to have been removed and Randall cleaned up after he was dead.

And Bert surmised who might have done that. And arranged the bodies to make them look like lovers.

Just a hunch. No real proof. But an old cop learns to trust his hunches.

Anyway, he knew the boy better than most, although he hadn't spent a whole lot of time with the kid. Couldn't stand to, because visiting with the boy meant encountering the mother, and the way Bert loathed her . . . Some of that loathing rubbed off on his feelings toward the youngster too. Unpleasant kid, totally spoiled and messed up. The only child, the youngster was the hub of the household and his parents' whole daytime world, for good or bad. Penny would get so mad at him she'd knock him across the room, and then she'd cry about it, and cuddle him, kiss him all over, buy him anything he wanted— and then, it seemed on purpose, the kid would make her mad again. Bert liked kids as a rule, but something about this brat repelled him, and his revulsion had grown stronger as the boy had grown into a teenager and took to slouching around all martyred and gloomy with black clothes on. Bert knew it was wrong for him to feel the way he did, but feelings don't listen to rules, and his wouldn't let him love the boy the way a grandpa should.

Nevertheless, the kid *was* his grandson.

Just the same, knowing what he knew, Bert hadn't taken young Blake to live under the same roof with him and his wife after the deaths of the boy's parents. He sure as heck didn't want to end up as suicide pact number two, dead in bed with his wife, wrists cut. Her diabetes and all the rest of it, health problems galore, had given her and him excuse enough. They had let the boy go to a foster home.

Bert kind of regretted that now that he was old and alone. Sometimes he thought he had failed in his duty to his family, and wondered whether he could have made a decent human being out of the boy, made a difference. Other times he regretted that he had failed in his duty as an officer of the law, felt the guilt of his silence. Girls had died because of his silence.

One regret pretty much balanced the other, and together they kept his mouth shut.

He wondered whether the kid even realized that he, Bert aka Grandpa, was still alive to tell what he knew.

"Really?" I breathed in the wispiest voice I could manage with my back against the wall and a knife wound in my arm. It was a good thing I didn't have the strength to give in to the nausea in my gut, or I would have puked. "Blake . . ." I forced my voice to caress the name. ". . . it really happened? Your mother and father died together in a suicide pact?"

"They did it to each other," he said without any emotion that I could hear or see. "They didn't do it to me."

What *had* they done to him?

I knew a little bit, but the rest I could only guess. If Juliet was to live at all, and if I lived through the next few minutes, it would be by guesswork and intuition.

I murmured, "But they—they slit each other's wrists? That is so—so unbelievably brave and loving and romantic."

I was beginning to know what I had to do.

No. Fever was making me think it. Lupus inflaming my mind as well as my body, that plus terror making me think sick things. Sick.

Don't do it.

But I had to.

I had to go ahead and be Candy, the first true Candy, because Blake was still Blake.

I had to try it, to save Juliet.

Do it.

What scared me the most was not that I had given myself permission. What really terrified me was that I had the darkness in me to understand, to empathize, and to act. Knowingly this time, I *could* do it. Go there. Into the wild, warped, vehement world of Blake Roman. It was hard to acknowledge how vulnerable I myself had been in my adolescence, a lonesome, needy loser raised by—face it—parents whose harsh religion verged on sadism. Parents who, even though still technically alive, had in a sense killed each other. Like Blake's.

Not that I fully believed what Blake was saying of his parents, that they had committed mutual suicide. Something about that messy double death rang true, but his tonelessness told me how much was hidden.

Weird intuition of my fevered mind told me what to ask next. "Blake," I ventured, "your knife . . ." As if acknowledging a third party in the conversation, I nodded to Pandora, mother of all castrating bitches, standing in the clutch of his hand. Reverently I asked, "Is Pandora the same knife they used?"

Something opened in his shuttered face. "Damn straight she is." His stony eyes actually widened. "Nobody ever . . . How'd you know?"

"Just . . ." I forced myself to smile a rather loony tunes smirk at that awful knife. "Just because of the way you love her."

"Oh, yeah. Pandora is a goddess." Something came alive, almost animated, in his face. "Pandora rules the world, you know? Whatever Pandora says, that's what you got to do. You never met such a sweet bitch. Cold like an Italian ice. Call her Mommy, she doesn't even hear. You got to call her Penny or Pandora."

Oh, my God.

Blake's voice sank so low I could barely hear him. "A few times I had sex with her."

Oh, my *God*.

But I didn't even blink, just said, "That's wild."

He grinned. "I like it wild."

Sick, sick, even sicker than my queasy, dizzy body. But my weakness helped to make it all seem like a fever dream, and anyway, there was no time to think, just blurt out another crazy hunch. "Is that when she cut your arms?"

"Cut me and laughed. It made her happy. Pretty red blood coming out of me. Beautiful bright blood."

Blood equaled sex equaled knife/mother equaled happy sweet candy equaled cherry red blood, round and round like the vertigo threatening my head. I wondered whether it had to be wrist blood.

"And your wrists?"

"That . . . um, no. That was later." He glanced downward and to the left, away from me.

I saw guilt in that glance.

Guilt? In Blake Roman? Lying didn't make him look guilty. Seduction, abduction, and rape didn't make him look guilty. *Murder* didn't make him look guilty. What in the name of—

Pandora.

Mother.

I knew where all *my* irrational guilt came from.

"Blake," I accused gently, almost teasing, "you haven't been doing it the way Mommy wants, have you?"

Instantly his face hardened. "You shut your fat mouth about her!" *Flip* went the mood switch, and he was all rage. "You don't know a freaking thing about her, you dumb fuck. And you lie. You're not—you're not—I don't know you. Fat bitch, you lie like a rug, all you tell me is lies, lies, lies—" Projecting his own guilt onto me, working himself up to a fury, he lifted the knife to lunge at me again.

And I was not afraid.

Because I had flipped a switch in my own exhausted mind, and now I could watch myself do whatever I had to.

I could watch myself be as ruthless as Blake. I could stand aside and watch myself be the Candy he deserved to meet. I had rejoined Blake in his bizarre world where blood was sex was love. I did not know what was going to happen next or whether I would live through this or whether I would ever be the same, but the only thing that frightened me was that I didn't care.

"My name is *Candor*," I told Blake. "Candor Birch White." Whether it was the force of my tone or the power of my name, he froze, then lowered his knife and stood like a stone man. "I am not a bitch," I scolded on, "and I am proud to be fat in normal places, not my head. And I do not lie."

Or not anymore.

Especially not to Sam. If, please dear God, I ever got to see him again.

I loved Sam. I had grown to love him with a deep, daily love with which no teenage infatuation could compare. I knew that now.

The romantic yearnings I used to have for Blake, my virginal willingness to be swept away by his perverse passions—the best thing I could do now was to recapture that lust unto death and use it.

"My name is Candor," I repeated more softly. "You used to call me Candy. This affliction is my punishment." With my hands I indicated the red and white crust of rash on my face, the hamster cheeks, the pinto spots of lost pigment on my bruised arms, the hippo hips. "My punishment for not doing it right, Blake." My parents had told me this so many times that I almost believed it, although the meaning Blake would take from my words was entirely different from the one my parents had intended. "I have been punished. And you will be punished too, Blake, because you haven't been doing it right either. Have you?"

I could actually see the blood ebb out of his face, leaving it chalky. He stood like white stone, his eyes staring into mine as if I had somehow hypnotized a blind man.

"Have you been doing what Pandora said, Blake?"

Like a wooden puppet's, his mouth cracked open. "I tried." His voice came out a hoarse whisper.

"But you didn't do it. All those Candies, and each time you didn't do it. You killed the Candies, but you didn't kill yourself."

"I . . . tried. . . ."

Nothing about his white stone face moved, but water ran down his cheeks. Like condensation dripping. I had gone harder than he was, so I did not perceive that moisture as tears.

"And now you've really messed up," I went on, relentless. "You've chosen a Candy who is your own daughter. You cannot join with her in blood or you will go to a worse hell than the one you're already living in. You cannot join with her in flesh or you will go to the ultimate hell designed especially for incestuous perverts. You cannot kill her because she is your daughter, and you cannot let her go because you will go to jail. What are you going to do, Blake?"

His wet stone face turned to sodden clay. He sobbed aloud. "Mommy," he wept, his voice cracking.

"What do you mean, 'Mommy'? You don't have a mommy. You never had a mommy."

"Pandora, please . . ."

I pushed myself away from the wall and stood as tall as I could, hardly even swaying, my stare locked onto his wet pebble eyes. I demanded of him, "What is my name?"

He whispered, "Candor."

I placed the palms of my hands flat on my cheeks, hiding rash and chipmunk cheeks, pushing them up and back. All eyes and lips, I demanded, "What else?"

He choked it out. "Candy . . ."

And as his raining eyes gazed into mine, that scarlet lightning electric connection flew between us again, stronger than ever. I know he saw me as if seventeen years had never happened, because that's the way I saw him, my demented weeping sweetheart, and right on cue I started weeping too.

"Blake," I cried, all the time watching myself from some disassociated place as if I were an actor on a stage, all the while silently coaching myself, *Good, Dorrie, good. Do whatever it takes.*

"Candy, it really is you, my love. I can only just barely believe it. . . ." Shakily he reached toward me. "You were supposed to stay, stay young forever with me in a red embrace, and you didn't obey, you were punished, we were both punished, but we're still . . ." He put his arms around me, embraced me, making the knife wound hurt like fire. "I'm sorry," he whispered, although I think he was not referring to my blood on his arm. "I'm so sorry. You're still my Candy, my first true Candy."

As he hugged me, I could feel the knife blade pressed to my
back.

*I am a skinny, trembling, shy teenager sitting on the sofa in the li-
brarians' lounge, my naked thighs clamped together. In my shaking
hand I clench the razor-sharp hunting knife. Blake kneels before me,
his pale underarm presented to me. That creamy skin looks as soft as
his penis does. I have never touched his penis with my hands, but I can
feel it right now fingering my knees. Presumably it's his penis that I
feel. I don't look. I don't want to look at his arm either. I keep my gaze
fixed on his face.*

"Cut me, Candy," he whispers.

*His voice is pleading and hypnotically powerful at the same time.
And his eyes—the passion and importunity in them—his gaze is so
naked that now I can hardly bear to look at his face either.*

"Cut me. Do it, Candy! If you love me, do this to me."

I whimper, "I can't."

"Once you do it, you'll love it, Candy. Do it!"

*When his voice takes on that vehemence of command, I cannot
resist him, even though I must use both quaking hands to lift the
knife. Barely able to control the wavering blade, I place its grinning
edge against the petal-soft skin with its blue shadow of a vein on the
inner side of Blake's elbow. Wincing, I slide the blade about an inch.
Bright, bright cherry red drizzle wells up from Blake's vanilla skin
to spiral in candy cane stripes down the side of his arm, then drip to
the dull linoleum floor. And the low sound that trickles from Blake's
wet mouth—I have never heard anything that stirs me so deeply, not
even the way he moans when he comes in me.*

*He is right. I love cutting him. I want to cut him again. I want
to hear that cry of utterly passionate, injured ecstasy again.*

And the fierce feral grinning knife, I want it for my own. I want to take it home and make my parents cry out in a red ecstasy that will have nothing to do with love or nakedness. I want to open them up and see whether they have blood inside them. I want to make them scream and be real.

I want to kill them.

I am terrified.

Not of Blake.

Terrified of someone savage and fearsome whom I have never met before.

I am terrified of my primal self.

This was what I had not wanted to remember.

Standing at the dead end of the dark passageway in Blake's embrace, with my lifeblood trickling from my arm while Pandora's blade pressed to my spine, I flashed back to that last day with Blake before my parents took me away, and I shuddered. That scene of the story, that brief red interlude, was the part I had blocked out with a white light in my mind. It was the reason I had wrapped myself in shining dreams of a true love all my life. It was the reason I had fantasized Blake as my prince, my darling, my angel, for all these years.

Because, if he was my prince, then I remained a princess, no matter what my parents called me.

And if he was my rebel angel, then, bearing his child, I was a rebel angel too.

But if he was—what he really was . . .

If I had done what I had done, and felt that sick thrill, and that even more fearsome urge to kill—then what was I?

Even now, I could barely face it.

Yet now I needed it as never before. As Blake held me close. As Blake eased his hands to my shoulders, his knife blade caressing the side of my neck, while he gazed into my face.

God only knows what he saw in my eyes. The red memory, intimation of the unthinkable, knifed through me for only one slashing flashback moment, then left me dazed and stupefied, like an accident victim attempting with difficulty to remember who I was and where I was and how I had gotten there.

Sam's first impulse was to obey Walker's summons, to go tell the Appletree police and the FBI guys about finding Dorrie's flashlight.

But then a leaden, stubborn feeling stopped him. Had they come running when he called? No. So why should he come running when they called?

Keeping his distance, Sam crab-walked his way back toward the building, casting about like a beagle hunting for rabbit spoor. He saw a clear plastic candy wrapper on the gravel, then another. They meant nothing to him, but in the ironically golden sunshine they sparkled, caught his attention, and led him on a kind of trail toward the back of the old library, where the antiquated concrete cellar entrance jutted out from the foundation. Near it, something else glinted in the sun. Sam headed over there to see what it was.

Standing beside the old-fashioned cellar entrance, a stairway into the ground covered by a metal door, Sam bent to see what the sparkly thing in the gravel was.

Some sort of kid's toy or bauble. Little, about the size of a triple-A battery, with some kind of blue cut glass—heck, probably molded plastic—some kind of lens or ornament on the end. It meant nothing to Sam. He didn't even bother to pick it up. With a grunt he began to straighten—

And found himself looking directly at the edge of a rusty old cellar door hinge. That is, the sloped concrete cellar entryway at this point rose to the level of his eyes, and the hinge lay on top. Mostly horizontal, because the heavy door—two doors overlapping, really—lay on top to keep snow and such out of the stairwell. They didn't make cellar doors like that anymore.

The remarkable thing about this hinge was that it had big round screwheads on top, but Sam didn't see any screws going through the metal into the concrete.

No screw shafts.

Just shadow.

The hinge was kind of hovering about an eighth of an inch above the concrete.

Sam blinked, peered, then looked at the other hinge on this side. But even before he moved his eyes, he knew.

The door looked like it was doing what a door was supposed to do, but actually it was just lying there on top of its concrete base.

Firmly padlocked, of course.

A wordless roar erupted from Sam's chest. He lunged, gripped, and flung the entire double door, padlock and all, off the cellarway in one heave, like a grizzly bear attacking a deadfall.

FOURTEEN

Bert saw Sam White begin to straighten, then freeze into a rigid fishhook, peering at the side of the cellarway.

Then he saw Sam White surge up like a tsunami, seize the door that lay on top of the cellarway, and hurl the whole damn thing to the side. He threw it on the gravel of the parking lot with a crash worthy of a demolition derby. Heads turned. Men shouted. Paula, the constable, screeched, "Oh, my *God!*"—her soprano voice the only one Bert could understand. Not that he understood much at the time. He just reacted, running forward.

He got there before anyone else, in time to see Sam White plunge down a steep flight of concrete block steps and slam into a closed door.

A vertical door this time, made of metal painted a dirty dark green, army green. Otherwise, featureless. Standing at the top of the cellarway, Bert scanned that door as Sam clawed at the damn thing. The poor guy literally couldn't get a handle on it. There was none.

Bert felt people, cops mostly, pressing all around him to gawk like a troop of monkeys, and he heard their voices unprofessionally babbling: *Holy shit, would you look at that, damn thing was just lying there all the time, wait till DC hears about this, neighbor lady said she thought somebody's been going in and out, who the hell is that civilian in there, where's the judge when we need a warrant.* Static. Static of radios and static of bureaucracy.

"Bert!" bellowed Walker's voice in his ear. "Get Mr. White out of there!"

Staring at the gloomy green door, Bert did not immediately respond. Not that conflicting orders bothered him—come here, go there—but the door at the bottom of the cellar stairs was not the entry he remembered from when he was a kid and worked at the cigar factory. And he couldn't imagine why the library would have put in a massive metal door like that, worthy of a fortress, just to keep people out of the basement—

"Bert!"

Asshole, Bert thought as he started to move, walking forward to wince his way down the concrete block steps, which were too steep for his aching old bones. Walker should do some of his own shithead work sometimes. At the dank, dim bottom of the stairs with Sam White, Bert laid a hand on the younger man's upper arm. "Come on, Mr. White. Out of the way, now."

Sam barely seemed to notice. Didn't even look at him. Just shook off the hand like a horse shaking off a fly, stood back, launched himself from the bottom step, and rammed the door as hard as he could with his shoulder.

He might as well have been ramming Hoover Dam. The metal door took no notice of him whatsoever.

Sam White looked a bit shook-up, though, and Bert took the opportunity to grasp him by the arm again. "Come on, Sam. Let the professionals—"

From some small distance above and behind him he heard Paula's voice yell, "The light just came on!"

Bert heard the hubbub up there increase. Heard Walker

yell, presumably at Paula, "What the hell are you talking about?"

"In that room with the broken window!" Paula screeched in reply. "I'm telling you, an electric light just came on in there!"

"We do it to each other," Blake was telling me huskily, a drizzle of tears on his combat-scarred face. Inches apart, we gazed into each other's humid eyes, and any sense of the real world receded into haze and shadows.

"Yes," I breathed. "Yes, darling. You and I."

"And Pandora."

"Yes. Yes, with Pandora. We do it together."

He nodded, blinking; tears trembled like dew on his eyelashes. "We take turns. I open your wrist. The left one, because that's where the blood runs straight from the heart. Then I give Pandora to you, and you open my left wrist. Then we press them together so the blood mingles."

"Oh, how beautiful," I whispered, gazing into his eyes, so close to him that I should have been able to see his soul if he'd had one.

"Yes." He swallowed hard. "It's my own dream of the . . . the ultimate way for two to become one, better than lovemaking, better than intimacy. Since I was a kid, I dreamed wet dreams at night and I dreamed this dream all the time. We press our slit wrists together and we press our bodies together. We join in blood and we join in flesh."

"It's poetry," I murmured.

"Yes. Yes, it's poetry. And to make it complete we slash the right ones as well, and join them in blood, and we embrace. . . ."

I heard a clashing, metallic noise from outside somewhere. At the far end of the building.

Blake heard it too. His gaze grew vague, worried, shifting away from mine. He said, "No. No, it's not right. We should be naked and we should be lying down."

"There's no time. They're coming." My God, were they coming? Not daring to believe that help could really be on the way, I stayed in role as the mother of all Candies, lifting my hand to Blake's face. I touched. Harsh wet skin, scars, hard flesh, hard bone. I pressed my palm to his chin, urging his gaze back to mine. As long as he looked into my eyes, deep into my eyes, gazing only at my eyes, bypassing my lupus-ravaged body and face, he seemed to know who I was. And he was mine again. Or I was his. And everything depended on my keeping it that way until Juliet was safe.

Blake begged, "But this is my last chance to do it right. Sweet, sweet Candy, help me do it right."

I actually felt sorry for him, but not sorry enough to change my plans. Keeping my Candy eyes wide and misty and innocent of any cynical thoughts, I said, "It's all right to keep our clothes on, because we have to hurry. The gestapo's coming, Blake. Hear them?"

He heard. Thumping sounds, and a metallic pounding.

I said, "Give me the knife. Give me Pandora. Quick."

"No, that's not right. The man has to do it first." He was crying again, my brutalized, vulnerable, wretched so-called prince. "It's like dancing. The man leads. Candy, give me your left wrist."

Thinking, *For Juliet*, I lifted my arm, palm up, and presented my wrist to be slashed.

When Sam White ripped the metal doors off the cellar entryway, both Sissy and Gerardo stood with their mouths open—*Airing my molars,* Sissy thought as she tried to get her jaw under control—staring as Sam plunged into shadows.

Wham, came the sound of his shoulder against— Jogging closer, Sissy could see green doors, metal ones, judging by the sound the impact had made.

And made again.

Wham.

Sissy saw Bert limping down what appeared to be steep steps, going after Sam.

Wham.

"No handle!" shouted somebody—a man's voice, and she never knew who. But Gerardo was the one who caught her by the arm to stop her, saying, "Better stay back. We don't know what the hell is going on."

Sissy for once did not bristle, did not mind that an authoritative male was protecting her, because she was in a sense his guest, and having been hustled out of bed in a hurry, she wore no uniform, no bulletproof vest, and carried no weapon. She stopped, but she had gotten close enough to stare down at the steep concrete block steps leading to the green door. She barely noticed Bert or Sam. Her perception caught on the massive metal barrier and the building behind it.

"He's in there," Sissy whispered.

Gerardo stared at Sissy the way she was staring into the shadows. "What did you say?"

"Blake Roman! He's *in* there."

"What makes you think that?"

"The door. Plus my gut. The way I read him. He's a creep, a twisted specimen of slime mold, but he thinks he's an outlaw. This place is an outlaw hideout he's made for himself—it's his hole-in-the-wall, his fortress. He's in there with his big bad knife, waiting."

"Why wait? If he's in there and he's a killer, how come he isn't shooting at us?"

"He *so* prefers his knife." Sissy was doing the shooting, firing thoughts straight out her mouth, trusting her instincts to hit a target she could not yet see. "And just an ordinary knife wouldn't be good enough for this guy, you know? He's conflicted. A knife's up close and personal, all face-to-face, bloody, and for some reason that appeals to him. But, being a psycho, he's also distant. Cold. Remote. Egotistic. A legend in his own mind, but at the same time he can't quite shake the feeling he's really a creepy pervert, so he'd like more respect, he'd like to be king, you know? Off with their heads. A sword is just an oversized knife."

"The light just came on!" some woman screamed.

Voices babbled. Agent Gerardo swiveled away from Sissy to see what was going on. "In that room with the broken window!" the woman screamed. "I'm telling you, an electric light just came on in there!"

Sissy's eyes widened, the light came on in her mind, and she grabbed Gerardo by the sleeve, shouting at him, "Remote control! That's why the door won't open, has no handle on the outside. That's why the light just came on for no reason. Your unsub has his hideout rigged so that everything is operated by remote control!"

Standing in that dark, dead-end passageway to nowhere, I felt more than saw the blood flowing from my slit wrist, aware of it as a fluid I gave for Juliet, much as I would have given milk if I had ever breast-fed my baby girl.

The unspeakable man who had once been the love of my teenage life gazed into my eyes. Salt water ran down his face;

tears were the fluid he gave. "Good, Candy," he said, his voice clotted with emotion. "Good."

The words meant nothing, but a sweet taste filled my mouth simply because I was still alive, aware, on my feet and able.

Blake demanded of me huskily, "You know what to do, don't you?"

I nodded. This was more deeply true than he could possibly imagine.

"Be my blood lover, Candy." Intent on me, he gazed into my face. "Help me. Help me finally do it right."

There is no telling what he saw in my eyes.

Or dreamed he saw.

And needed. No telling the depth of that need.

Hesitating, he reached toward me, the knife lying in his slack hand.

Pandora.

The mother of all knives.

The weapon with a woman's name.

I reached out for her, took her in my hand, and her thick black handle fitted into my palm like a fat baby into a cradle. Hefting her, I felt more than heard something click as my hand tightened around her hilt. I saw a golden glow spring up like a candle flame at the far end of the dark passageway. No, more than candle flame, far brighter, greater. It was as if God or some angel had turned on the sun down here.

Let there be light. Electric light in the room where Juliet sat helpless.

Juliet. Kidnapped, abducted, captured, imprisoned. Duct tape binding her to a chair. Duct tape sealing her mouth.

Juliet, my daughter.

Our daughter.

Blake startled as the light flowed onto us from behind us,

and for a moment I cringed. But Blake kept his focus; his face grew yet more rapt. "Good, Candy, good!" he breathed. "I need to show you something before we die." He grabbed the knife back from me.

Oh, God, I hated my own clumsiness. I felt all my strength quite literally bleeding out of me. I'd lost my chance—

Swiftly Blake slit his left sleeve from wrist to shoulder, then opened it, throwing it over his back like a hero's cloak. Then he turned slightly so that I could see—a tattoo.

Sickening.

Dedicated to me.

I had never liked tattoos, and I found this one even more hideous than most. Into the flesh of Blake's upper arm were inked red lines in the shape of a bloated, oversized mouth, wide open like that of a hungry suckling. Within the mouth melted a red heart. And in dark blue script across the heart flowed the word "Candy."

"Candy, do you see? Do you understand?" Speaking, he almost sobbed. "It's always you. All my life, it's always been for you, my Candy, my sweet, my love. Now do it. Join us. Join us in the final embrace."

And he handed the knife back to me.

Once more, almost in disbelief, I hefted the deadly weapon in my hand.

Villain in silhouette, Blake might have been a youth again, masterful and romantic, as he reached toward me, presenting his naked left arm to me, his wrist awaiting me, his hand turned up toward heaven.

Was there a heaven?

Was there a hell?

In that moment I knew what it meant to have a soul and I knew what it meant to face judgment. A red river of Jordan flowed from my wrist and I felt faint. Reeling, I lifted the knife in my right hand, and yes, yes, I knew what I must do, but I didn't know whether I was going to be strong enough.

Dark cellar entryway. Green metal door, no handle. Dorrie was in there, Sam knew without knowing how he knew. He didn't understand much of what was going on. Barely comprehended the bony hand on his arm and the gritty voice in his ear:

"Mr. White, you're trespassing. You can't get in there and you don't know what's in there if you did. You're in danger of getting yourself killed."

Oh. Bert.

"Go away," Sam muttered, lurching toward the remorseless metal door to tackle it again.

Bert's grip on his arm tightened with surprising force for such an old guy, restraining him. Bert's voice turned stern. "Mr. White, you come on out of here before I have to put the cuffs on you."

Sam shook his head, tried to shake away Bert's steely hand. "I have to get in," he said thickly, struggling against Bert's grip, straining to launch himself against the door again.

"Mr. White—"

Inside, someone screamed so horribly that it cut off all the noise from Bert and the others, slicing through the moment like a knife. Sam felt his heart stop. The shriek ended too sharply, bursting into silence like a bubble of blood, and the very silence screamed. For a moment Sam stood as rigid as a pillar of salt. He couldn't move. He couldn't tell whether that awful noise had come from a child, a woman, or a man. But it had sounded human and it had sounded like someone was dying.

In the screaming silence, all the church bells of Appletree began to toll the call to Sunday morning early worship.

FIFTEEN

Gradually a red mist of panic and rage cleared from Sam's eyesight. Blinking, he found himself standing in that selfsame infernal gravel parking lot while several different kinds of cops and fire department volunteers and emergency personnel swarmed all around him. At some point an ambulance had materialized, and a ladder truck, and swerving around the corner that moment came a white van with a bright TV logo painted on its side. Reporters. For all the good they'd do. Sam tried to look down the concrete steps at the green door, but he couldn't see it; the cellar stairwell was a bobbing sea of heads in black fire helmets, yellow hard hats, blue police caps.

Standing there, Sam felt his heart pounding. Felt wetness on his face. Fear. Tears. He tried to lift a hand to clear his eyes.

Couldn't. Something made of cold metal clamped his wrists behind his back.

Despite a bruised and aching feeling throughout his body, Sam only vaguely remembered having been forcibly removed from the stairwell. Evidently they had handcuffed him.

But . . . but handcuffs were for criminals. Their steely grip renewed Sam's panic.

"Hey! Get these damn things off me!" he yelled. If ever in

life there was an occasion for swearing, this had to be it. Struggling, wrenching against the handcuffs, Sam felt them skinning his wrists, but they wouldn't let go. He wasn't strong enough. "Somebody get these goddamn things *off*!" he bellowed, but none of the swearwords he knew were strong enough either.

No one paid any attention to him. No one even looked at him. Except for the ones who were running back and forth with camcorders and microphones, they were all running in circles and yelling at one another: *Bring the Jaws of Life! No, everybody get back till the SWAT team gets here. Hell, what do they plan to use, dynamite? Bring a pry bar, get the plywood off one of the windows. Nobody go near any of the windows. Try one of the windows around the other side. Everybody's supposed to get back. We're going in. Not there, you idiot. Too small. Upstairs. Bring the ladder. Get the ladder away from the window. Bring the ladder, Goddamn it, sometime before we all get too much older.* Orders, countermanded orders, revised orders, contradictory orders, total lack of order.

Instinctively, like a trapped animal, Sam tried to move, and found that even with cuffs binding his hands behind his back, he could still walk. Weaving through the chaos around the back of the old brick building, he saw a familiar craggy oldster in a blue uniform. "Bert," he begged, "get these handcuffs off me."

But Bert responded only with a stare that passed right through him without any apparent comprehension.

Sam looked around for another blue uniform. Who the heck were all those people on the sidewalk? Most of them wearing their Sunday best, they had been on their way to church, Sam surmised, but were enjoying live entertainment instead. Uniformed police officers were trying to keep them and the news reporters back, giving the parking lot space to more important police officials such as the men in suits. Vaguely Sam recognized the FBI agents from the Phillipses' dining room; now they clustered in a football huddle at the corner of the building. Along with them stood a burly blue back. Sam approached it.

"Excuse me," he said, his courtesy a plaintive throwback to the way life used to be a day ago, "could you please take these handcuffs off?"

The cop turned, scowling. It was Walker. "What the hell you doing here? I told them to put you on ice!"

"What are you holding him for?" demanded one of the FBI Men in Suits, a tough-looking guy with ice blue eyes.

"Interfering with a police officer in the performance of his—"

"Bullshit. Let him go."

"You trying to tell me what to do? We been through this before and we're going to keep going through it until you feds get a clue. Read my lips. I Hold Jurisdiction Here."

"You are holding back from us, is what you are holding. Where's Officer Roman?"

Sam heard this without interest or comprehension. "My wife's in there," he said, the words coming out of him compulsive, inane. "Her car was here. Her purse is here. I don't know whether that was her screaming. I never heard anybody scream like that."

"Bert!" Walker roared, turning his back on the FBI. "Get your rear in gear over here! Agent Gerardo wants to talk with you."

"I don't know whether she's all right," Sam said.

Walker had already stalked away. Bert appeared not to have heard his boss's order; he stood staring at something that apparently only he could see. Sam gave a gaze of mute appeal to the FBI guys, but they headed toward Bert. His wandering glance caught on a familiar caramel-colored face.

She saw him at the same time. Officer Chappell from Fulcrum. Not in uniform. Out of place here. Didn't seem to know what to do any more than he did. She ran over to him like a frightened kid. "Mr. White! Mr. White, that awful scream, who was it?"

"I don't know." Because he liked her and felt he could trust her, he added, "I pray it wasn't Dorrie."

"Did it sound like her?"

"I just don't know. Would you take these handcuffs off me?"

"Handcuffs! What did they cuff you for?"

"For trying to get in, I guess."

"But somebody's got to get in!"

"I know. Could you take them off?"

"Mr. White, I don't have the authority to remove your handcuffs. Of course I've probably already lost my job. But I don't have the key either."

Sam barely heard any of what she was saying except the gist. What mattered to him. She couldn't help him.

Time to face it.

Nobody was going to take the handcuffs off.

Sam turned his back even though Sissy Chappell was still speaking to him. He no longer heard her. Like a locked-out puppy trying to get into the house the only way it knows, he headed back toward the rear of the building, toward the place where he'd been as close to Dorrie as he'd gotten yet.

The green door.

The cellar entryway stood empty now. The men in black helmets and yellow hard hats and blue caps had swarmed around to the side of the building where the light had come on.

Sam looked down the concrete steps. With its green paint

somewhat scratched now, the metal door still stood there, relentless, inscrutable, impregnable.

Carefully, a bit off-balance with his hands cuffed behind him, Sam descended the steps. It was cold down there. Dank. Shadowed. A chill hell. He stood staring at the door.

Dorrie. Behind it somewhere. Sure as a compass pointing toward the north, he could feel her presence in there.

Maybe alive.

Maybe dead.

The thought made him gulp and bow his head. Tears burned his eyes. He'd never felt more helpless than he did at that moment, with the people who were supposed to help him playing power games, nobody giving a damn about Dorrie. . . . For lack of a friendly shoulder, Sam leaned against the strong, cold metal door.

CLICK. From inside its metal torso.

The door swung open.

SIXTEEN

Bert was still trying to connect with things flying in all directions—Blake's name zinging at him like a bullet out of nowhere, a dark green door without a handle, a light springing on, somebody's agonized scream—he was still trying to figure out what devilment was getting milled in the middle of all the chips shooting this way and that when he heard Walker yell his name.

"Bert!"

Actually he heard his name hanging in the air for a moment after it was yelled.

In kind of a delayed reaction, Bert took in the order after it was issued. Oh. Damn. They'd made the connection. The feds wanted to talk with him.

Focusing, then slowly turning his head, Bert saw two things: the FBI agents heading toward him, and Sam White striding across the parking lot, heading toward the steep concrete steps down to the basement and the inscrutable green doors. It took Bert no time at all to decide he preferred Sam's company to that of the FBI. He sure didn't want to answer a lot of nosy questions just because his last name happened to be Roman. However, it took him a moment to get himself moving. His stiff old arms and legs didn't want to work right these days. As quickly as he could, he limped after Sam.

As Bert shambled along, he tried to reason a way out of this mess. The way Bert's mind worked, he couldn't just let the chips fall wherever; he had to try to line them up in some way that made sense. And the way to do that was to start with the facts of the case: The White woman was missing and the girl Juliet Phillips was missing. Sam White said the girl had been abducted by some guy in a van and Dorrie White had followed. Walker said Dorrie White had abducted the girl. He was still saying it and he wanted to go busting into the old library and get both of them. For some reason, though, the FBI had changed its thinking. Now the suits thought there was a dangerous felon, a serial rapist/killer, holding both the woman and the girl in that building. The FBI wanted to set up a command post, establish communications, bring in the sharpshooters and the listening devices and the expert negotiators, and in general hold off until the cavalry arrived.

Bert did not know the identity of this putative serial rapist/killer.

But he did know that Blake Roman had been profiled as one.

And he did know that Sam White had suggested Blake Roman's name to the FBI, and so had that Fulcrum police officer who really should mind her own business.

What he still didn't get was *why*. Why pick on his grandson? What was the connection?

"CANDY GOT LAID HERE," read the wall.

Okay, so what? Blake had taken advantage of half the girls in town when he was a young buck. In his way, after his parents had died, Blake had become as notorious as they had been. Bert had heard rumors about the kid fooling with girls under the stairs in the school, back in the stacks in the library, under bridges at night, wherever. Candy, Candor, Dorrie, whatever her name was, had been only one of many. So now, close to twenty years later, this Dorrie Birch White character had gone missing, so what? Why drag Blake in?

Well, maybe it was kind of peculiar that Blake kept renewing the writing on the wall. But even so—

Bert broke off his attempt to line up some thoughts in a row, because he saw Sam White descending the basement stairs to the locked door.

Damn strange, a door without a handle. Not the way any normal person would choose to shut out unwelcome company. But it sure had worked. That door wouldn't budge—

Bert blinked. The green door was moving.

Sam White had barely touched it this time, but the green door swung open.

Wide open.

Silent. Inward. Dark.

Bert stood rigid, staring, not likely to yawn again anytime soon. His mind struggled against what he was seeing, but his gut comprehended it completely.

Nobody had been able to open that door before.

But now somebody was in control.

Somebody inside.

Inviting Sam White into a trap.

And it had to be Blake.

Bert knew this instantly, with bone-deep intuitive certainty, because he remembered too clearly: Blake, damn brilliant kid in his freaky way, when he was only ten years old already putting together gadgets for his crippled daddy. Remote control coffeepot, remote control microwave clicker. Remote control switches for fans, lights, heaters. Door openers, door locks.

Blake.

Good son. Clever. Clever son of a bitch.

Bert felt as if his insides had turned to soup. He couldn't move or he'd slop himself, watching Sam White, hands cuffed behind his back, walk into the darkness behind the yawning door.

God. The guy was either incredibly brave or two eggs cracked in his dozen. Or both.

Sam peered into the basement behind the open door. He saw only shadows.

In those shadows somewhere he would find Dorrie. He felt stark certain of it.

But he didn't know whether he would find her alive.

He walked in slowly, testing each step with his big feet. Couldn't even feel his way with his hands, because they were locked helpless behind his back. Didn't know what he was going to do if he needed to rescue Dorrie from some creep with a gun; tell the guy, *Wait, excuse me, don't shoot, don't hit me until I get close enough to trample you*? Sure. A lot of good he'd do Dorrie by getting himself killed.

Yet Sam considered that he had no alternative but to walk into this shadow hole.

After a few shuffling steps he began to hear someone crying.

Or he thought he did. It was hard to tell when his frightened body insisted on gasping like a guppy out of water. Sam stood still for a minute, held his panicky breath, tried to tune out the pulse yammering in his ears, and listened.

Yes. He could hear it, off to his right. It sounded like—Sam had hardly ever heard Dorrie cry, and never like that. He didn't think it was Dorrie. Too young, too soprano. It sounded like a girl, maybe the missing girl, the Phillips girl, moving around and making a choked-down panicky sobbing sound, as if she was trying not to be heard but she couldn't hold back her whimpering.

Turning toward the sound, Sam realized his eyes were adjusting to the dark and he was beginning to be able to see. That vertical shadow line ahead was a corner, and somewhere beyond it, a yellowish electric light was sending a few rays his way.

Sam sidestepped until his shoulder bumped against the wall; then, using that contact for guidance, he walked forward. Slow steps. Three. Four. Five.

Six. Sam edged around the corner and found himself blinking at a stretch of shabby hallway—shredded carpet, or had somebody dumped garbage? Splotches and blotches of something on the floor. It was hard to see through tears and harsh light and harsher shadow, hard to put the picture together with an exhausted, stricken mind. Hard to comprehend paneled walls with sections missing, lying splintered—or were those sharp things shadows, or parts of the door?

A broken door. An old-fashioned wooden door with a big hole busted right through its rectilinear middle, as if this insane place were a circus and the door was made of tan tissue paper a lion had plunged through.

The light issued through that hole. From behind that door.

It had to be the door to a room.

Where someone was crying.

Sam walked forward to see why.

I struggled along a dark passageway, so shadowed, so far under so much weight of earth and mortality and transience, a straight and narrow tunnel rife with angel cries and devil shouts and thunder gong noise. Bells, bells, bells. A silver shining presence accompanied me—a crescent of moonlight? An angel, a devil? Or a shaman, a psychopomp, a guide? The journey felt long, long, perhaps beyond my strength. I staggered, I fell, I crawled, I fell farther, I hitched, I crept on my elbows while the companion shaped like a silver fish swam in my blood, while I swam in my own blood toward—nearer, yet too far—the end of the tunnel of travail where light shone, and the name of the light was love.

In his mind Sam wanted to stop, go back, stay away, never know. But his big blundering feet insisted on carrying him forward.

To the shattered door.

Its breach, a jagged oval, framed the jumble of images within so that he saw it as a grotesque vignette, not something he had to quite believe, not yet. For an instant he just saw objects overlapping in confused juxtaposition:

Table shoved into a corner. Overturned chair. Drips and puddles of red on the floor. Brown coat lying there. No. Brown coat was Dorrie. Covering Dorrie, or Dorrie's body. Girl, teenager, kneeling over Dorrie with thick ribbons of something silvery gray hanging off her hands and feet. Broken glass. Beer cans. Big hunting knife on the floor. Knife same color as metallic ribbons. Weeping girl wrapping and wrapping the silver gray stuff around Dorrie's left wrist. Red mess on Dorrie's arm, her hand, her clothes.

Blood.

Dorrie.

Oh, my God.

At the sound Sam made, the crying girl screamed, snatching the hunting knife from the floor, crouching over Dorrie with it as her stare darted to the door, the invader. Her wild wet eyes fixed on Sam, and for a hallucinatory moment he thought she *was* Dorrie, a disheveled new butterfly Dorrie that had just emerged from the dead brown cocoon Dorrie lying on the floor. The next moment sanity returned, and he recognized her: Yes, it was the missing girl. Juliet Phillips.

"I won't hurt you," he said, pushing against the door with his shoulder. Something heavy—oh. Sofa. Sam forced the door open a couple feet anyway and edged in. "Is she—is she . . ." With all his hammering heart Sam wanted to rush to Dorrie and help her, hold her, will her to live. But damn the handcuffs, the best he could do was waddle toward her.

Raising the knife, the girl cried, "Who are you? What do you have behind your back?"

Crashing to his knees on the hard floor, Sam said, "Handcuffs."

"You're a—you're a prisoner?"

Intent on Dorrie, Sam didn't answer. Unable to feel for a pulse with his hands, he did it with his face, mouth to her throat, exploring with his lips like a baby.

Yes. Yes! He found a pulse. He felt her breathing.

"She's alive!" he cried, straightening to face the girl across Dorrie's unconscious body. "She's *alive*," he informed her earnestly.

She met his gaze, and within an eyeblink she'd decided he was harmless; he saw her face dismiss any fear of him. She let the knife drop to the floor. "But I can't get the *bleeding* stopped," she wailed, clenching Dorrie's wrist between both her hands.

The silver gray ribbon stuff, Sam saw, was duct tape. Juliet had been bandaging Dorrie's wrist with it. But blood flowed from under the tape.

Sam stared at the tape, the blood, just barely comprehending. He blurted, "Who did that to her?"

"*Him,*" the girl said with a note of hysteria in her voice. "She cut the tape off me before she fainted, but I don't know where *He* is. He could come back any minute. And she's bleeding to death!"

"No, she's not. She's *not.*" Not with an ambulance parked outside. Reeling like a drunk, the handcuffs throwing him off-balance, Sam struggled to his feet, intending to go yell in Walker's ear until he got through. But once upright, he discovered he could not leave Dorrie's side. Could. Not. A kind of gravitational force bound him to her, stronger than the steel binding his wrists.

So it was up to him to fix her. Practical. Mechanical. "Find something to tie real tight around her arm," he told the girl.

"A tourniquet! Duh!" With frenzied haste Juliet Phillips grabbed for a shoe box lying nearby, snatched from it something red—thong panties? She tied the fabric, whatever it was, around Dorrie's upper arm, then stuck the knife handle through it, twisting to tighten it.

"Oh, God," she whispered, eyeing the flow of blood from Dorrie's wrist, "please stop."

Oh, God, thought Sam, *what else can I do?* Lurching closer to the broken window, he lifted his head and bellowed, "Help! We need help down here! Send the medics!"

But he couldn't tell whether his words were heard, because the sound of his voice was punctuated by an explosion far stronger than any exclamation. *CRACK*, like the crack of doom, a blast from somewhere close at hand, in the basement, so near that Sam could feel the concussion in the air.

Gunshot.

Hanging on to Dorrie and her makeshift tourniquet, Juliet screamed.

SEVENTEEN

S eeing Sam push open the green basement door and enter,
Bert had known from his training what he should do. He
needed to get on his radio, inform Walker, alert the FBI.

But he didn't. Instead, his hand, as if acting on its own, went
to his belt and presented him with his sidearm.

Bert snapped the safety off the pistol. For once, his aging
body needed no coaxing. It moved forward on its own, toward
the cellar entryway.

Headed down the steep steps.

Toward that open door.

And into the dark.

With no idea whose side he was on.

Silently, cautiously, Bert slipped into the dark basement.
Taut, with his handgun at the ready, he stopped at the first
corner to listen. He heard the girl crying. Heard a man's voice
make an inchoate sort of croak. Whipping around the corner
with his weapon leveled, Bert saw that the sound had come
from Sam White, who was blundering into a room with a broken door.

Bert lowered his gun. Obviously Blake wasn't in that room,
or Sam White would be dead.

Bert knew he ought to head in there, assess the situation, render assistance, take Sam White into custody.

Nope.

For the first time, Bert acknowledged in his own mind that he was not just following Sam White. And he was not doing his duty as a police officer either. He was not trying to arrest a perpetrator or rescue the Phillips girl or anyone else. And he was not going to radio for backup.

He was looking for Blake.

His grandson.

Silent, like an old gray cat, Bert reached the doorway Sam White had entered and passed it. A long, dim hallway lay ahead, partly illuminated by a blast of electric light from what appeared to be another shattered doorway.

With impatient bravado he strode down there, knowing that the moment he entered that lit area, he would be a plain target for anyone—not necessarily his grandson—any armed and dangerous perp lurking in the darkness beyond the area he could see. But letting the chips fall wherever, Bert stepped into the light anyway, peering into what turned out to be a bathroom with a watery mess on the floor and two stalls hanging open, empty. Nowhere else in there for anyone to hide. Ceiling light shining like a son of a bitch. Bert flicked it off.

He gave his eyes a moment to adjust to the darkness before he tackled the next stretch of hallway. Should have given them several minutes more, but by acting like a badass TV cop he had scared himself, and his heart wouldn't stand the wait. He could feel the old pump pounding fit for a coronary. Could feel the sweat popping out on his forehead. Couldn't stand himself much longer. Swallowing hard, Bert raised his pistol, strode out of the bathroom, and headed on down the hallway.

Walking into darkness. Couldn't see where he was going.

But anybody down there would see him coming, silhouetted against the light that still shone, not from the bathroom, but from the other room at the far end of the hallway.

Anybody, not necessarily his grandson.

Even if it was Blake, the boy wouldn't know it was his grand-daddy coming to get him.

And if he did know, would he care?

Bert shied away from answering that question, yet made himself a moving target by sidestepping, taking a few strides, sidestepping again, then back the other way, at irregular intervals.

Stalking along the unlit hallway, Bert tried to remember the layout of the building. He thought he should be coming to a corner, then a doorway to a stairwell. As his eyes struggled with the darkness, making shapes of the shadows, he thought he actually saw the vertical line of the corner ahead, and he quickened his stride to get behind it. . . .

Something large blocked his foot. He stumbled hard, falling, throwing his hands up to catch himself, but instead of sprawling on the floor, he slammed into a wall. Not a proper wall but a barrier made of rough wood, which should not have been there.

He turned, panicked, to point his gun in the direction of the thing that had tripped him up. Just by the feel of it under-foot he knew what it was: a body. But he had no idea whether it was dead or alive.

Facing back toward the distant light, squinting into the gloom, he could make out the dark shape lying across the passageway.

A man.

Playing possum?

Bert stood waiting, gun at the ready, willing the form to move. Stand up. Curse him. Knife him.

Get up, damn you.

But it just lay there. Stone still.

Hurt?

Unconscious?

Bert felt his sweaty hands start to lose control. This was not the way it was supposed to be. His grandson was not supposed to meet him lying down. Grandfather and grandson were supposed to converge face-to-face. Their eyes were supposed to lock. Their fists were supposed to lift. And something was supposed to happen. Some kind of justice or comprehension, and then Bert would know what he was made of because he would know what to do. Maybe shake hands. Maybe hug Blake, maybe kill him. Or maybe his grandson was supposed to kill him instead because he had been such a poor excuse of a grandpa. Or if not that, then maybe he, Bert, was supposed to understand what was wrong with himself.

Bert's gun hand quaked so hard he couldn't steady it. But he kept it up in the air. With his other he fumbled for his flashlight, finally got it out of its holder on his belt with its business end wavering toward what seemed to be the head of the dark manifestation on the floor. It took his arthritic fingers three tries to get the flashlight flicked on.

And he saw.

Blake Roman lay there with his eyes wide open, but not looking at anything in this life.

The flashlight illuminated Blake's head with a white aureole of light, and from that halo Blake gazed up with the look of a child, not a man, with the look of a boy who has been utterly betrayed. Like a storybook prince on bended knee mutely begging, *Love me, love me, why won't you love me?* A prince wearing a cloak of blood red tied with a crimson ribbon at his throat.

Bert flinched, swallowing hard, staring at Blake's throat slit clear across from shoulder to shoulder, at Blake's blood running down to the floor and spreading like a crimson cape. But then Bert's gaze locked with the empty gaze of his grandson's eyes, supposedly the window to the soul that should have inhabited the body his grandson used to walk around in. In the corpse lying at his feet Bert saw nothingness, and he stopped trembling. He knew who and what he was. And he knew to his marrow that he was finished, through, done. Done with being a cop. Done with Appletree; there were other places on earth. Or maybe done altogether.

Not conceptualizing much of this, just reacting, Bert fired a bullet into the body on the floor as if driving a stake into a vampire.

A moment after the gunshot finished echoing through the dark basement, Sam heard footsteps impending down the hallway toward him. Not welcome footsteps. Not running, the way rescuers would have done. These footfalls drummed out the relentless rhythm of a desperate man.

Inwardly cursing all handcuffs ever manufactured, Sam blundered toward the door to place his large self between whatever was coming and his wife. He couldn't fight with steel bracelets binding his wrists, but maybe he could stop a bullet or two.

Juliet, he saw as he scuttled past, had seized the knife again as she huddled over Dorrie. But that eight-inch blade wasn't going to do her much good against a gun—

A hard hand slammed the door aside, sofa and all. Hard-faced, the gunman strode in, pistol at the ready.

Sam exclaimed, "Bert!"

But the old man showed no sign of hearing. He didn't even seem to see Sam, although for a moment—Sam's heart stopped—Bert's gun barrel's single black-hole eye stared straight at him. Then it passed on like a tornado, sparing him. Sam swiveled to watch, gawking, as Bert blew past him. He saw Bert cast an expressionless glance at the woman lying uncon-scious on the floor, the girl cowering over her with knife in hand. Then Bert strode past them, coiled, and hurled his pistol with great force and accuracy through the window. Shattering glass flew like fountain spray. Sam heard shouts and screams from outside.

Turning his back on the sounds, Bert strode over to Sam, grabbed him by the elbow, and spun him around as if spinning a display stand at the end of a drugstore aisle, as if he were looking for aspirin or something. No, make that handcuffs. It was handcuffs Bert was after. Sam felt Bert jabbing at them none too gently with some kind of key or tool. Then, blessedly, he felt the cuffs snick off him.

For a moment Sam blinked at his own hands, which had gravitated forward and up in front of his face to greet him like long-lost friends. The next instant, they led him urgently to Dorrie. Folding to the floor beside his wife, Sam gathered her upper body into his lap and his arms, cradling her, hugging her to his chest, kissing her lidded eyes, her temple, her forehead. He could barely sense her shallow breathing.

"Dorrie, it's Sam. I'm here. Dorrie," he begged, "don't leave me."

He caught sight of a silvery circular blur. Bert seemed to be amusing himself by spinning the handcuffs. No. Bert wanted something else to throw. Like an aging David facing his final Goliath, Bert whirled the handcuffs and let go, sending them winging through the window amid more shouts and flying glass.

This time Bert seemed inclined to respond to the shouts. He clawed at his old radio.

"Walker, you asshole," he grated in his gravelly voice, "get your fat cowardly backside in here. Or what would do more good, send the medics. Woman and girl need help. Tell the FBI they can put the flash-bang grenades away. Their serial killer is lying dead with his throat cut."

Sam heard Juliet gasp. Horror, relief, shock, release. But Sam felt no reaction. Hugging Dorrie, whispering to her to stay alive, please live, please stay—hanging on minute by minute, Sam cared about nothing except his wife, his love.

This time I journeyed not in a dark tunnel but in a luminous lake of prismatic light. This time I did not need to struggle, suffer, fight my way toward love; the light was made of love, and I floated in it. The love was made of timelessness, not a swift stream of moments to sweep me along, but a vast pool of eternity in which to drift. Perspective had splayed like my poor lupus-hexed carcass sprawled below on a dingy linoleum floor, and I relaxed without pain in the sunlight near the smashed window, I lazed as if on invisible eiderdown, luxuriating in an unimaginable freedom. Freedom from the strait and narrow progression of seconds, moments, hours. Freedom from lupus. Freedom from myself.

Outside any context of my life's minutes ticking away, I saw my bloodied body being cradled in the arms of a man I barely recognized at first: an unshaven man with a harrowed, bruised face. A man in a business suit but wearing no tie, his shirt collar all sweat, his slacks ruined with dirt, his jacket soiled as if he'd been spelunking in it, rumpled as if he'd slept—no, not slept in it. Sam looked as if he hadn't had any sleep—

Sam?

Sam! Here!

Sam, embracing me in his arms, talking to me—I could see him talking but I could not hear him. Sam, a real man. Sam, a real hero. And Juliet. I could see her kneeling on the other side of my body from Sam, clutching herself, her thin shoulders shaking. Juliet, my daughter. I barely knew her, yet in some atavistic way I loved her more than—

More than life.

No romance novel I had ever read, no classic movie I had ever watched, began to explain the bone-strong, marrow-deep way I loved my daughter.

Far, far more than I had ever loved Blake.

Although as a girl I had loved him with all my silly heart.

And he—even as a felon, in some sick, insane sense of the word, Blake had loved me. He had looked like a man, but he had never gotten over being a boy. This I knew because he had handed me the knife.

I killed him.

Would hell's fire someday burn me because I had slashed that man-boy's throat? Killing, even to save Juliet, was a dreadful thing. And to kill someone who had once been my prince—

From a presence that floated with me in the lake of light came a gentle reply. *Think, rather, that you closed the eyes of a dream long dead.*

Of course I had an entity keeping me company and giving me guidance, but this time it was not a silver swimming blade named Pandora. This time my companion was—all names, no names, it was in the golden light and of the white light. It was the light. Some people might call it angel. Some might call it God.

I gave what my parents had taught me to give to God: guilt to the hilt in my own heart. *He wasn't my dream man. He was a real person. And I killed him.*

Instantly the presence responded, *Think, rather, that you put an end to his misery.*

I didn't knife him to be merciful.

Again, reassurance reached me without hesitation. *Neither did you do it to be cruel.*

This being was very different from the pitiless God my parents had taught me. This was no He-God, no Jehovah. Neither was this a She-God. But it was utterly a Person conversing with me inside my mind, a stranger residing deep within me like an old, forgotten friend.

It instructed me, *Think why you did what you did.*

That was simple enough. *For Juliet.*

I saw her clutching at my hand as the paramedics shoved her away. I saw Sam standing over me, praying, as she stood beside him, watching the ambulance people work on me.

Sam. I loved him.

I really loved him. As a real person.

I loved him so much.

But would he still be able to love me now that he knew about me? If I returned to my body . . .

Understand that every ending is a beginning, whispered the white-light presence that accompanied me.

I understood only that I hovered on the cusp of an enormity.

Sam felt the girl tugging at his sleeve, but he had to keep his eyes on Dorrie, unconscious on the floor. Officious people in white coats intruded, getting in the way; he couldn't see Dorrie's face.

Weeping, the girl demanded, "Who *is* she?"

Sam mumbled, "My wife." He could still see Dorrie's corduroy skirt. And there was a glimpse of her hair. Good. Good. With his heart in his gaze Sam hung on to her. As long as he could see Dorrie, even only glimpses of her, she couldn't really leave him.

The Phillips girl cried, "She's not just your *wife*. Who *is* she?"

As if Candor Birch White were a comic-book heroine, Sam thought, Super Wife, with a secret identity. Sam had always known there was a mystery, a distance, about Dorrie, but he had never wanted to face it.

"Um . . ." Sam did not want to be rude, but he wished the Phillips girl would leave him alone. Couldn't she see Dorrie might die? Couldn't she see he was trying to pray?

"Her name is Dorrie White," someone answered Juliet, "and she is a hero." Sam recognized the gentle voice, and peripherally glimpsed a familiar caramel-colored face. Sissy Chappell stood with one arm around Juliet, trying to comfort her.

"She came out of *nowhere*," the girl cried. "How did she know my name?"

"We aren't sure. But she knew you were in trouble."

Juliet turned to Sam. "Mister, *how did she know me?*"

Desperately trying to contact the Almighty, Sam didn't answer. Starting in childhood he had been taught the right way to pray: First you thank God for specific blessings in your life, and then you ask God in a general way to be with you and your loved ones, keeping the moral hygiene up to par, and then you ask God to help with any specific problems on your mind, and then you say that, notwithstanding any of the above, Thy Will

Be Done, Amen. Sam knew all this, but he couldn't do it. All he seemed to be able to pray was *Stay with me, Dorrie, stay, please God, please let her stay with me, please don't let her die.* Over and over. Just at the time it mattered the most, he couldn't format the prayer properly, couldn't focus, and if he couldn't even pray right, he certainly couldn't give this weeping girl his attention. He couldn't think what she wanted from him. It was hard to understand her words, choked with sobs. Heck, it was hard to understand anything that was happening.

That officious jerk Walker popped up out of someplace and grabbed the girl by the elbow. "Juliet Phillips? Come with me."

"No!" Juliet pulled away from the man.

As if interpreting for the girl, Sissy Chappell said, "Take it easy, Captain. Wait a couple minutes until we see whether Mrs. White is okay."

"I don't have a couple minutes, miss. I am an officer of the law, and—"

"And you didn't save me," Juliet flared at him. "*She* saved me." Heads turned; even Sam turned to look as she shouted at Walker, "She saved my *life.* A hundred ways, a hundred times. She didn't leave me and I'm not leaving her."

"I'm not in uniform, but I am an officer of the law also, Captain Walker," said Sissy quietly, "and this girl—"

Sam stopped paying attention. He wanted Dorrie. What were they doing with her? Through the interstices between white coats, blue uniforms, and gray suits, Sam saw Dorrie seemingly levitate onto the gurney that would take her to the ambulance. He saw the people around her begin to move in unison, like a multilegged insect, toward the door, with their arms waving aloft like feelers, trailing plastic tubes, wires, scary-looking paraphernalia.

Sam heard Walker say loudly, "Miss Officer of the Law

Also, I don't give a rat's ass that the kid is from your jurisdiction. She's in mine now."

"Then you had better call my boss, Chief Angstrom, and arrange—"

"Bull crap! You're just trying to stall me!"

And succeeding, Sam thought. But Walker's tone of voice and the way he was treating Juliet made Sam feel like throwing a punch at him—a thought he could not afford to entertain right now when Dorrie needed all his attention. He followed the medics as they rolled his wife toward the door, but Juliet broke away from both Sissy and Walker to grip his arm, begging, "How did she know I needed her? Why did she save me?"

Having no answers for her, barely able to speak if he did, Sam took her hand as softly as if it were his own child's to remove it from his arm. He had to go with Dorrie. Couldn't let her out of his sight or she might cease to be, leave him, die. He trotted after the gurney rolling out the door.

Behind him the girl called, "Mister, wait!"

Sam felt her cry hit him like a smack from God. He had to do something for her. He couldn't stay with her, had to get on the ambulance with Dorrie, but he grabbed the cell phone from his pocket and turned back just long enough to see Juliet Phillips straining to follow him, Sissy trying to talk to her, Walker's ungentle grip on her arm restraining her. Sam tossed the phone to her. "Here!"

She snagged it one-handed. Excellent catch. This girl was no stranger to baseball.

"Call your parents!" he yelled to her, running to follow the gurney up the steep concrete-block stairs and out of this accursed place.

EIGHTEEN

Several hours later, after driving Sam White's Silverado back from Appletree, Sissy parked it in his driveway and got out.

Car doors slammed up and down the street, and people with microphones started to run toward her. Goddamn, the news freaks were staking out the Whites' private home now. And they'd been thicker than ticks in sheep dip at the police station back in Appletree. Dorrie White was going to be a big story.

So tired that it was not hard to stay silent and flat-faced, Sissy started walking, straight-arming reporters out of her way without even looking at them. After following her for a couple of blocks they gave up, and she continued, her feet dragging, on her way to the nearest bus stop. Once she got home, she would phone the Fulcrum hospital to check on Dorrie White. A medical helicopter had rushed Dorrie White there, to the Fulcrum Trauma Center, the area's primary emergency medical facility, but the helicopter that had brought Sissy to Appletree hadn't taken her back home, not when she wasn't a priority anymore. It had taken Juliet Phillips to reunite with her parents instead.

So Sissy Chappell had been caught for a while in the bureaucratic chaos that was to be expected after a major crime—she and Sam White. Not allowed on the medevac copter with his wife, Mr. White had been so upset that for once the local police and the feds were of one mind: This man was too distraught to be allowed behind a steering wheel. Sissy had offered to drive the Silverado, and Sam had been persuaded to give her the keys. The FBI had helped Sam duck the news-media crowd, tucked him into their big sedan, and headed for Fulcrum. The Appletree police, or rather Captain Walker, had relieved Bert Roman of duty and detained him on charges of insubordination, withholding evidence, abuse of a corpse, and whatever else they could think of.

That was pretty much the end of Appletree's involvement in the Juliet Phillips/Dorrie White case.

Sometime after Bert's arrest but before arrangements had been made for Sam White, Sissy had sighed deeply, straightened her shoulders, and phoned Fulcrum PD to speak with Bud Angstrom. She had barely started to tell him she was in Appletree and why before he shouted loud enough to traumatize her eardrum, "I said you'd be fired and you're fired!"

It had, of course, been well worth it.

Just the same, all the long drive home from Appletree, Sissy had worried about being without a job. It had been hard enough to find the first one; would any other police department ever hire her without Angstrom's recommendation? Or would she end up as a security guard at a shopping mall? Walking out of the housing development where Sam White lived, Sissy was still worrying, and hoping her car had not been towed out of the Fulcrum PD parking lot; when Angstrom was mad, he could get pretty mean.

Finally she reached a main street, a block down from a bus stop.

It took the right bus seemingly forever to come. But once on it, heading for home but finding no seats available and barely able to hang on as she stood in the aisle, Sissy knew for sure that nothing was going to keep her from sleeping. Worry could wait until morning.

In her apartment at last, after her phone call to Fulcrum Hospital (no word on Dorrie, still in surgery), a quick meal of scrambled eggs, and an even quicker shower, Sissy snuggled into bed and almost instantly slept.

For about an hour and a half.

Then her phone rang.

It was déjà vu.

The phone rang persistently beside Sissy Chappell's bed. Facedown in her pillow, groping for the source of the noise, she brought the phone to one ear and mumbled, "'Lo?"

"Sistine Chappell?"

Sissy recognized the voice as that of Frank Gerardo and sat up in a panic. "Please, please don't tell me that Dorrie White died."

"No, no, she's about the same. Still on the operating table. Did I wake you up? Again?"

"Well, yes, kind of."

"Maybe you'd rather we talked another time—"

"No, right now is *fine*." Worry might not keep Sissy from sleeping, but she knew curiosity could. What did Gerardo want?

He said, "Okay, um, Miss Chappell, Agent Harris has told me you've lost your position at the Fulcrum PD due to our interference, and—"

"How in the world did Agent Harris know?"

Gerardo gave a quiet chuckle. "Through the grapevine. Several persons besides yourself could hear Angstrom shouting on the phone, Miss Chappell."

"Oh." Duh. Sissy added hastily, "It's nice of Agent Harris to take an interest."

"Agent Harris has a great deal of respect for you and your work."

"That's good to hear," said Sissy, trying hard to muster some enthusiasm. "Is it possible—I mean, do you think either you or Agent Harris could talk Angstrom into taking me back?"

"I doubt it. But I'd much rather talk you into coming to work as a consultant for me."

Sissy had never woken up so fast, or responded so enthusiastically, in her life. "That would be great! Consulting about handwriting?"

"Sometimes, I'm sure, but right now I have a specific job of a different nature in mind for you. Go back to sleep and I'll get in touch with you tomorrow, okay?"

"Okay. Yes. Um, thank you. Good-bye."

After that, it was pleasantly difficult for Sissy to get back to sleep.

The next morning, Monday, Sissy dressed in her favorite chambray shirt, khaki slacks, and Converse high-tops. Heading downtown on foot to the Fulcrum PD to give her shield and sidearm back to Bud Angstrom, she found herself noticing birdsong and a blue sky and the occasional wildflowers that had forced their way through the pavement. Her car, in the parking lot right where it belonged, seemed to twinkle a headlight at her. Breezing into the building where she had worked for less than a year, Sissy found herself smiling at sour faces and shrugging off the sympathies of friendly ones. After cleaning out her desk, she tapped on Chief Angstrom's office door, determined to be so pleasant she would give him heartburn. She would have done this in any case, but Agent Gerardo's phone call made it much easier.

Angstrom roared, "Enter!"

Sissy did so, singing out, "Good morning!" as she placed her pistol, shield, and departmental hat on his desk. Her uniform she had paid for, and she would keep it, for all the good it might ever do her.

Angstrom scowled at the items on his desk. His formidable eyebrows, Sissy noted, adhered firmly to his forehead today. She wondered why he did not invest in a matching toupee for his bald head.

He growled, "What's all this?"

"I'm fired," Sissy reminded him, making a great effort not to smile.

"Oh. That. How's about if I dock you two days' pay instead." He plunked her pistol and badge into her hat, making a receptacle out of it, and lifted it in her general direction, his attention on some papers on his desk. "Get back to work."

How sweet life could be sometimes, albeit at long and unpredictable intervals.

Sissy did not lift a hand to accept her job back. "No, thanks," she said. "I have another offer. The FBI is hiring me as a consultant."

A kind of lightning flash reflected off Angstrom's shiny pate as his head jerked up, and a kind of thunder sounded as the hat and its cargo fell from his slackened grip into his metal waste can. "You *what*?" he yelped. "*What* effing FBI?"

"Agent Gerardo—"

Angstrom's next bellow brought him to his feet, knuckles on his desk to stick his face into Sissy's. "Gerardo! So you're quitting on me! If you go with pretty boy, don't you ever try crawling back here!"

"Very best wishes to you too, sir," Sissy said, turning to hide her grin as she headed out the door.

Once outside and in her car, Sissy phoned the number she had already programmed into her cell.

Two ringtones, then, "Gerardo."

"Chappell reporting for duty, sir."

"Good Lord, don't 'sir' me, Chappell. Can you meet me at the hospital third-floor lounge? Intensive care?"

"Yes, si— Um, what am I supposed to call you?"

"Franklin Delano Gerardo. Or whatever."

"Um, okay. On my way."

News cameras scanned the hospital entrance, but as nobody knew Sissy was anybody, she entered without interference.

A few minutes later, her new boss was briefing her over coffee: Mrs. White was in grave condition, heavily sedated and barely conscious. She had nearly died from loss of blood before reaching the hospital. During the fairly long and serious operation to repair her injuries, both the slashed arm and the slit wrist requiring reattachment of nerves and blood vessels, she had required multiple transfusions. No sooner was she out of surgery than complications had started setting in; Dorrie's wounds showed signs of infection, and her lupus was ravaging her body.

Sissy's assignment was simple but important: be available to question Dorrie White if and when she became lucid. Neither Chappell nor Gerardo dwelt long on the grim possibility that she might not survive, although as professionals they had to accept it. Both hoped for a happier outcome.

In any event, Sissy would keep vigil at the hospital for days, perhaps even weeks, until she had all the necessary information for an official deposition to close the case.

"I've been in touch with the home office," Gerardo explained, "and they agree that my men and I could better spend our time elsewhere. They've faxed paperwork for you to fill out, and once you're sworn in by a judge, Harris and I have to head back east. We agreed we would rather turn the case over to you than to anyone else we've met locally, and we take responsibility for providing you with a future in the FBI. After this case is wrapped up, we'll find you work somewhere else, or perhaps you'll want to apply for a more formal position? Might you consider applying to the FBI school at Quantico? Maybe even eventually becoming a profiler?"

Sissy told him that yes, indeed, she very much might consider it.

Sam White dealt one minute at a time with the unthinkable: None of Dorrie's doctors could honestly reassure him that she would not die. In a day or two they would know more, they said. A day or two! Sam did not know how he would make it through the night. From a hospital pay phone, he called his parents in Colorado; utterly shocked by the unshed tears they heard in their son's clotted voice, they promised to be on the next airplane to Fulcrum.

Next, Sam knew, he should call Dorrie's parents, but he could not bring himself to do it. Instead, he phoned Pastor Lewinski, hoping he might do it for him.

"Wait," said Lewinski's young voice as Sam attempted to explain what had happened to Dorrie. "Whoa. One crisis at a time. She's hurt? You're at Fulcrum Hospital? Stay put; I'm coming over."

Only thanks to Pastor Lewinski and, later, Mom and Pop White, did Sam sleep or eat at all for the next few days. The first night, Lewinski managed to make Sam sit down in the lounge rather than hover outside his wife's intensive care cubicle. He listened to Sam compulsively talking about events that he, Sam, apparently had experienced but even so was having difficulty believing. He brought food from the hospital cafeteria and coaxed Sam to eat some of it as he told a story very much disjointed by distress. He got Sam to stretch out on the sofa by promising that he, Lewinski, would not leave intensive care for a moment without alerting Sam.

Mom and Pop White, the cavalry that arrived at dawn, exerted more authority. Pop took Sam home and made him shower and change clothes while Mom sat in Dorrie's cubicle and Lewinski stepped out for breakfast. Then, feeling guiltily that he really couldn't put it off any longer, he went to make a pastoral call on the Birches.

Knocking on their front door, thinking that it could have and should have been painted almost any color except the same drab brown as the house's shingles, Lewinski mentally prepared himself—belay that. There was no way to prepare for dealing with these particular parishioners.

He was just lifting his hand to knock again when the door was opened by Mr. Birch, who said utterly without expression, "Reverend Lewinski. You're up early today." He stood aside to let the pastor into a narrow passageway, then opened another dark brown door to a dim room that appeared to be a formal parlor, normally unused.

Lewinski stood feeling awkward, as if he should have a hat to remove and hold in his hands. "Would it be possible for me to see Mrs. Birch also? I'm afraid I have bad news."

"She's dead, then?" asked Mr. Birch without any apparent emotion.

"No! No, can you be thinking that Dorrie—your daughter—" As happened all too frequently when he spoke with the Birches, Lewinski found himself babbling. With an effort he stopped to try again. "What have you heard?" He found it incredible that they remained here, at home, if they knew their daughter lay near death in the hospital.

Mr. Birch's mouth tightened into a straight and lipless line, like a mail slot. He seemed about to answer when Mrs. Birch came in, wearing an apron and followed by the aroma of bacon. She greeted him with no more smile than her husband, yet with hospitality. "Pastor Lewinski. Would you like to join us for a bite to eat? I have some fresh-baked coffee cake."

"No, thank you." He successfully controlled his voice, and his thoughts about the appropriateness of coffee cake under the circumstances. "You've heard about your daughter?"

Mrs. Birch's voice became as starchy and colorless as her collar. "We have been scandalized to hear Candor's name on the news, not only radio but television. We have been given to understand that she has disobeyed us, and she has sinned, and she is being punished."

"But—but what Dorrie did was heroic, not a sin!"

"We ordered her never to go back there," said Mr. Birch.

"We would rather not talk about it," said Mrs. Birch.

The two of them stood shoulder to shoulder, facing their spiritual leader, in the middle of the dark parlor. No one had invited Lewinski to sit down.

"Of course we will pray for her," Mr. Birch added.

Lewinski could see quite clearly that they wanted him to leave before their bacon and eggs got cold. Actually, he had to control an impulse to flee. But he made himself say, "Let us pray for her together." Before they could refuse, he bowed his head and started speaking to God. In no way could they refuse to lower their heads also, and listen.

In his prayer Lewinski likened Dorrie's self-sacrifice for the sake of another to the sufferings of sacred martyrs, stopping only a hair short of declaring her Christlike. He extolled the virtues of her quick mind and generous heart, then requested the Almighty's aid in restoring her with due speed to health. He also implored the Almighty to soften the hearts of those who had grown hardened in their belief and remind them to judge not lest they be judged. He closed by calling for blessings on families of the faithful. He noticed without surprise that the Birches did not echo his "amen."

He shook hands with them anyway, met their chilly stares with a smile, and left their home with a sigh, shaking his head.

Three days later, to Sam's great relief, Dorrie was declared out of danger. Her sepsis was under control; her medications had been lightened; she was more alert and even, occasionally, able to talk. Sam felt hopeful and pleased when the hospital staff moved her out of ICU, but astonished when they put her in a generously proportioned private room. They shrugged off his questions as to whether his insurance would cover it. The father of the girl whom Dorrie had saved, they explained, insisted that Dorrie should have nothing less than the penthouse of hospital suites, and he had legally committed himself to pay for whatever expenses Sam's insurance would not meet.

This felt a bit hard on Sam, and when Lewinski came in— Pastor Lewinski was a dependable daily presence, as much so as Mom and Dad—Sam told him about it and asked anxiously, "What do you think?"

"I think you need to put your pride aside," Lewinski said firmly. "Dorrie deserves whatever goodness and consolation the world can bestow on her."

Sissy, who had received frequent accurate reports of Dorrie's condition thanks to the authority of the FBI, heard about her release from intensive care with almost as much relief as Sam. She decided it was time to get started, even if that meant no more than showing her face.

Dressed like the human being she preferred to be (T-shirt, jeans, Chucks), Sissy walked softly into Dorrie's small kingdom, which included no less than three easy chairs. She was not at all surprised to find Sam White occupying one of them, at Dorrie's bedside, like a permanent installation, but he did look taken aback to see her. Struggling to his feet, he inquired, "Officer Chappell?" as if he thought she might be a hallucination. Mentally, Sissy gave him points for remembering her name at all. She wondered whether he had made the acquaintance of a bed in the past three nights. He looked like a study in sleep deprivation.

"I'm not an officer anymore," she replied, shaking his hand. "Please call me Sissy."

"Um, okay, Sissy." With a gesture he introduced her to another person in the room—she had walked right past his chair without seeing him. Despite chaotic red hair, he still managed to have that kind of self-effacing personality. But as he stood up to smile and shake her hand, she noticed with great approval that he wore Chucks—an old, obviously cherished pair, faded blue with white checks.

"You're not an officer anymore?" Sam asked her. "What happened?"

Sissy decided to skip the Bud Angstrom unpleasantness. "I've been hired as a consultant by the FBI." She tried to keep pride out of her voice. "I've been authorized to take your wife's deposition when she's ready. No rush, but I thought I'd come in today just to see her. May I?"

"Of course!" Sam guided her toward the bed where, covered by a white blanket, Dorrie lay very still, intravenous tubes in both arms. Circumnavigating the drip stands, Sam stood on one side of Dorrie and Sissy on the other as if at a shrine.

What Sissy saw was not what she expected. When a person is lying with her eyes closed, you don't expect to see pus-filled blisters on her *eyelids*, let alone the rest of her face. "What's wrong with her skin?" she asked, embarrassed that her voice came out as a startled squeak.

"Lupus. It's not usually that bad, but skipping her meds on top of—well, you know—"

Sissy nodded to assure him that she understood.

"Her ordeal has caused one doozy of a flare, and it's all over her, sores popping up on her scalp and in her mouth and ears and—and even more miserable places."

"I hope it doesn't feel as bad as it looks."

"It would be uncomfortable, but her injuries where that bastard cut her with the knife would hurt worse. The doctors are keeping her bung full of pain meds and sedatives."

"Can she hear us? Dorrie, my name's Sissy; can you hear me?" Sistine reached for one of her hands, then saw that they too were encrusted with oozing sores. "Never mind," she said, ashamed of calling on this woman to make the slightest effort. "It doesn't matter."

Sam said, "She can hear us."

Dorrie responded to his voice with a slight movement of her head.

"That's my brave wife. Don't try to smile, sweetheart. Just rest and pretty soon you'll feel better."

Dorrie was going to be okay, Sissy knew in that moment. Dorrie had a wonderful, big warm husband and Sissy bet she had a wonderful family too. She'd be fine.

NINETEEN

Sissy started to say, "Well, I should be going—"

The sound of the door opening rather hard interrupted her. Turning, Sissy saw entering Dorrie's room a man and woman dressed in old-fashioned black, looking eerily like Grant Wood's *American Gothic* come to life—if one were to place a narrow-brimmed black hat in the man's hand instead of a pitchfork, and a black prayer bonnet on the woman's head.

Sam stepped forward quickly but did not offer to shake hands. Rather, he seemed to stand between them and Dorrie as if to guard his wife. "Mother and Father Birch," he said in a carefully neutral tone. "Long time no see. I trust you've been sleeping well?"

These were Dorrie's parents?

Instantly Sissy revised her rosy ideas of a moment earlier. She sensed family trouble, which was none of her business. "Um, I'd better be going," she said, meaning it this time, and she started toward the door. But to her surprise, the young redheaded man, Pastor Lewinski, stopped her by grasping her wrist for a moment.

"Reinforcements," he murmured very quietly, so that only she was likely to hear him.

Meanwhile, Mrs. Birch, who carried a plate swaddled in

aluminum foil, sidled past Sam and advanced on Dorrie's bed. "Candor," she said loudly but without emotion, "I've brought you some cookies. Your favorite kind. Hermits."

Whether Dorrie responded in any way, Sissy could not see.

"Thank you, Mother Birch," said Sam, his tone a bit warmer than it had been before.

"Yes, Mrs. Birch, thank you. It seems God has answered my prayers." Pastor Lewinski sounded as if, like a happy golden retriever, he had received his reward.

But neither of Dorrie's parents answered him. Simultaneously they gave him a disgusted glance.

Sam went to take the plate of cookies from his mother-in-law. "Dorrie can't eat these yet. Her throat is too sore, so she's being fed intravenously."

"Just as I expected," said the old woman harshly.

Sam's eyebrows shot up. "Expected?"

She gave him a look that said any other response wasn't necessary. Meanwhile, Mr. Birch stood at the foot of Dorrie's bed, regarding her with profound disapproval. Indeed, Mr. Birch seemed to swell with negative fervor like a male grackle puffing its feathers at a rival.

Suddenly, "Candor Verity," he proclaimed like a tent-revival preacher to a congregation, "we have come to bear witness of our condemnation of your behavior."

"You have dragged our good name into the public cesspool," Mrs. Birch joined in as her husband drew his next breath. "We have heard mention of you, our daughter, on the radio, the television—"

"Mr. and Mrs. Birch!" Pastor Lewinski exclaimed. "Think upon the mercy and humility of our Lord!"

He might as well not have spoken. They seemed not to hear

him. Mr. Birch thundered, "You disobeyed us and now you are being punished."

"—but we don't watch the news. We don't wish to know the extent of your iniquity."

"Mr. and Mrs. Birch!" Pastor Lewinski tried again. "Examine yourselves. Are you without sin?"

Sissy watched and listened, dumbstruck. How had Dorrie survived being raised by such a pair of fanatics? Sissy made a mental note never to complain about her own mother and father again.

Mr. Birch flung his next verbal stone at—under the white blanket on the bed, Dorrie lay so still that she might as well have been made of wood. A target. "It is our misfortune that you were born to be a woman and disgrace us."

"Stop it. Stop it!" Sam tried to forced Dorrie's parents away from the bed, but he was only one person, and the pair of them sidestepped him relentlessly.

Whipping the air with his black hat, Mr. Birch thundered, "Candor Verity, we ordered you never, ever to go back to Appletree. It's your own fault you experience the Lord's vengeance."

"We pray for you constantly," added Mrs. Birch in tones of martyrdom.

Sissy saw a nurse peek in, then hustle away, probably to summon security. Sissy hoped. Although it might be better not to wait. She figured she could handle the old man if Lewinski would subdue the woman. She eyed him. But he seemed too shocked and distressed to take action.

Mrs. Birch stabbed at a vase of roses with her forefinger and demanded, "Who sent you such expensive flowers? What a waste."

"Flowers, bah!" echoed Mr. Birch. "Perfume the air all you like, Candor, we can still smell the putrefaction of your soul."

"Dorrie's *injured*." Shaking his head, with his lips pressed into a grim line, Sam grasped his father-in-law by the arm, trying to usher the old man away from the foot of Dorrie's bed. "And she's having a severe lupus flare. You're supposed to be helping her."

Pulling away from Sam without even looking at him, Mr. Birch intoned, "We have helped her. God saved her unworthy life because of our prayers."

And while Sam was distracted, Mrs. Birch had advanced to lean over the bed. "Why the private room?" she shrilled almost directly into Dorrie's ear. "Good money up a puppy's rectum!"

The nurse reappeared and strode in, speaking to the Birches. "Sir, ma'am, please lower your voices or I will be forced to call security. This is a *hospital*."

Neither of them so much as looked at her; a mosquito would have received more attention.

Dorrie's father thundered, "Candor Verity, you have disobeyed us and disobeyed us unto the gates of Hell, and now you *must* listen."

"Listen and repent," Mrs. Birch exhorted.

Mr. Birch continued, "We absolutely forbid you to go near that illegitimate—the Phillips girl ever again. Not—"

Then it happened.

The drip stands supporting the intravenous tubing clattered and nearly fell, Dorrie sat up so forcefully. With strength she should not possibly have possessed, Dorrie reared forward in her bed and flared at her parents, "You two vultures are not my family anymore. Get out of this room. And get out of my life." Her voice, so powerful it seemed almost supernatural, made Sissy think of a flaming sword. Dorrie's puffy eyes opened as wide as they could to blaze. "And stay out! Don't ever come near me again. Never!"

For a moment of silence so profound it seemed nearly miraculous, Dorrie stared down her startled parents. Sissy watched the old woman's face go cane-sugar white but far from sweet; the old man's turned heart-attack red. But Sam moved first, three long steps to sit with Dorrie and support her in his arms. And he spoke first. "I would take great pleasure in throwing you heartless freaks out of here with my own hands," he said, his voice low and intense, "but I have to ask Officer Chappell and Pastor Lewinski to do it for me."

"Glad to," said Lewinski.

"Likewise." Sissy stepped up to confront Mr. Birch, assuming the authority of a uniform even though she wore none. "You have been ordered to leave these premises at once. I advise you to go now, quietly—"

"Jezebel!" shrieked Mrs. Birch. So much for quiet.

Expertly Sissy seized Mr. Birch, spun him, and, with his arms twisted behind him, propelled him out of the room. Glancing over her shoulder, she saw that Lewinski was handling Mrs. Birch simply by towing the old woman, his hands gripping her elbow.

Sissy wished she had a slightly more expert assistant, and was relieved when hospital security met them before they reached the first elevator.

"We resign from your church!" Mr. Birch, restrained by a security guard, shouted at Lewinski.

"Good," said Lewinski.

"Go to hell!" screeched Mrs. Birch. A real-life witch could not have invoked the curse more virulently.

"If that happens, I'll see you there."

Sissy did not engage in any repartee. She could not forget

the old couple quickly enough. Running, already halfway down the hall, she wanted only to see how Dorrie was doing.

Back in the room, she found Sam still tending to his wife, gently easing her back to lie down in bed, smoothing her hair as he settled her head on the pillow, talking to her, dropping tiny kisses on her anywhere there was some unblistered skin. He kissed her hairline, her ear, her nose. "I'm so proud of you, Dorrie," he whispered, kissing her. "So very, very proud of you. What a woman."

She opened her eyes slightly and answered him with an exhausted smile. She whispered, "Give those cookies to the nurses, would you, sweetie?"

I drifted back into myself over a period of days. I don't remember a thing about the ambulance or the helicopter or the emergency room. I don't recall any climactic moment of waking up to find myself alive with Sam by my side. I think it happens like that only in movies. For me, it was more like a series of dreams and vignettes, and I couldn't always tell the vignettes from the dreams.

Sometimes it was Juliet in a ballet tutu or a clown wig with a sapphire blue flasher stuck in her nose, Juliet saying, "Mommy, Mommy, Mommy!"

Sometimes it was a man or a woman in a white coat bending over me, murmuring, extracting fruit punch from one arm as they added milk to the other.

Sometimes it was a soft female voice asking questions. What had I seen at the mall? How had I followed the van? What had happened to my Kia? What had happened in the gravel parking lot?

"I broke the van and the alarm went off," I explained not very lucidly.

"Did you put anything up the tailpipe?"

"Oh. Yes. Kleenex. I forgot." I opened my eyes. She was a youthful black woman with such ineffably sweet concern in her caramel face that I did not think of her as an ordinary human being. Instead, I thought of her as God taking notes. "I killed Blake," I said.

"With the knife?"

I nodded. "I threw all my strength into slashing his throat. I couldn't risk letting him live."

"Yes."

"It is terrible to kill like that, blood spurting and his eyes so surprised and hurt."

"Yes."

"Do you think I will go to hell for killing him?"

"No. I think you can be proud. You saved the world from a rapist, a murderer."

"I killed Blake with the mother of all scary castrating bitches," I said.

"Really?"

"Yes. Her name was Pandora."

"Oh."

"So if I could do that," I added, closing my eyes again, "I guess I can get over being afraid of knives."

"How did you get the knife away from Blake?"

"Pandora? He handed her to me."

"Excuse me?"

"We had a suicide pact. I was supposed to slash his wrist. The way he did to his parents."

"His *parents*?"

"He murdered them." I had not known this until the moment I said it, yet I had known it back then in my adolescence too. Every time I had wanted to kill my own parents, I had known, then repressed, what Blake had done to his. I told the gentle being who was questioning me, "They made him crazy and he killed them. Or he killed them and then he went crazy. Whatever." Humbly I asked, "God, do you think I'm going to go crazy from killing him?"

She said gently, "I think you need to go back to sleep and I'll talk with you again tomorrow."

I slept, sometimes with my eyes open, amid limpid whiteness. The white-light presence abided with me, drifting into oneness with me as I drifted back into myself, meanwhile engaging me in important conversations. About the meaning of my name. Candor Verity: honest truth. Ironic, considering the life I had lived so far.

Sam stayed with me almost as constantly as the presence. Mostly silent, holding my hand in both of his. So warm, his hands. I remember once waking up to ask him in genuine surprise, "You're still here? Why aren't you slaving away at the machine shop?"

His reply was vehement and remarkable. "Screw the machine shop. I love you."

Remarkable because I had never heard him use the verb "to screw" in any sense except its most literal one.

And even more remarkable because he hardly ever said "I love you" except on Valentine's Day or our wedding anniversary.

Which meant he too knew this was more important. I told him, "Sam, when I decided to live, it was for you. To give us another chance."

"Decided to live?" he repeated blankly. Typical Sam, stuck on a detail while the gist sailed right past him. "You *decided*?"

I closed my eyes for a moment, because it hurt, remembering how I could have floated forever at peace on the wide horizon of eternity, and I had elected to return to the painful straits of time instead. When I opened my eyes, Sam was still there, still staring at me.

"I married too young, maybe. Up till now I haven't given you the love you deserve," I told him, watching his face. How had I ever thought he was just an average-looking man? He was strong, rugged, handsome in his quiet way.

He turned his head. Not looking at me, he said as if we were dealing with a forgotten grocery item, "Don't worry about it, Dorrie. You do okay. I mean, shoot, look what you grew up with. Look at the parents who raised you."

"Oh." The mention of my parents distracted me from the odd way Sam was acting. I lay thinking. "I remember . . . am I dreaming, or did I really tell them to go jump in a lake?"

"Indeed you did, although not in those exact words." Sam leaned over me and kissed me gingerly on one of the few places not encrusted with an ulcerating rash: my forehead. "You told them to get out of your life and stay out. They had to be physically removed from this hospital and they're not allowed back in." He watched my eyes. "Are you okay with that?"

"Okay?" My heart felt like a winged thing, a once-caged bird free at last, ready to sing. All my beepy machines began to chorus like spring peepers, and I popped some lupus blisters by grinning. "I'm better than okay. I could dance, or fly. I'm free. I'm out from under all that black. Do you think we can make the old killjoys stay away from the house when I get home?"

A nurse rushed in to check my machines before Sam could

answer, but I could tell by the warm feel of his hand on my forehead and hair that his answer was yes. Yes.

Later, Sam told himself, much later when Dorrie was much stronger, he would tell her what her parents had done. The same day Dorrie had ordered them out of her life, they had put their narrow brown-shingled house and its contents up for sale, loaded some personal items into their old green sedan, and left Fulcrum without telling anyone where they were going and without leaving a forwarding address.

Sam did not think Dorrie would be very hurt by their final gesture of rejection. He himself hoped never again to see them. But it was hard to tell what Dorrie might feel deep down. Parents were parents.

Even though Dorrie was looking better every day, Sam still kept reminding himself not to question her, not to mention Appletree or anything that might upset her. His own feelings, which were pretty well mixed up between wonder and hurt and awe and shock and love and jealousy and fear, were going to have to wait. First things first: Dorrie needed time to recuperate. Even Sissy's questioning had been limited to five minutes a day. Now, more than a week after it had all happened, Dorrie was conscious, talking some, and the doctors said she was in stable condition, but Sam had decided that any discussion of Juliet Phillips, or more specifically how Juliet Phillips had come to be born, was out of the question unless or until Dorrie raised the subject herself.

Dorrie was peacefully napping and Sam was in his customary bedside chair, thinking along these lines, when the door of the private hospital room opened. "Mr. White," called a nurse, "there's a gentleman out here who would like to speak with you."

Sam got up from his chair, glancing back at Dorrie over his shoulder as he went out. Who would want to talk with him? Any doctor would have come into the room. If Dad was in perplexities trying to run the machine shop, he would have called, and if Mom wanted to discuss dinner plans, she would have just popped in. So who—

He saw the man, although it took him a moment to place him.

Oh. Don Phillips.

Don Phillips?

This was odd, the district attorney and gubernatorial hopeful, three-piece suit and briefcase and all, a man with lots of things to do, waiting in the hospital hallway.

"Sam." Don Phillips took Sam's hand and grasped it more than shook it. Sam could have sworn it wasn't the gesture of a politician. The man seemed off his stride, poise in abeyance for some reason.

But then, the district attorney seemed to be studying him with similar sympathy. "You look like hell," Don Phillips said.

"I'm fine. Things are getting back to normal." Somewhat. Mostly thanks to parents who insisted that their son eat, shower, change clothes, sleep. "Dorrie's resting comfortably."

"Your wife deserves a medal for what she did. I intend to nominate her for the Carnegie Heroism Award." Don Phillips steered Sam down the hospital corridor toward one of those little closed-off lounges the hospital provided for families to confer in—crying rooms, Sam called them. Following him in there, Sam tried to think what might be on the guy's mind. Juliet Phillips's statement had cleared Dorrie of any wrongdoing. The police and FBI were busy with the artifacts in Blake Roman's shoe box, which had already enabled them to link that unspeakable punk to the rapes and/or murders of seven young women in California, Wyoming, Indiana, Michigan, and Ohio. They were also happily preoccupied with the guy's customized knife, which featured remote control panels in the hilt. They surmised that either Juliet or Dorrie had pressed the one that had opened the green metal door, probably without even knowing it.

On top of all that, they had old Bert Roman's ravings to sift through. Appletree PD had dropped all charges except such as were necessary to keep Bert in the psychiatric wing of the local hospital, because he had been acting mighty strange since he had shown himself to be a possible danger to himself and others by discharging his gun. But the coroner said Blake Roman's body had already been dead when Bert Roman had plugged a bullet into it.

That had been a doozy of a surprise, finding out that the serial killer had been the old guy's grandson.

Not the scariest surprise, though, to Sam.

"You sure you're okay?" Don Phillips asked, closing the door of the crying room behind Sam and him.

Sam clenched his teeth. What the heck did this guy want from him? "I'm not sure of anything."

"I know the feeling." Don Phillips reached into his suit jacket pocket and produced a cell phone Sam vaguely recognized. "Juliet thanks you very, very much for the loan of this," the DA told him, handing it over, "and asked me to return it to you."

"She's very welcome. How is she doing?"

"Wonderfully." Don Phillips sat down on an unlovely tan vinyl sofa, his facial expression not reflecting what he had just said. Yet he repeated it. "Wonderfully. She's just tired and a little confused. Barely traumatized at all." Don Phillips raised a haunted gaze to Sam's face. "I can't stop thinking what would have happened to her if it weren't for your amazing wife. I can't get over it."

Sam sat down on a tan vinyl chair facing the matching sofa. He didn't lean back; he perched on the edge of the stiff square cushion, elbows on his knees and his big hands dangling, waiting to see what this was really about.

Don Phillips sighed and met his eyes. "Have you talked with your wife at all about Juliet?"

Oh. That was what this was about. Whether Dorrie got to be a mother.

Which, by God, she deserved after all she'd been through for that girl's sake.

"No. Not yet," Sam replied levelly. "Have you talked with Juliet at all about Dorrie?"

"No. But I know Juliet wants to see her just as soon as the doctor will permit it. I wish—I truly wish I could just let nature take its course, but I can't."

"Why not?"

"Because the adoption . . ." Don Phillips continued to study the soiled beige carpeting. "Morally I don't think Pearl and I have done anything wrong, but legally, um, the adoption agreement is, um, somewhat questionable. . . ."

"I don't blame you," Sam said. "I know what it is to pray for a child."

"Thank you." The DA met his eyes with visible relief. "But not everyone is going to be so understanding. Your wife's parents have threatened to ruin me if anything is made public."

Sam sagged back into his chair. He felt his mouth hanging open and struggled to close it. "That's just the sort of thing they would do," he said when he could speak. "Old buzzards. But they've left town in a snit, did you know that?"

"No. But it doesn't really matter. They can still get me into a lot of trouble."

"All right. So we want to keep you out of trouble. So how many people know about Dorrie and Juliet?"

"Quite a few, actually, but they are police or FBI, and they're with me on this."

I bet they are, Sam thought. This guy had clout.

"Angstrom told his people it was all a mistake, the idea that there was anything suspicious about Dorrie's involvement. They'll forget about it. End of story."

"Which leaves me and Dorrie," Sam said. And Sissy Chappell, but he felt no need to mention her. Sissy wanted only the best for Dorrie.

Don Phillips nodded. "Did you personally tell anybody?"

Sam gave the question some thought. He hadn't told his parents a thing except what they could read in the newspaper: A heroic woman named Dorrie White had seen a teenage girl being abducted, had followed and confronted the abductor, and had ultimately gotten his knife away from him and killed him in self-defense, then freed the girl, and was now recovering from her injuries.

Trying to remember whether he had said anything more to anyone else, Sam reviewed the past week and a half in his mind. The early days seemed like a bad dream to him, his memories of them fading, but he didn't think he'd told anyone. . . . Bert? Had Bert made the connection that Juliet was his great-granddaughter? As far as Sam could tell, no, the old guy had not. Moreover, Bert seemed not likely to make connections of any kind anytime soon.

And Phillips wouldn't make the connection with Bert either. Besides Dorrie, only Sam himself, as far as he could tell, knew the whole story, and it made him feel sick just to think about who Juliet's father was—or had been. But Phillips didn't know. And Juliet didn't know. And for the sake of all mercy and sanity it should stay that way.

"No," Sam replied to Don Phillips, "as far as I can remember, I didn't tell a soul. No reason I should."

Don Phillips requested humbly, "May I ask you to continue that policy? Don't tell a soul?"

Sam liked it that Don Phillips was being man-to-man with him, not acting like a politician or any sort of superior being. He liked it that Phillips had not once mentioned his contribution to paying Dorrie's considerable hospital bills. Heck, he liked the guy, period. He said, "I don't have a problem with that."

"Thank you." Don Phillips looked and sounded genuinely grateful. "I knew you wouldn't wish any harm on me." Don Phillips consulted his lower lip with his teeth for a moment, then asked, "Now, here is where I feel like I have no right even asking—how is your wife feeling?"

How was Dorrie *feeling*? Sometimes she cried. Other times she lay there looking so frail that Sam wanted to protect her forever, yet in her face he saw something so stark strong it frightened him, such potency in a woman; what if she ever turned against him? Yet other times she seemed far away, her open eyes dreamy, looking at something only she could see. And still other times she focused on Sam and smiled at him with a brave tilt of her chin that he'd never noticed in her before.

But none of this was what Don Phillips really wanted to know.

Sam took the bull by the horns. "You haven't told Juliet."

Looking at the floor, the DA conceded, "My wife and

I talked it over and agreed we had no choice." With a visible effort Don Phillips raised his head to face Sam. "We told Juliet we didn't know who your wife was or why she did what she did."

In other words, they'd lied. Sam pressed his lips together to keep from saying so.

Don Phillips went on, "Apparently, your wife didn't tell Juliet anything differently during the time they were together."

Sam allowed himself to retort, "I imagine they didn't get much chance to talk."

"Exactly." Don Phillips leaned forward, his expression one of sincere appeal. "And I'm sure your wife will agree that, under the circumstances, it will be better for Juliet if we just leave things that way."

Your wife, your wife, your wife, Sam thought. Not once had the DA referred to Dorrie by name.

Don Phillips went on, "Will you please talk with her, tell her what I've told you, and request her—"

"I ought to punch your lights out."

Considerably startled, Phillips squeaked, "I beg your pardon?"

"You think I'd tell Dorrie what to say to her daughter? I ought to brain you. I'm not going to mention a word of this conversation to her. But just so you can stop fussing, I think Dorrie has her own very strong reason for keeping things the way they are."

"Oh. Um, then that takes care of it, I guess." Possibly never had a DA sounded less certain, but reaching for his briefcase seemed to give him back some of his aplomb. "Just one more thing." Setting the briefcase on a chair, he opened it and pulled out something flat protected by a paper bag. "Will you return this to your wife for me? And please see that no one else looks at it?"

Accepting the parcel, Sam nodded, because, almost as if the color pink were leaching through the paper to give him hives on his fingers, he could tell without looking what was in it.

TWENTY

I was sitting up in bed, bored now that Sam's parents had gone home and Sam had gone back to work, wondering whether there might be anything worth watching on daytime TV, when the door of my hospital room shot open and Juliet flew in, her entrance so impetuous it was as if she were being carried away by a huge bouquet of helium balloons, their yellow, turquoise, pink, and violet ribbons gathered into one hand.

So many times I had thought what I would say to her, but when my mouth opened, all that came out was a banal, "Oh! I love balloons."

Juliet did better. She ran straight to me and put her arms around me, carefully, as if I might bruise. "Thank you for what you did," she said close to my ear, her voice vibrant with emotion. "Thank you, thank you, thank you." She kissed the side of my head.

My arms had gone around her, of course. A Supreme Court injunction could not have kept me from embracing her.

Even though I knew what I had to do.

I patted her strong young back, but a clotted feeling in my chest made it difficult to speak. I managed only another banality. "I'm just glad you're okay."

"Me!" Juliet let go of me and stepped back, her face flushed, her eyes sparkling. "You're the one who got knifed. Do you really like balloons?"

"I adore them. They make me feel good. Too many flowers, it's like a funeral."

"I totally concur." She glanced around the small room crowded with funereal flora. "Where—"

"Tether them right here beside me, on this table thingie."

She did, tying the ribbons around the gooseneck stand, then sat down on my bed, as close to me as she could get.

I knew what was coming. I'd tried to prepare myself for this moment, but no amount of forethought seemed like much help right now.

Juliet looked me straight in the eye. "Please," she requested firmly, "who are you, really?"

Here it was. The moment of my dreams. The moment when I could have looked deeply into her eyes and said, "I'm your birth mother."

And I wanted to, I longed to, I yearned to; my heart burned with wanting to say, "I'm your mother."

But I must not. Because if I did, then someday, maybe not today, but too soon, she would ask, "Who is my father?" And she must never know. Never ever.

Feeling my way through the quandary, I quipped, "Who am I? As opposed to Maria Montessori?"

"That was cute." She allowed me a half smile. "I can't believe that self-kissing psycho creep didn't know who Maria Montessori was."

That psycho creep. Her biological father.

I asked, "Do you have nightmares about him?"

"Oh, yeah. Majorly." She shuddered. "But I'd be having a lot worse nightmares if I was raped or dead." Despite the obvious whimsy of this statement, she did not smile. She gave me a no-nonsense stare from under her strong dark eyebrows. "You saved me. I want to know why."

I said slowly, "Well, you know, Juliet, I have no children of my own—"

She broke in. "That's another thing. You told me you had a daughter in school with me, and you don't."

Oops.

"And you knew my name," Juliet went on, leaning toward me, passionately earnest. "My parents are trying to tell me you're just a nice lady who happened to be passing by, but they're lying."

I'd expected her parents wouldn't tell her too much. Such prominent people were likely to be protectors of the status quo. Although I hadn't thought they'd outright lie.

I wondered why, but Juliet gave me no time to conjecture, speaking on in a rush. "I can tell they're lying. Anyway, I'm not stupid. Nice by-passer ladies might call the police, but they don't go chasing after the creep and they definitely don't climb into his van. They don't hang around distracting him, they don't get in his face, and they don't take a knife . . ." Juliet faltered, gulped, breathed deeply.

I said, "Sweetie, it's not that big of a deal."

"It is too. It's huge. Ginormous. You got wounded and somehow you got the knife away from him and killed him."

"I had to."

"You didn't have to do any of it. You should have been home taking your lupus medicine. Instead you're crawling down the hallway to cut the duct tape off me before you pass out. No big deal, my ass. It's humongous. Extreme. It's *crazy*. Unless . . ."

Once again my chance to say it.

No. NO. She must never ask about her father.

"Sweetie." I couldn't look at Juliet or I might not have been strong enough. Instead, I looked at the balloons she had brought me, sunlight from my hospital room window glorifying them into a celestial celebration of—some tender rainbow-colored event, a wedding, a baby shower, a prom. . . . I wondered whether Juliet had a date to the prom, whether he was the boy of her current dreams, whether she would be wearing a gown she adored, what style, what color. . . . Maybe someday we'd have a chance to girl-talk about things like that.

Please, God.

I took a deep breath and looked her in the eye. "Sweetie, okay, you're right, I did know your name beforehand. And I was kind of keeping an eye on you that day at the mall."

The rapture on her face . . . I could only just bear it. Emotions opening to the light. A pink rose blossoming. She breathed, "Like a guardian angel."

I said softly, "More like a lonely, neurotic woman who ought to see a therapist. I have problems you don't know about, honey. So do your parents, most likely. Juliet, do your parents love you?"

The sudden question caught her off guard, with her shield of adolescent coolness lowered. She blurted, "Of course."

"Yet you say they're lying to you. Why would they lie?"

The shield went up. She rolled her eyes. "To be *stupid*. Probably something to do with my father. Politics."

"Or could it be because they love you and want to protect you from something?"

Out came the pubescent pride. "I don't need protection!"

"Really? I sure do. Most of us do." Especially from our own families, I thought, trying not to wince as I thought of my parents, grandparents Juliet could definitely do without. I told my daughter quietly, "But you're right just the same. Nobody should lie to you. I want *never* to lie to you, Juliet. Never ever."

With a gasp that was not quite a sigh she leaned toward me, gazing into my face, rapt. Her lips parted.

Tenderly I told her, "So, the question you're about to ask, please don't."

Her dark eyes went wide, shadowed, but I did not allow myself to flinch away from facing her. I willed her to understand. For a moment, despite bright balloons and sunlight, it was like that nighttime first meeting in the van, with unspoken communication flying between us: Be strong, be smart. We're in this together. We'll handle this our own way. You know the truth as well as I do.

Trust me.

And she did; she trusted me. She gave a gasp that was not quite a word, and her eyes misted over with tears, but she didn't ask the question that would have forced me to lie. My heart squeezed. I wanted to cry with her, for her. But I must not.

She had leaned so close to me that I could pull her into my arms, and I did that. I whispered, "Hush. Shhhh," and I didn't mean just her weeping. I stroked her back, patted her head, memorizing the feeling of hugging my . . . my daughter.

She relaxed into my embrace. I felt her breathing shudder, then steady.

"One thing I will say," I murmured into her dark hair. "I care about you. I care so much."

I felt her head nod against my shoulder before she gathered herself and sat up, trying for a shaky smile. "Duh," she told me. "I never would have known."

"Your parents are the ones who have earned the right to say they love you."

"I think you have too."

"I . . . I'd feel presumptuous. But . . . Juliet, sweetie, may I come see you? I'd like to meet your parents."

"Of course."

"And will you come see me?"

"Yes," she said, and I could tell it was a promise she made with all her heart, as if she were declaring "I do" in front of an altar.

Sam came in. "I met Juliet in the hallway," he said as he sat in his customary chair.

Very tired, I managed a smile at him as I reclined the bed so I could lie down.

Sam said, "She looked kind of teary."

I nodded.

"So I gave her a hug and asked her what was the matter."

"And?"

"She said, 'Nothing, really. I think everything's going to be okay.' Then she stepped back from me and lifted her chin like a little soldier and said, 'Actually, everything *is* okay.'"

I breathed out.

"She's a great kid," Sam said.

I nodded.

Sam peered at me. "Are you all right?"

"Yes." I meant it. My future was looking a lot brighter than it had a week ago. I felt well enough to give Sam a teasing glance. "You saw her come in and you were waiting down the hallway, weren't you?"

He's cute when he gets sheepish.

"Well, yes, I did and I was." Sam loosened his tie and his belt, leaning back in the chair as if he meant to stay a while. "So, Juliet's coping. What did you tell her?"

"Just that I couldn't tell her." I turned my head on the pillow so I could watch Sam's face, so gently contoured yet solid, like a mountain's weathered summit. "But she knows who I am, and she knows I know she knows. It's just that we're not going there."

Sam nodded. "Because you don't want her to find out who her father was."

It took my breath away. I had been wanting to tell him, had been trying to figure out how to tell him, but I had no inkling he already knew.

"Blake Roman," he confirmed. "I found the notes, and then I just kind of read the writing on the wall."

It shocked my heart, the stark way he said that. Tears filled my eyes, spilled down my temples into my hair. Sam leaned forward and took my limp, cold hand between his. "Now, what are you crying about?" His hands were warm, but his voice wasn't, not very.

"You," I whispered. "You're hurt."

"I'll live."

"Can you forgive me?"

"For what? For being human?"

"Don't try to tell me it doesn't bother you."

"No, I admit, it does." Slowly he let my hand slip out of his grasp. He sat back. "You were in love with that pervert."

"Not anymore."

"But you were. For years." Just trying to verify data, his tone said, not accusing. "Weren't you?"

"I was living in a dreamworld. If you want to call that love, then yes."

"And you thought about leaving me?"

"No. You're my real world. I never wanted to leave you."

He exhaled a long, slow breath. "Well, then I'm a fool," he murmured.

"No, you're not. You sensed I was keeping my distance. Sam, up till now we've barely been married. We've just been two people sharing a house and a business, because up till lately, I didn't know what honest love was."

Silence, during which I breathed in the fragrance of too many flowers, listened to rainbow balloons rustling.

"But I've grown to love you more than I knew until . . . Sam, in that awful basement, I was looking down from the ceiling, and you were holding me, you were dirty and rumpled and freaked-out, and you were *there* for me. So I came back."

"God, Dorrie, you're scaring me." He turned his head away. "Don't look at me like that."

"Like *what*?"

"Like a—like an angel with a fiery sword, like a dragon slayer. You killed your dream to save Juliet."

"And to save myself. And us."

He nodded, but I could see him thinking hard about something. Then he faced me and took a deep breath. "Dorrie, I've been waiting for the right time to tell you something, and I'm not sure this is it."

"Go ahead, tell the dragon slayer," I reassured him.

"Well, if Blake Roman was just an empty dream, Mother and Father Birch were a real live nightmare, and, bless your fiery sword, you've gotten rid of them too. Your parents have left Fulcrum and I don't think they mean for you to see them ever again."

It took me a moment to absorb this. Then I felt angry. The old crows, they had done it to hurt me, I knew. But almost immediately joy took over, because rejection by those two didn't hurt, and freedom felt so long overdue. "Good," I said.

"Good? Are you sure?"

I nodded. "Good."

Sam studied my face.

I studied his. "What about you? How are you, Sam? Really?"

I saw him take a deep breath as he forced himself to tell me, although not quite steadily. "I'm kind of a mess, honey. Everything's changing, and I'm off-balance. I'm so uncomfortable, it's like I'm sitting on a knife's edge."

A rush of empathy made me smile. Leaning toward him, I told him earnestly, "Sam, I've been there too, but now I'm not afraid anymore. Not of knives. Not of living. And I'm not afraid of loving you."

I reached out. He hesitated only a heartbeat before he responded. Our hands clasped.

"It's going to be all right," I told him the way I had told Juliet in the van.

We gazed at each other as if touching for the first time.

Nancy Springer has written fifty novels for adults, young adults, and children, in genres that include mythic fantasy, contemporary fiction, magical realism, horror, and mystery—although she did not realize she wrote mystery until she won the Edgar Allan Poe Award from the Mystery Writers of America two years in succession. *Dark Lie* is her first venture into adult suspense.

Born in New Jersey, Nancy Springer lived for many decades near Gettysburg, Pennsylvania, of Civil War fame, raising two children, writing, horseback riding, fishing, and bird-watching. In 2007 she surprised her friends and herself by moving with her second husband to an isolated area of the Florida panhandle, where the bird-watching is spectacular and where, when fishing, she occasionally catches an alligator.

CONNECT ONLINE

nancyspringer.com
facebook.com/nancyspringernovelist